ELIZABETH TAYLOR

(1912–1975) was born E█████████████ The daughter of an insu███████████████ the Abbey School, Read███████████████ as a governess and, later █████████. At the age of twenty-four she married John William Kendall Taylor, a business-man, with whom she had a son and a daughter. She lived much of her married life in the village of Penn in Buckinghamshire.

Elizabeth Taylor wrote her first novel, *At Mrs Lippincote's* (1945), during the war while her husband was in the Royal Air Force. This was followed by *Palladian* (1946), *A View of the Harbour* (1947), *A Wreath of Roses* (1949), *A Game of Hide-and-Seek* (1951), *The Sleeping Beauty* (1953), *Angel* (1957), *In a Summer Season* (1961), *The Soul of Kindness* (1964), *The Wedding Group* (1968), *Mrs Palfrey at the Claremont* (1971) and *Blaming*, published posthumously in 1976. She has also published four volumes of short stories: *Hester Lilly and Other Stories* (1954), *The Blush and Other Stories* (1958), *A Dedicated Man and Other Stories* (1965) and *The Devastating Boys* (1972). Elizabeth Taylor has written a book for children, *Mossy Trotter* (1967); her short stories have been published in the *New Yorker*, *Harper's Bazaar*, *Harper's* magazine, *Vogue* and the *Saturday Evening Post*, and she is included in *Penguin Modern Stories 6*.

Critically Elizabeth Taylor is one of the most acclaimed British novelists of this century, and in 1984 *Angel* was selected as one of the Book Marketing Council's "Best Novels of Our Time". Virago publishes eleven of her sixteen works of fiction.

VIRAGO
MODERN
CLASSIC
NUMBER
236

THE
BLUSH
AND OTHER STORIES

ELIZABETH TAYLOR

WITH A NEW INTRODUCTION BY
PAUL BAILEY

To
WILLIAM MAXWELL

Published by VIRAGO PRESS Limited 1986
41 William IV Street, London WC2N 4DB

First published in Great Britain by Peter Davies 1958

British Library Cataloguing in Publication Data

Taylor, Elizabeth, *1912-1975*
  The blush.—(Virago modern classic)
  I. Title
  823'.914[F]   PR6039.A928

  ISBN 0-86068-672-8

Printed in Finland by Werner Söderström Oy

Contents

Introduction

In "The Ambush", the first story in this collection, Elizabeth Taylor has a character voicing what sounds to me like her own artistic credo. Mrs Ingram, a middle-aged woman of great refinement, is describing the work of a young painter named Freddie to Catherine, the girl she had hoped would be her daughter-in-law. Freddie's painting, she remarks, has "that detestable ingredient, virtuosity". She continues:

"It allows one to see how clever he has been, and that should never be. I don't want to see the wheels going round or to feel called upon to shout 'Bravo' as if he were some sweating Italian tenor. One should really feel, 'How easy it must be! How effortless!' I should think — don't you, Catherine? — that an artist must seem too proud to have tried, too careless to have thought of succeeding."

Elizabeth Taylor is not an obvious virtuoso, detestable or otherwise. Her best writing has that effortlessness Mrs Ingram admires. The short story is an art form that cannot accommodate effort, and its finest practitioners are wary of cleverness: the trick endings of O.Henry stand as an awful warning. The twelve stories in *The Blush* are not effortful and not obviously clever, which is why they have retained their freshness over thirty-five years. They are free from the tricks of the trade, yet they contain plenty of surprises. The beautiful ending of "The Ambush" is a case in point. What depths of feeling and personality it hints at, in four sentences.

"Not a tale here fails to expand in the imagination of the reader", wrote Elizabeth Bowen of *The Blush* on its appearance in 1951. It is the praise of one expert to another, for Elizabeth Bowen knew better than anyone how much artistry is required to achieve a story that expands. The masters of the short story are masters of omission as well as suggestion: it is what they leave out that often makes for their most devastating effects. From the very beginning of her career, Elizabeth Taylor quietly exhibited this particular skill. Look at the way she manages it in the delicious "The True Primitive", where she brings a self-admiring old windbag to vivid life with an economy of means. We know immediately that Mr Ransome is a bore, but his creator never allows him to bore us. It is enough for her to show Mr Ransome through the sometimes drowsy eyes of the unlettered Lily. This is how "The True Primitive" begins:

Lily had not considered culture — as a word or anything else — until she fell in love. As soon as that happened it, culture, descended on her. It was as if all the books Mr Ransome had ever read were thrown at her one after the other — Voltaire, Tolstoi, Balzac — the sharp names came at her, brutal spondees, brutally pronounced. She thought, though, that she hated Dostoievski most of all. "Yes, Dad," Mr Ransome's two sons continually said, agreeing to rate Zola higher than Dickens if he wished them to, promising to remember what he had told them about Michelangelo. Painters' names were part of the attack, but Lily thought they sounded gentler. She had felt curiosity about someone called Leonardo when first she heard him mentioned and had wondered if he were Harry's cousin. When she asked Harry he laughed and referred her to his father, which meant three-quarters of an hour wasted, sitting in the kitchen listening, and then it was too late for them to go for their walk. Trembling with frustrated desire, she had learnt her lesson; she asked no more questions and sat sullenly quiet whenever the enemy names began again.

It's an exemplary paragraph: informative, funny, revealing of two characters who have not been accounted for in conventional chunks of description. Lily and Mr Ransome are both *there* — she in her resentful frustration; he in his sage-like complacency. "She thought, though, that she hated Dostoievski most of all" is a marvellous conceit, sneaked in with this author's habitual cunning. The joke doesn't patronise Lily. It is plain that the preposterous name, often repeated, would inspire hatred in the unfortunate girl who is wild about Harry.

Perhaps the funniest story in *The Blush* is "Perhaps a Family Failing", which is also concerned with frustration. The newly married Beryl has waited months to experience her first night of wedded bliss. She has studied the women's magazines with attentiveness, and has bought the recommended "filmy, lacy, ribboned lingerie" in order to "tease and entice her husband". While Geoff is downstairs in the bar at The Seaferry Arms making lots of new friends, Beryl is upstairs in the bridal suite "provocative in chiffon". The Taylor combination of sadness and hilarity informs the closing pages, as Beryl continues to be provocative and Geoff's capacity for friendship leads him to an act of ludicrous heroism.

The simple Beryl is likely to survive her humiliation. The sisters, Ursula and Melanie, in "Summer Schools", have reached middle age scarcely without knowing it. They are locked in a combat of sorts, and have become inseparable in their near-contempt for each other. This is an extremely subtle piece of writing, with much left pointedly unsaid between the two unhappy women. A strange means of survival is of the essence here, and Elizabeth Taylor only suggests it. The suggestion is enough.

It has been recently revealed by Robert Liddell, in his short memoir *Ivy and Elizabeth*, that the story "The Letter-Writers" is partly autobiographical. For many years, Elizabeth Taylor, who lived in the Thames Valley, corresponded with Robert Liddell, who lived in Egypt and Greece. The writers admired each other's books. After a while, they became wary of meeting. The personalities revealed in the letters were charming and witty and observant: the real people might turn out to be disappointing. So Elizabeth Taylor feared, and "The Letter-Writers" is an expression of that fear. She even went on a cruise to the Greek Islands and contrived to avoid seeing him. When, eventually, they did meet, the fear expressed in the story proved groundless. Even so, "The Letter-Writers" survives as a gentle study of a peculiar friendship, a surviving relationship that satisfies its two participants. It is a study in the contentment that certain people find in isolation. Their best friends are always abroad, out of harm's way.

I don't know if Elizabeth Taylor chose to call this collection *The Blush* because she considered "The Blush" the best of the twelve stories, but I can guess that she must have been proud of it. It deals with deception, as so many of her later stories do. What causes Mrs Allen to blush is almost comic in its nastiness, though the misery of the deluded man who supplies her with the unpleasant information is conveyed, as always, compassionately. The deception is, of course, of the everyday variety, and all the more dreadful for being so. The quotidian is Elizabeth Taylor's province, where the ordinary are to be found extraordinary, as she thought they should.

Paul Bailey, London, 1986

The Ambush

A FEW weeks after the funeral, Catherine went back to stay with the Ingrams. Uncertain, during those weeks, how much grief was suitable to her—for she and Noël had not been officially engaged and in the eyes of the world she saw her status as mourner undecided—she had shown no sign of sorrow, for one tear might release the rest and one word commit her to too many others. Her fortitude was prodigious, even alone after the funeral when all that she had keyed herself up to was over. She avoided the drawer where his letters were; the air about her, at the art school by day and with her parents at home, was full of warnings and tensions. She felt jolted and stunned, as if she had been in his car at the time of the accident, and she walked about slowly and carefully, suffering from a stiffness of her limbs and a sensation of vertigo. By the end of the first month her effort had told on her—the energy spent in fending off other people and the sympathy they might offer, the holding back of tears, left her weak and apathetic. The boredom of her grief was not its easiest part to bear—the irritation of having nothing but her loss ever enter her mind now, when once she had had so many thoughts, dulled all her days and her dreams at night. Her parents were thankful when she took herself off to the Ingrams and they could come down from their tightrope and relax.

Mrs Ingram met her at the station. Catherine saw her first, standing on the platform, scanning the carriages as the

1

doors began to open. She was wearing a mauve gingham frock and her white hair was blown back from her forehead and from that plane below her high cheekbone which Noël had had, too, and which made, Catherine thought, those two faces the most beautiful she had ever known.

"I am here," she said, setting down her suitcase for a moment while she was kissed.

"Dear Catherine, I am so glad you came before it was dark." Her seemingly meaningless phrases were often found, later, to have some meaning after all.

A soldier, for Mrs Ingram's sake, not Catherine's, had lifted the suitcase and was carrying it out to the station-yard. A wake of devotion always followed her and Catherine joined her own homage to the rest.

They got into Mrs Ingram's tinny little shopping car and drove away through the red-brick Thames-side village and down darkening lanes scented with elder-blossom.

"Esmé is still with us," Mrs Ingram said. "I wanted you to come before his leave was over."

Esmé was Noël's elder brother, adored first-born, whom Catherine had heard of for years, resented somewhat on Noël's account and seen fleetingly at the funeral, to which he had come from abroad.

"You will be someone young for him," Mrs Ingram said.

She drove as if she were a goddess in a chariot, her white hands confident, her head erect. Sometimes she waved to children who pressed back against the hedges, staring.

They turned through iron gates into the tunnel of trees leading up to the house; a haze of gnats danced under the bitten leaves; cow-parsley was grey in the shadows. The drive ended suddenly and they were under the high façade of the house with its rows of Georgian windows diminishing in height at each storey and the panelled door and rounded fanlight. Lights were on on the ground floor and a young

man came out of the house and down the steps towards
them.

Not quite up to the shock of seeing even a slight resemblance to Noël, Catherine was obliged to look up at what
she had steadfastly at the funeral ignored. This brother had
the same eyes, shrewd and alert, lines from laughter
beneath them—for as a family they seemed to have laughed
a great deal. When Mrs Ingram did so, she became even
more beautiful—a rare thing in a woman; laughter en-
livened her features and never disorganised them. Esmé
was heavier than Noël; his features less defined; his colour
paler. The beautiful flatness under the cheekbone he
lacked. Catherine could imagine him in middle-age rather
puffy under the eyes and stout and inactive and even, later,
gouty as his father had been.

Catherine saw the house in the last of the light—
perhaps its most magical time. It was ashen and flat against
the dark trees. Beyond the lawns the river slid by and she
could hear and smell the tumbling water at the weir. Moths
followed them into the lighted hall. Damp had drained
colour from great patches of the crimson walls, but the
room was in brilliant contrast to outside. The tall clock only
tocked, never ticked, Noël had said. On a table was a disarray
of flowers and baskets and vases, for Mrs Ingram had left
for the station in the middle of building a great pyramid of
honeysuckle and peonies. She now, leading Catherine to
her room, looked back regretfully at her interrupted work.
Could not Esmé have fetched me, then? Catherine wondered, apologetic as always. Or wouldn't he?

From her bedroom's two long windows she would be able
to see the river when it was daylight again.

"I hope the weir won't disturb you," Mrs Ingram said,
as if Catherine had never stayed in the house before. "I
never hear it now."

When Esmé had brought in the suitcase and gone, Mrs

Ingram embraced Catherine again. "So lovely that you are here," she murmured. "Come down soon and have a drink after your long journey."

She looked round the room, pulled at a curtain and rearranged some white geraniums in a pewter mug before she left Catherine alone.

The girl had the most extraordinary feeling of dizziness from so much sudden beauty—the beauty of Mrs Ingram herself whose footsteps were now light and hastening on the oak staircase, and the house and garden and this room scented with pinks and sounding of the river.

On the wall above the writing-table hung a water-colour drawing of Esmé and Noël as children—vaguely done, insipidly pretty and not worthy of their mother's room. They sat on a sofa together and had a picture-book open across their knees. The smocking on their blouses was painstakingly tinted in and Esmé's tawny curls were carefully high-lighted though nothing much could be made of Noël's straight black hair. His eyes were round and unseeing and bright as forget-me-nots. Fond drawing by a relative, Catherine thought. She herself had never drawn Noël, either fondly or objectively. The nearest she had got to that, she reflected, was once sketching his foot when he was lying on the lawn after swimming. She had been drawing the gable of the boathouse and branches of a chestnut-tree and, for some reason turning to look at him, began on a corner of the paper to draw his foot with its bony ankle and raised veins. Then he had slapped one foot against the other to chase off a fly. She had rubbed out the sketch, blown at the paper and quickly covered up the smudge with a clump of rushes. She had trembled as if hoping to hide some misdemeanour, but was calm again when he stood up and came to look at her drawing. She had added an imaginary dragon-fly above the rushes and then, at his request, a heron. What became of the drawing she could not now recall.

Mrs Ingram was in the hall when Catherine went downstairs. The uncarpeted staircase could be an ordeal, so much of it exposed to the hall, and now Mrs Ingram looking up and smiling as she stripped leaves from the peonies. Voices echoed here, and whatever Esmé said as he came from the library carrying a decanter was lost to Catherine.

She took her glass of whisky and Esmé pulled a chair out from the table for her where she could watch Mrs Ingram's flower-arranging. A pale greyhound lay on a window-seat, and Esmé sat down beside it, fingering its silky ears.

"Other women I know do the flowers in the morning," he said.

"You need not stay with me."

She tore some leaves from a stalk with an asperity to match her voice, an asperity Catherine had never heard before, but which she always had felt to be a dreaded possibility in people as decisive as Mrs Ingram.

Esmé sat far back in the shadows stroking the dog's ears, not replying.

This hall was at the heart of the house—open to the garden in fine weather, a place for casual conversations and chance meetings. The last time Catherine was there it had been filled with wreaths, cushions of carnations propped against chair-legs, Mrs Ingram's hoop of roses and camellias lying on the table. It had had a drab symmetry about it, with its suggestion of flowers bought by the dozen and Catherine had seen the glance it received, the weary contempt with which it was put aside as beyond improving.

Now Mrs Ingram carried the big soup tureen of flowers and stood it against the wall, stepped back to view it while Esmé yawned and clapped his hands, then called to his dog and went out into the garden.

Mrs Ingram sank into a chair the moment he had gone as if she had no need now to be busy.

"I shall send you to bed soon," she told Catherine. "You

look tired after your journey;" and then as Catherine was
obediently finishing her whisky she asked, "How are you
getting over Noël?"

At home, no one had dared to say this name and Catherine
was unprepared to hear it and could think of no reply.

"Don't defer it, or try to pay off in instalments," Mrs
Ingram said. "One only pays more in the end." She sat so
still with her elbow among the litter of leaves on the table
and her cheek resting on her hand. "I knew you would take
it in this way, poor Catherine, and that is why I asked you
to come here." She gave the smile that was always so
much remembered when Catherine had left her and was
trying to reassemble the look of her, feature by feature, in
her mind. The smile was the only uncertain thing about
her, wavering, pleading; deep lines broke up the smoothness
of her face and her regality—the Blue Persian look, Noël
had called it—vanished.

I love her, Catherine thought. I could never withstand
her, no matter what she wanted of me.

When she was in bed, she wondered why such a thought
had come to her, when there was no longer anything Mrs
Ingram could want of her, no longer anything she could
ask her to relinquish. Strangeness and the physical beauty
of the place overtook her. She was under this roof again, but
the old reason for being there was gone. Listening to the
weir, lying in the flower-scented room, between the cool
sheets (Mrs Ingram's linen was glassier than anyone else's,
she thought), she fell under the spell of the family again,
although the one of it she loved was dead. Missing him, it
was in this place she wanted to be, no other.

She heard Esmé crossing the gravel again and calling in a
low voice to the dog.

*   *   *

In the morning, the garden, drenched with dew, flashed

with rainbow colours; the meadows on the other side of the river gently steamed. The sun had already warmed the carpet under the windows. Catherine stood there barefoot looking down on the dazzling scene. She could hear the grating sound of oars in rowlocks before Esmé appeared round the river-bend under the silvery willows. She watched him coming up from the boathouse. His footprints were dark on the dewy grass and the dog's paw-prints ran in circles about them. He was especially tender with his dog, would be with all animals and with children, as some bachelors are, she guessed.

When Catherine had stayed in the house on other occasions, Mrs Ingram had always had breakfast in bed. She had a clever way of not being seen coming downstairs, but of being discovered later very busy about the house, at her desk or coming from the kitchen with a list in her hand, as if she had been about since daybreak, the reins gathered in her hands for hours. This morning, Catherine, coming downstairs, was surprised to hear Mrs Ingram and Esmé talking in the dining-room. "If you object, I can go to *his* place instead." That was Esmé. Then his mother said quickly, "I don't object . . ." and paused, as if she were about to add a second clause that would take the meaning from the first. She got as far as saying 'but' and then heard the footsteps in the hall and Catherine came into the room to a tense silence and rearranged expressions.

Mrs Ingram was standing by the window, drinking coffee. Esmé rose from the table and, doing so, scattered some pages of a letter over the carpet. His mother glanced, then glanced away. She really does look as if she has been up since dawn, Catherine thought. Perhaps *she* doesn't sleep, either.

The warmth of Mrs Ingram's smile welcomed her and Catherine regretted the stiffness and timidity of her own that answered it. She felt full of a jerky vagueness, and the beginning of a fear that the house with its associations might undermine her and expose some nerve in an intolerable way. She was constantly alarmed at the possibility of behaving badly and trembled to think of the presumption of not holding back a grief that Mrs Ingram herself seemed able to contain. The strain was not merely of never being herself, but of not knowing who she any longer was.

She took a chair opposite Esmé's and Mrs Ingram came back to the table to pour out coffee, but without sitting down.

"Are you going out sketching this morning?" she asked Catherine; for that was how she had spent her mornings on other visits.

Catherine stared down at her boiled egg as if she were wondering what curious object she had been given, so dismayed was her expression. Esmé, who had put away his letter, looked across at her but wished that he had not. There was a sign of a crack in her sedate composure.

She said: "Yes, I think I will do that."

"Then we shall all meet at luncheon."

Mrs Ingram was brisk, as if now Catherine was disposed of for the morning. This was unlike her, Esmé thought: but his mother was definitely up to something and he wondered for whom ill was boded, Catherine or himself. Some wonderful ill, no doubt, he thought; done for one's good; a great, bracing, visionary ill. Even if I want to paint again, Catherine thought, I don't want to be in the painting *mood* —so exposed and inviting. She had brought her painting materials with her and knew that she must rouse herself to work again and better here, perhaps, than at her own home with its too patent watchfulness, the irritating parental concentration upon her and all her doings and the secret discussions she could imagine just as if she had overheard them. "Now she is painting again. Such a good sign. We will pretend not to have noticed."

So after breakfast she went down to the river and along the bank until she reached the lock. Much about the Thames Valley is Victorian—the canopied steamers and the red brick lock-keepers' houses and the little shelters with spiked edges to their wooden roofs like miniature railway platforms. The garden beds of marguerites, calceolarias, were edged with whitewashed stones and slung about with whitened chains; all was neat and two-dimensional, like a primitive painting, captivating, bright and unconvincing.

Beyond the lock was a stretch of river, darkened and smothered by dusty, summer chestnuts; the oily, olive-green water slid by, was brown when the sun went in; a boat tied up in the rushes had no reflection. The other bank, in contrast, was silvery with aspens and willows, with shifting white leaves and light.

She sat on the bank and unpacked her water-colours. The sun was strong now, the light banal, she thought fretfully, narrowing her eyes to blur what she saw too sharply and with too many irrelevances. She felt a deep reluctance to begin painting on this lulled and buzzing mid-morning, and felt too that she had been expelled, excluded from Mrs Ingram's presence where she wanted to be, and sent off to do her painting as a child might be sent to practise scales.

She slapped at the horse-flies biting her bare legs. They were always a plague—the towing-path flies—and on other summer days Noël had sat beside her and waved them away with his handkerchief while she painted. Her irritation suddenly heeled over into grief and she dropped her brush, stunned, appalled, as the monstrous pain leapt upon her. Her painting—the faint washes of grey and green which had lifted the paper—dried in the sun, the jar of water was scarcely coloured. She rested her elbows on the drawing-board and covered her eyes with her hands, waiting for this moment to pass. Esmé, going along the tow-path to the pub, saw her before she heard his footsteps and would have turned back, but as he hesitated he thought that she had heard him. He was a reticent man but could see no reason for turning his back on sorrow, so against his inclination he went over to her. His dog, following him, sniffed at the paint water and stretched himself out in the shade of some rushes.

Catherine kept her head bent, and began to pack up her painting things as Esmé sat down beside her. She had not been crying. Her face was pale, but her cheek-bones were red where her hands had pressed against them. In a few seconds this colour receded and she seemed more in command of herself.

She unpinned the drawing-paper from the board and tore it across.

"Not a good morning?" he asked.

"I am bitten to death by horse-flies."

"Come with me to the pub and have a drink. I will carry all the paraphernalia."

He had Noël's voice, though he talked too rapidly and stumbled over words. His tongue was not quick enough to keep up with his desire to have the words done with and his part of the conversation over. His manner of speaking was, from nervousness, over-decisive and just when he meant to be tender he sounded stern.

They walked along the towing-path in silence until they reached The Rose and Crown—there, the bar was empty until a woman came through from the kitchen, drying her hands, to serve them. She drew the beer and went back to her cooking. Catherine and Esmé sat on the varnished window-seat and looked out at the river. Conversation was uneasy between them. What they had in common was felt by both to be taboo and he, from lack of interest and living abroad, had no idea of what sort of girl she was. This morning, he began to be moved by her forlornness and blamed his mother for letting her mope: something

strenuous and gay should surely have been arranged—
though he could not think what.

"Would you like to play darts?" he asked her. She did
not in the least want to play darts and did not know how,
but his solicitude was so masked, his voice was so abrupt that
she timidly agreed. He was patient and encouraging as her
darts struck the brick wall, once a tin lamp-shade, but
rarely the board, until, as part of her haphazard throwing—
and she had no idea that such a thing could happen—two
darts landed together in the bull's-eye. She glowed at his
amazement and praise. He called in the landlord's wife to
draw them some more beer and to see Catherine's score and
said that he had never done such a thing in his life and
would never do it.

"But I didn't *know*," Catherine said happily. "They
might just as easily have gone out of the window." She could
not have imagined that doing something well in a game
could be so stimulating.

They left the pub and walked back along the towing-path.
Mrs Ingram was sitting on the steps in the sun and she, too,
listened to Esmé's account of Catherine's first game of darts
and she smiled radiantly, as if this was the nicest, gayest
thing that could happen. At luncheon, the three of them
were drawn together : by some simple magic, which Catherine
could not understand, Mrs Ingram no longer seemed cross
or embarrassed with her son, but rather as if she were
acquiescing to some delightful plan he had for the future.
Only when they were drinking coffee on the terrace and
Esmé suggested an afternoon on the river did she detach
herself from them again, making too many excuses—a little
headache and a letter to write and a vague notion that one of
her friends might call. She would not let them delay one
moment. They must go alone and if they wanted tea it
could be packed for them.

Catherine was disappointed, for it was Mrs Ingram she

loved and admired, not Esmé; and Esmé himself looked
sulky again. He watched his mother going away from them
along the terrace and his eyes were full of contempt, as if
he knew some secret she had, which he despised. He stood up
and said "Well, then," in a hearty voice, trying to seem
gaily anticipatory, but not managing it.

Mrs Ingram had a small motor launch which was used
for visiting her friends up and down the river, and in this,
sitting beside one another in wicker chairs, Esmé and
Catherine drove sedately under the summer darkness of the
trees. The easy gaiety had gone and Catherine felt helplessly
that Mrs Ingram had pushed her off alone with Esmé
against his inclination, and she was puzzled to think what
motive she could have for doing such a thing. If it was
simply to be rid of her, then she need never have invited
her; that she might be trying to lay the foundations of
something deeper between Esmé and Catherine than this
slight acquaintance they had was not in character with her
rôle of possessive mother. Noël had once said: "It is lucky
for you that you love me, not Esmé. Mamma never allows
any girls within yards of her darling. They are just to be
devoted to one another." Equally, that Mrs Ingram simply
had, as she said, a headache was unthinkable. She was not a
woman who would be likely to have headaches or confess to
such frailty if she had. She was ordinarily so proudly direct
that excuses were alien to her. She would not deign to
dissemble or explain. When she did so, Catherine felt uneasily compelled to wonder why.

Some cloud was between mother and son. In other
circumstances, Catherine would have thought that it
gathered from Mrs Ingram's jealousy. Her coldness might
have been caused by Catherine and Esmé wishing to escape
together, not from the reverse. For the second time that day
Esmé set out to dispel the melancholy his mother had
induced in Catherine. She recognised along the river

features of the landscape she had discovered with Noël, and
Esmé pointed them out to her as if she had never seen them
before. Soon, his discourse became more than a commentary
upon the river banks and the late Victorian and Edwardian
houses, gabled and balconied, the rustic summer-houses,
the lawns with urns of geraniums and flag-poles, and
weeping copper-beeches, and began to be an excursion back
through time; for here, he said, Noël had rammed the boat
into the mooring-posts, ("Yes, he told me," Catherine
whispered) and on that island disturbed a wasps' nest in a
hollow tree.

They were held up outside the lock, and at last the
keeper came out and opened the gates. The peace and heat
inside the lock were intense. As the water went down,
Catherine, grasping a slimy chain looked long at Esmé who
stood up with the painter over a bollard and was lighting a
a cigarette. The most veiled of men, she suddenly thought
him; his in some ways handsome face expressionless with
discretion, the speed of his talk overcoming his reluctance
to talk at all, and his easiness, his courtesy—with the lock-
keeper at this moment—proclaiming almost that beyond
this he was far removed and could not love, be loved, or
have any exchange at all that courtesy or kindness did not
dictate.

Beyond the lock, she found herself thinking: We shall
have to come back through it, in an echo of the triumph
with which she used to say this aloud to Noël. Each lock had
prolonged their aloneness, as indeed it prolonged her time
with Esmé, but it was so much as an echo of an old thought
that it came to her that she found herself telling Esmé now
how once it had been.

At first, she thought his courtesy had deserted him. "Oh,
look, a kingfisher," he said.

She looked in the wrong place and it was gone. "Another
thing about the river," he said. "We can quite safely bring

our unhappiness here. No one can reach it or be contaminated by it, as on dry land. I have felt that I was in
quarantine with it these last weeks."

"But at home . . .?" Catherine began.

"No, I don't think we can be safe there," he said rapidly.
"I mean that other people would not be safe from *us*."

"I wonder if your mother wishes now that she hadn't
invited me."

"My dear little Cathy, what an odd thing to wonder. Or
should I not call you 'Cathy'?"

"I liked to hear it." She had blushed with pleasure and
surprise. "I wondered if the sight of me depresses her," she
said humbly. "I suppose that we have only Noël in common.
By the fact of just being myself I can only go on and on
reminding her of him."

"You remind her of yourself and that she loves you. The
dead can become too important, just by dying. Any ordeal
is yours surely? Coming back to the house and the river and
so much obviously that only you and Noël knew about." He
spoke rather aloofly, to imply that being in love was not in
his province, though he acknowledged it in hers. "But I
understand," he added, "that it was probably now or
never."

"I shouldn't have liked it to be never. I love it here,
being with your mother and seeing the house again—the
beautiful house . . ."

"Yes, I think it is the only nice one on the river," he
said. He turned the boat round in mid-stream. "All of those
rose-red villas with their fretwork balconies and the con-
servatories and so much wistaria . . . yet I miss it when I'm
away, and it comes at me with a dismaying, not wholly
depressing rush, when I return. Living in one place all of
one's youth makes being an expatriate very difficult. I
think I shall go and live in London for a bit before I go
abroad again. Go by instalments, as it were. It may halve the

pains of departure. I must tell Mamma. Until I have done so, know nothing of it, please."

"Of course not," Catherine whispered.

*   *   *

"Has Esmé said anything to you about leaving here?" Mrs Ingram asked Catherine a day or two later.

"No."

'Wide-eyed surprise, poorly done,' thought Mrs Ingram. "I know he feels concerned about leaving me and may not like to mention it; but he will have to go in the end. He mustn't be tied to my apron-strings for ever."

'Apron-strings' had too homely a connotation altogether —Esmé and his mother were not just pottering cosily about a kitchen. So fine that they were invisible were the threads with which she drew him to her: it was by the most delicate influence that she had had him break off his long-ago engagement and had later tried to stop him from going abroad, though seeming all the time to speed him on his way. I know that she sometimes does wrong, Catherine thought. But I love her and I should be happy if she cared to dominate me, too. She had wanted to be her daughter-in-law and part of the enchantment. She and Noël would have lived nearby, and come often to the house. "The children are coming to luncheon," Mrs Ingram would say. Once, the summer before, Catherine, sitting out on the steps in front of the house had heard Mrs Ingram in the hall, telephoning a friend. "Do come over. I shall be alone. The children are going to the cinema." Bliss had flowed through Catherine. She had shut her eyes, feeling the sun, hearing the sounds of the garden—the birds and insects and the weir. Yes, it was bliss in those days, she thought, and she still sensed the magic of this quieter house, though the river was more melancholy to her and the family diminished and Mrs Ingram's composure no longer completely holding.

Someone called Freddie began to be talked of—a friend of Esmé's, a painter, of whose painting Mrs Ingram disapproved. She compared it unfavourably with Catherine's. It had, she said, that detestable ingredient, virtuosity. "It allows one to see how clever he has been, and that should never be. I don't want to see the wheels go round or to feel called upon to shout, 'Bravo', as if he were some sweating Italian tenor. One should really feel, 'How easy it must be! How effortless!' I should think—don't you, Catherine?—that an artist must seem too proud to have tried, too careless to have thought of succeeding." Esmé said nothing, so Catherine could not judge if he agreed.

Freddie was expected for luncheon, but did not come.

"Perhaps he didn't feel hungry today," Mrs Ingram said.

So Freddie himself was out of favour along with his paintings, Catherine thought. Mrs Ingram had glanced at Esmé when she had spoken and his face betrayed him by its impassivity.

In the afternoon, Catherine made another attempt to paint, in a tangled part of the garden behind the old stables. In the shade, the nettles and docks were a dark and bitter green and this greenness seemed to tinge the curdy white flowers of elder and cow-parsley. She became gradually absorbed in the shapes and the textures of the leaves—the feathery, the ribbed and spade-like, the giant fern weighted down by a heavy snail. She was pleased with what she was doing and just painting in a bright poppy among the green and silvery green, for contrast, when she saw a snake lying on the path before her at the edge of the shade. It was green, too, of an olive-green to enhance her picture and in a curious way she realised this before she took fright, tiptoeing backwards away from it until she felt safe to turn and run.

She sped up the steps and into the hall, calling for Esmé, then the wonderful sunny slumbrance of the house checked her and she felt disconcerted. A young man came to the drawing-room door, saying, "I wanted Esmé, too."

Oh, I am glad, for Esmé's sake, that he came at last, thought Catherine, pulling up too suddenly and slipping on a rug.

"Scatter-rugs they call these in America," said Freddie, coming to steady her. "A good name. I should like to scatter them all in the river."

He seemed a very neat young man at a first glance. His suit exactly matched his fawn hair and his blue bow-tie matched his pullover and socks. His voice and his Cockney accent were pert and gay, his small eyes very bright. A second impression revealed his bitten nails and dirty shoes and the fact that his slight build and his clothes made him seem more boyish than he was.

"You sound as if you wanted Esmé in a great hurry," he said.

"Yes, I saw a snake round by the stables and I think it is an adder."

"Isn't there a gardener or something?" Freddie asked, looking vaguely out at the terrace.

"I just thought of Esmé first. I left all my painting things there."

"I shouldn't think a snake would harm them. Did you want me to kill it or something?" he asked reluctantly.

"You see, I am sure they are deadly."

"Is that supposed to encourage me?"

He went into the back hall and chose a walking-stick from the umbrella-stand. "Oh, dear, this isn't really up my street. I just hope it's gone away by now. It would have been much better if you had asked a gardener."

They set out towards the stables and he said: "My name is Freddie Bassett. I was expected to lunch. Was there much hard feeling?"

"I am a guest. It isn't for me to say."

"So there was! I ran out of petrol miles from anywhere. So what could I do?"

"You could have telephoned, I suppose."

"Splendid! I knew I was right to try the story out on you first. You spotted the flaw as Mrs Ingram would have done. How can I get round that one? I telephoned, but the silly girl at the exchange said there was no reply. I don't know what these girls are coming to."

"No one would believe you."

"Mrs Ingram will not dare to say so. All right, then, I lost my way."

"This way," said Catherine coldly, taking another path.

"As a matter of fact, I did." He seemed surprised to find himself speaking the truth. "I stopped for a quick one and fell in with a little party. You know how that can be done—complete strangers, but something happens, there is some clemency in the smoke-haze, so that they seem the dearest companions one ever had, one almost weeps with gratitude that they are so sympathetic, so much one's own sort. So helpful in helping one to forget anxiety. I could not tear myself away from them and now I have forgotten them and shall never see them again—only similar ones. When it was closing-time we stayed on, because the landlord was the same sort as well. I felt dreadfully guilty about Esmé, and they were all so sympathetic and so full of condolences and advice about what his mother would say. They came out to see me off and wish me good luck. Then I took the wrong road."

"Wouldn't it have been better not to have come at all?"

"Surely not? I can stay to dinner instead."

Catherine felt frightened. I am not his accomplice, she thought. It is nothing to do with me.

"Do you know when Esmé went out?" he asked. "I want to say that I arrived the minute after."

"I didn't know that he had gone."

"He has taken his mother to a meeting. I hope it is a nice long one and that my head will feel better before she comes back."

They crossed the stables courtyard and Catherine peered through the archway at the path where her painting things were lying beside her folding stool.

"Have I really got to?" Freddie asked. "Oughtn't I to be wearing puttees or something? I am sure it has kindly gone away."

But the snake had only moved farther into the sun. Catherine shrank back and for some strange reason put her hands over her ears. "Oh, Lord!" grumbled Freddie, going forward with the stick held high. Catherine stayed in the courtyard. She heard the stick beating the ground and Freddie swearing, but she would not look. When he came back, he was carrying the stool and the drawing-board and his face was white. "I take it you don't want to go on with this at the moment," he said, handing her the unfinished water-colour without glancing at it. "I just left it there— the snake."

"You did kill it?"

"Yes, I suddenly went mad with fear. It was a dreadful thing to ask someone from London to do. Are you the girl Noël was engaged to?"

"We weren't engaged."

"And now, I understand, Mamma wants you to marry Esmé?"

"I think you are rude and absurd," Catherine said. "It is none of my business, but I don't know how Esmé can tolerate you."

She hurried on ahead of him and turned the corner of the house. There was Esmé walking on the lawn, his head down, his hands in his pockets. He paced up and down dejectedly. When he saw Catherine he smiled and then his smile warmed and he came forward eagerly, quite transformed by the sight of Freddie trailing behind, carrying the folding stool.

*   *   *

"It was a poor grass snake," Mrs Ingram said. "It would have done no harm to anyone and great good to the garden."

"I am just a Cockney. How should I know?" said Freddie. "I did as I was told."

Catherine could only keep saying how sorry she was.

"I am surprised at you," Mrs Ingram said teasingly. "So meticulous in your painting, and to make such a mistake."

It seemed to be Catherine who had failed. Freddie was triumphantly eating dinner instead of lunch, although Catherine would have staked a great deal against such a possibility. She had listened to his long apology with outraged astonishment . . . "tramping along in the blazing heat with my little petrol can in my hand. . . . I went all round some village looking for the Post Office. Wonderful honeysuckle all over it and jars of bull's-eyes in the window. I should have thought there would be some regulation against calling them that, when they are nothing of the kind . . ."

He is putting off the weak part of his story, about the telephone, Catherine thought with interest.

". . . the phone-box was just outside the door and the exchange itself just inside by the bacon-slicing machine. The same pop-eyed old codger who was selling the bull's-eyes went to the switchboard. Twice he got the wrong number. 'Skates the Fishmongers here' was one. The third time I truly thought would be lucky, but there was no reply. 'There is always someone there. There are hundreds of servants. They are moneyed folk,' I said. 'Comfortably *placed*, as you might say.' 'I daresay,' he said, sarcastically, as if I were a child, or drunk. 'All the same, they're not answering.' "

Esmé bent down and stroked his dog, trying to hide a smile.

"You *might* have answered," Freddie whined complainingly. "After I had trudged so far and had such a horrible time and my hands were so *sore* with carrying the petrol can." He glanced at them, wincing.

"It *is* only pretending, isn't it?" said Mrs Ingram, her voice as sweet as honey. As if she thought that Freddie was over-exciting himself, she changed the conversation.

So Freddie triumphed. He triumphed over his headache and he stayed to dinner and Catherine thought that he would manage to stay the night as well. Esmé was quiet and full of a peace that Catherine could understand. She remembered the contentment of saying those words to herself, "We are under the same roof." She had known how beautiful it can be to come to the close of the day and lie down in bed, thinking those words. Then the house itself became haunted, enchanted, spellbound with love.

Her heart began to ache again and her throat almost shut. The flesh is endlessly martyred by grief, humiliated by nausea and vomitings, bothered and alarmed; breath checked and the heart belaboured; the eyes stabbed viciously until they unload their tears and the tongue as bitter as if it had tasted poison. 'This Freddie does not know,' Catherine thought, and she felt pity for Esmé and kinship with him.

*　　　*　　　*

Dinner was soon over, for there was hardly any conversation to prolong it. Once Mrs Ingram said to Freddie: "Catherine paints, too," and Freddie answered, "So I saw."

Beset by midges they drank coffee out on the terrace above the steps. "An irritating noise," Freddie said, referring to the weir, and Catherine thought, So it is. The sound is what you are yourself at the moment: if you are in despair, it sounds despairing; tumultuous if you are angry; romantic when you are in love.

Esmé and Freddie never exchanged remarks or glances and when Mrs Ingram went indoors Catherine felt herself so much in the way that she followed her and was conscious of their nervous silence as she walked away.

Mrs Ingram came from the back hall carrying a bunch of roses. "I was going to ask you if you would like to come, but don't if you aren't up to it. To Noël's grave, I mean. No, you would rather not, I am sure," she said quickly. "It is difficult to guess how other people feel about such a thing. I know it is old-fashioned and unimaginative of me, but I feel comforted when I go there."

Catherine did not know herself how she felt or would feel, but she went with Mrs Ingram and carried the roses for her. They walked slowly along the scented lane to the church by the river; then through the lych-gate under the limes. She began to be afraid. She remembered the church-yard carpeted with wreaths and the raw earth mounded up ready for its dreadful purpose; the groups of black figures standing, as if stunned, among the graves and the lime-trees only just in leaf which now were ready to flower. She wondered if she would have to face some overpowering monument, for death is alien enough in itself without some of the things which are done afterwards as being appropriate. She hung back on the gravel path as she had done once before and Mrs Ingram, humming peacefully, her pink cardigan hung over her shoulders, stepped quickly across the grass. Following her, raising her eyes only to look at a safely eighteenth-century headstone with a cherub's head and wings and saffron rosettes of lichen all over the crumbling stone, Catherine saw the name 'Ingram' with a sense of shock. But there were groves of Ingrams, among them Noël's father, who was to share the roses. Unlike most of the other riverside families, this had kept its bones in one place for at least two hundred years. The last Ingram had, Catherine was relieved to find, only a simple white wooden cross with his name painted in black. She faced this steadily, feeling that she had been spared an awkwardness. "Only until the ground has sunk," Mrs Ingram said, throwing away stale water and going to fetch fresh.

Catherine took a step back, as if she might otherwise sink with the earth. She felt obscenity, not peace, around her.

"I suppose that little liar will be staying the night," said Mrs Ingram, returning from the water tap. "I can't pretend that I fancy having him under my roof."

She knelt down and began to strip leaves off the roses and break off the big blood-red thorns.

When her plans have failed, there are always the flowers to do, Catherine thought. The night I arrived, I suppose that she left them until late as an excuse for sending Esmé to the station—to make us be together from the start. But Esmé wouldn't fall in with the plan—a new habit in him, I should think.

Then the words 'my darling Noël' broke across her reflections. For a second, she wondered if she had said them aloud, caught on the in-breath of a sob. But Mrs Ingram finished the flowers calmly and then they walked home along the towing-path. The river was bronze in the sunset and the fluffy meadow-grasses filled with a pinkish light.

Esmé and Freddie were still sitting on the terrace. Freddie was now in Mrs Ingram's wicker chaise-longue, his hands clasped behind his head and his legs stretched out comfortably. Esmé sat, rather awkwardly, with his grey-hound across his lap. They both struggled to rise when they saw Mrs Ingram and Catherine crossing the lawn, but Mrs Ingram ignored them and went round the house by a side-way and Catherine followed her.

*   *   *

Catherine went up to bed and stood by the open window, looking out into the dark garden. A misty moonlight furred the grass, like rime, and white ghosts rose off the weir. 'I have been to the churchyard,' she thought, 'and now I have had enough.'

She drew one of the heavy velvet curtains round her like a cloak. 'I cannot *not* feel when I am here,' she thought. 'Especially when I am so *meant* to feel.' Was not Mrs Ingram, she wondered, trying to make her realise the extent of her loss, as if nothing could be accomplished until this was done or any other part of her plan proceeded with.

Mrs Ingram came in to say good night and found Catherine wound up in the curtain.

"So Freddie went—as if he overheard me and meant to prove me wrong."

She came to the window and they both looked out at the garden, listening to the weir.

On the blanched terrace below Esmé's greyhound appeared, then Esmé. He went down the steps and was lost in the dark garden. Sometimes he reminded Catherine of his brother. Family likenesses in gestures are stranger than those of feature or build and often more poignant and she had sometimes been moved by such a slight thing as the inclination of his head as he walked, so mysteriously the same as Noël.

"He is going away next week," Mrs Ingram said.

"And I," said Catherine quickly. "I must go too." She was struggling with tears and her voice was rough and abrupt. She breathed very steadily and presently the tears receded and she said: "I must get back to work, you know. I must. . . ."

"What makes it difficult for living here may make it good for painting," Mrs Ingram said.

"Too beautiful," Catherine began. She put her hands over her face and tears ran down her wrists and the insides

of her arms. Mrs Ingram waited, as if she were measuring
the fall of tears and knew when the limit of grief was
reached and only then put out her hand and touched
Catherine's shoulder.

"You see, I can't stay. You do see?" Her heart had been
twice ambushed in this house and now she was desperate to
escape. Yet did Mrs Ingram understand? She said nothing.
She simply took Catherine in her arms and kissed her—but
with a welcoming, a gathering-in gesture as if to one who
has come home at last rather than to someone preparing to
go away.

The Blush

THEY were the same age—Mrs Allen and the woman who came every day to do the housework. "I shall never have children now," Mrs Allen had begun to tell herself. Something had not come true; the essential part of her life. She had always imagined her children in fleeting scenes and intimations; that was how they had come to her, like snatches of a film. She had seen them plainly, their chins tilted up as she tied on their bibs at meal-times; their naked bodies had darted in and out of the water-sprinkler on the lawn; and she had listened to their voices in the garden and in the mornings from their beds. She had even cried a little dreaming of the day when the eldest boy would go off to boarding-school; she pictured the train going out of the station; she raised her hand and her throat contracted and her lips trembled as she smiled. The years passing by had slowly filched from her the reality of these scenes—the gay sounds; the grave peace she had longed for; even the pride of grief.

She listened—as they worked together in the kitchen—to Mrs Lacey's troubles with her family, her grumblings about her grown-up son who would not get up till dinner-time on Sundays and then expected his mother to have cleaned his shoes for him; about the girl of eighteen who was a hairdresser and too full of dainty ways which she picked up from the women's magazines, and the adolescent girl who moped and glowered and answered back.

My children wouldn't have turned out like that, Mrs Allen thought, as she made her murmured replies. "The more you do for some, the more you may," said Mrs Lacey. But from gossip in the village which Mrs Allen heard, she had done all too little. The children, one night after another, for years and years, had had to run out for parcels of fish and chips while their mother sat in The Horse & Jockey drinking brown ale. On summer evenings, when they were younger, they had hung about outside the pub: when they were bored they pressed their foreheads to the window and looked in at the dark little bar, hearing the jolly laughter, their mother's the loudest of all. Seeing their faces, she would swing at once from the violence of hilarity to that of extreme annoyance and, although ginger-beer and packets of potato crisps would be handed out through the window, her anger went out with them and threatened the children as they ate and drank.

"And she doesn't always care who she goes there *with*," Mrs Allen's gardener told her.

"She works hard and deserves a little pleasure—she has her anxieties," said Mrs Allen, who, alas, had none.

She had never been inside The Horse & Jockey, although it was nearer to her house than The Chequers at the other end of the village where she and her husband went sometimes for a glass of sherry on Sunday mornings. The Horse & Jockey attracted a different set of customers—for instance, people who sat down and drank, at tables all round the wall. At The Chequers no one ever sat down, but stood and sipped and chatted as at a cocktail-party, and luncheons and dinners were served, which made it so much more respectable: no children hung about outside, because they were all at home with their Nannies.

Sometimes in the evenings—so many of them—when her husband was kept late in London, Mrs Allen wished that she could go down to The Chequers and drink a glass of sherry and exchange a little conversation with someone; but she was too shy to open the door and go in alone: she imagined heads turning, a surprised welcome from her friends, who would all be safely in married pairs; and then, when she left, eyes meeting with unspoken messages and conjecture in the air.

Mrs Lacey left her at midday and then there was gardening to do and the dog to be taken for a walk. After six o'clock, she began to pace restlessly about the house, glancing at the clocks in one room after another, listening for her husband's car—the sound she knew so well because she had awaited it for such a large part of her married life. She would hear, at last, the tyres turning on the soft gravel, the door being slammed, then his footsteps hurrying towards the porch. She knew that it was a wasteful way of spending her years—and, looking back, she was unable to tell one of them from another—but she could not think what else she might do. Humphrey went on earning more and more money and there was no stopping him now. Her acquaintances, in wretched quandaries about where the next term's school-fees were to come from, would turn to her and say cruelly: "Oh, *you're* all right, Ruth. You've no idea what you are spared."

And Mrs Lacey would be glad when Maureen could leave school and "get out earning". "I've got my geometry to do," she says, when it's time to wash-up the tea-things. "I'll geometry you, my girl," I said. "When I was your age, I was out earning."

Mrs Allen was fascinated by the life going on in that house and the children seemed real to her, although she had never seen them. Only Mr Lacey remained blurred and unimaginable. No one knew him. He worked in the town in the valley, six miles away and he kept himself to himself; had never been known to show his face in The Horse & Jockey. "I've got my own set," Mrs Lacey said airily.

"After all, he's nearly twenty years older than me. I'll make sure neither of my girls follow my mistake. 'I'd rather see you dead at my feet,' I said to Vera." Ron's young lady was lucky; having Ron, she added. Mrs Allen found this strange, for Ron had always been painted so black; was, she had been led to believe, oafish, ungrateful, greedy and slow to put his hands in his pockets if there was any paying out to do. There was also the matter of his shoe-cleaning, for no young woman would do what his mother did for him—or said she did. Always, Mrs Lacey would sigh and say: "Goodness me, if only I was their age and knew what I know now."

She was an envious woman: she envied Mrs Allen her pretty house and her clothes and she envied her own daughters their youth. "If I had your figure," she would say to Mrs Allen. Her own had gone: what else could be expected, she asked, when she had had three children? Mrs Allen thought, too, of all the brown ale she drank at The Horse & Jockey and of the reminiscences of meals past which came so much into her conversations. Whatever the cause was, her flesh, slackly corseted, shook as she trod heavily about the kitchen. In summer, with bare arms and legs she looked larger than ever. Although her skin was very white, the impression she gave was at once colourful—from her orange hair and bright lips and the floral patterns that she always wore. Her red-painted toe-nails poked through the straps of her fancy sandals; turquoise-blue beads were wound round her throat.

Humphrey Allen had never seen her; he had always left for the station before she arrived, and that was a good thing, his wife thought. When she spoke of Mrs Lacey, she wondered if he visualised a neat, homely woman in a clean white overall. She did not deliberately mislead him, but she took advantage of his indifference. Her relationship with Mrs Lacey and the intimacy of their conversations in the kitchen he would not have approved, and the sight of those calloused feet with their chipped nail-varnish and yellowing heels would have sickened him.

One Monday morning, Mrs Lacey was later than usual. She was never very punctual and had many excuses about flat bicycle-tyres or Maureen being poorly. Mrs Allen, waiting for her, sorted out all the washing. When she took another look at the clock, she decided that it was far too late for her to be expected at all. For some time lately Mrs Lacey had seemed ill and depressed; her eyelids, which were chronically rather inflamed, had been more angrily red than ever and, at the sink or ironing-board, she would fall into unusual silences, was absent-minded and full of sighs. She had always liked to talk about the "change" and did so more than ever as if with a desperate hopefulness.

"I'm sorry, but I was ever so sick," she told Mrs Allen, when she arrived the next morning. "I still feel queerish. Such heartburn. I don't like the signs, I can tell you. All I crave is pickled walnuts, just the same as I did with Maureen. I don't like the signs one bit. I feel I'll throw myself into the river if I'm taken that way again."

Mrs Allen felt stunned and antagonistic. "Surely not at your age," she said crossly.

"You can't be more astonished than me," Mrs Lacey said, belching loudly. "Oh, pardon. I'm afraid I can't help myself."

Not being able to help herself, she continued to belch and hiccough as she turned on taps and shook soap-powder into the washing-up bowl. It was because of this that Mrs Allen decided to take the dog for a walk. Feeling consciously fastidious and aloof she made her way across the fields, trying to disengage her thoughts from Mrs Lacey and her troubles; but unable to. "Poor woman," she thought again and again with bitter animosity.

She turned back when she noticed how the sky had

darkened with racing, sharp-edged clouds. Before she could reach home, the rain began. Her hair, soaking wet, shrank into tight curls against her head; her woollen suit smelt like a damp animal. "Oh, I am drenched," she called out, as she threw open the kitchen door.

She knew at once that Mrs Lacey had gone, that she must have put on her coat and left almost as soon as Mrs Allen had started out on her walk, for nothing was done; the washing-up was hardly started and the floor was unswept. Among the stacked-up crockery a note was propped; she had come over funny, felt dizzy and, leaving her apologies and respects, had gone.

Angrily, but methodically, Mrs Allen set about making good the wasted morning. By afternoon, the grim look was fixed upon her face. "How dare she?" she found herself whispering, without allowing herself to wonder what it was the woman had dared.

She had her own little ways of cosseting herself through the lonely hours, comforts which were growing more important to her as she grew older, so that the time would come when not to have her cup of tea at four-thirty would seem a prelude to disaster. This afternoon, disorganised as it already was, she fell out of her usual habit and instead of carrying the tray to the low table by the fire, she poured out her tea in the kitchen and drank it there, leaning tiredly against the dresser. Then she went upstairs to make herself tidy. She was trying to brush her frizzed hair smooth again when she heard the door-bell ringing.

When she opened the door, she saw quite plainly a look of astonishment take the place of anxiety on the man's face. Something about herself surprised him, was not what he had expected. "Mrs Allen?" he asked uncertainly and the astonishment remained when she had answered him.

"Well, I'm calling about the wife," he said. "Mrs Lacey that works here."

"I was worried about her," said Mrs Allen.

She knew that she must face the embarrassment of hearing about Mrs Lacey's condition and invited the man into her husband's study, where she thought he might look less out-of-place than in her brocade-smothered drawing-room. He looked about him resentfully and glared down at the floor which his wife had polished. With this thought in his mind, he said abruptly: "It's all taken its toll."

He sat down on a leather couch with his cap and his bicycle-clips beside him.

"I came home to my tea and found her in bed, crying," he said. This was true. Mrs Lacey had succumbed to despair and gone to lie down. Feeling better at four o'clock, she went downstairs to find some food to comfort herself with; but the slice of dough-cake was ill-chosen and brought on more heartburn and floods of bitter tears.

"If she carries on here for a while, it's all got to be very different," Mr Lacey said threateningly. He was nervous at saying what he must and could only bring out the words with the impetus of anger. "You may or may not know that she's expecting."

"Yes," said Mrs Allen humbly. "This morning she told me that she thought. . . ."

"There's no 'thought' about it. It's as plain as a pike-staff." Yet in his eyes she could see disbelief and bafflement and he frowned and looked down again at the polished floor.

Twenty years older than his wife—or so his wife had said —he really, to Mrs Allen, looked quite ageless, a crooked, bow-legged little man who might have been a jockey once. The expression about his blue eyes was like a child's: he was both stubborn and pathetic.

Mrs Allen's fat spaniel came into the room and went straight to the stranger's chair and began to sniff at his corduroy trousers.

"It's too much for her," Mr Lacey said. "It's too much to expect."

To Mrs Allen's horror she saw the blue eyes filling with tears. Hoping to hide his emotion, he bent down and fondled the dog, making playful thrusts at it with his fist closed.

He was a man utterly, bewilderedly at sea. His married life had been too much for him, with so much in it that he could not understand.

"Now I know, I will do what I can," Mrs Allen told him. "I will try to get someone else in to do the rough."

"It's the late nights that are the trouble," he said. "She comes in dog-tired. Night after night. It's not good enough. 'Let them stay at home and mind their own children once in a while,' I told her. 'We don't need the money.' "

"I can't understand," Mrs Allen began. She was at sea herself now, but felt perilously near a barbarous, unknown shore and was afraid to make any movement towards it.

"I earn good money. For her to come out at all was only for extras. She likes new clothes. In the daytimes I never had any objection. Then all these cocktail-parties begin. It beats me how people can drink like it night after night and pay out for someone else to mind their kids. Perhaps you're thinking that it's not my business, but I'm the one who has to sit at home alone till all hours and get my own supper and see next to nothing of my wife. I'm boiling over some nights. Once I nearly rushed out when I heard the car stop down the road. I wanted to tell your husband what I thought of you both."

"My husband?" murmured Mrs Allen.

"What am I supposed to have, I would have asked him? Is she my wife or your sitter-in? Bringing her back at this time of night. And it's no use saying she could have refused. She never would."

Mrs Allen's quietness at last defeated him and dispelled

the anger he had tried to rouse in himself. The look of her, too, filled him with doubts, her grave, uncertain demeanour and the shock her age had been to him. He had imagined someone so much younger and—because of the cocktail-parties—flighty. Instead, he recognised something of himself in her, a yearning disappointment. He picked up his cap and his bicycle-clips and sat looking down at them, turning them round in his hands. "I had to come," he said.

"Yes," said Mrs Allen.

"So you won't ask her again?" he pleaded. "It isn't right for her. Not now."

"No, I won't," Mrs Allen promised and she stood up as he did and walked over to the door. He stooped and gave the spaniel a final pat. "You'll excuse my coming, I hope."

"Of course."

"It was no use saying any more to her. Whatever she's asked, she won't refuse. It's her way."

Mrs Allen shut the front door after him and stood in the hall, listening to him wheeling his bicycle across the gravel. Then she felt herself beginning to blush. She was glad that she was alone, for she could feel her face, her throat, even the tops of her arms burning, and she went over to a looking-glass and studied with great interest this strange phenomenon.

The Letter-Writers

AT eleven o'clock, Emily went down to the village to fetch the lobsters. The heat unsteadied the air, light shimmered and glanced off leaves and telegraph wires and the flag on the church tower spreading out in a small breeze, then dropping, wavered against the sky, as if it were flapping under water.

She wore an old cotton frock, and meant to change it at the last moment, when the food was all ready and the table laid. Over her bare arms, the warm air flowed, her skirt seemed to divide as she walked, pressed in a hollow between her legs, like drapery on a statue. The sun seemed to touch her bones —her spine, her shoulder-blades, her skull. In her thoughts, she walked nakedly, picking her way, over dry-as-dust cow-dung, along the lane. All over the hedges, trumpets of large white convolvulus were turned upwards towards the sky— the first flowers she could remember; something about them had, in her early childhood, surprised her with astonishment and awe, a sense of magic that had lasted, like so little else, repeating itself again and again, most of the summers of her forty years.

From the wide-open windows of the village school came the sound of a tinny piano. "We'll rant, and we'll roar, like true British sailors," sang all the little girls.

Emily, smiling to herself as she passed by, had thoughts so delightful that she began to tidy them into sentences to put in a letter to Edmund. Her days were not full or busy and the gathering in of little things to write to him about took up a large part of her time. She would have made a paragraph or two about the children singing, the hot weather—so rare in England—the scent of the lime and privet blossom, the pieces of tin glinting among the branches of the cherry trees. But the instinctive thought was at once checked by the truth that there would be no letter-writing that evening after all. She stood before an alarming crisis, one that she had hoped to avoid for as long as ever she lived; the crisis of meeting for the first time the person whom she knew best in the world.

'What will he be like?' did not worry her. She knew what he was like. If he turned out differently, it would be a mistake. She would be getting a false impression of him and she would know that it was temporary and would fade. She was more afraid of herself, and wondered if he would know how to discount the temporary, and false, in her. Too much was at stake and, for herself, she would not have taken the risk. "I agree that we have gone beyond meeting now. It would be retracing our steps," he had once written to her. "Although, perhaps if we were ever in the same country, it would be absurd to make a point of *not* meeting." This, however, was what she had done when she went to Italy the next year.

In Rome, some instinct of self-preservation kept her from giving him her aunt's address there. She would telephone, she thought; but each time she tried to—her heart banging erratically within a suddenly hollow breast—she was checked by thoughts of the booby-trap lying before her. In the end, she skirted it. She discovered the little street where he lived, and felt the strangeness of reading its name, which she had written hundreds of times on envelopes. Walking past his house on the opposite pavement, she had glanced timidly at the peeling apricot-coloured plaster. The truth of the situation made her feel quite faint. It was frightening, like seeing a ghost in reverse—the insubstantial suddenly solidifying into a patchy and shabby reality. At the window on the first floor, one of the shutters was open; there was the darkness of the room beyond, an edge of yellow curtain and, hanging over the back of a chair set near the window, what looked like a white skirt. Even if Edmund himself threw open the other shutter and came out on to the balcony, he would never have known that the woman across the road was one of his dearest friends, but, all the same, she hastened away from the neighbourhood. At dinner, her aunt thought she might be ill. Her visitors from England so often were—from the heat and sight-seeing and the change of diet.

The odd thing to Emily about the escapade was its vanishing from her mind—the house became its own ghost again, the house of her imagination, lying on the other side of the road, where she had always pictured it, with its plaster unspoilt and Edmund inside in his tidied-up room, writing to her.

He had not chided her when she sent a letter from a safer place, explaining her lack of courage—and explain it she could, so fluently, half-touchingly yet wholly amusingly—on paper. He teased her gently, understanding her decision. In him, curiosity and adventurousness would have overcome his hesitation. Disillusionment would have deprived him of less than it might have deprived her; her letters were a relaxation to him; to her, his were an excitement, and her fingers often trembled as she tore open their envelopes.

They had written to one another for ten years. She had admired his novels since she was a young woman, but would not have thought of writing to tell him so; that he could conceivably be interested in the opinion of a complete stranger did not occur to her. Yet, sometimes, she felt that without her as their reader the novels could not have had a fair existence. She was so sensitive to what he wrote, that she felt her own reading half created it. Her triumph at the end of each book had something added of a sense of accomplishment on her part. She felt it, to a lesser degree, with some other writers, but they were dead; if they had been living, she would not have written to them, either.

Then one day she read in a magazine an essay he had written about the boyhood of Tennyson. His conjecture on some point she could confirm, for she had letters from one of the poet's brothers. She looked for them among her grandfather's papers and (she was never impulsive save when the impulse was generosity) sent them to Edmund, with a little note to tell him that they were a present to repay some of the pleasure his books had given her.

Edmund, who loved old letters and papers of every kind, found these especially delightful. So the first of many letters from him came to her, beginning, 'Dear Miss Fairchild'. His handwriting was very large and untidy and difficult to decipher, and this always pleased her, because his letters took longer to read; the enjoyment was drawn out, and often a word or two had to be puzzled over for days. Back, again and again, she would go to the letter, trying to take the problem by surprise—and that was usually how she solved it.

Sometimes, she wondered why he wrote to her—and was flattered when he asked for a letter to cheer him up when he was depressed, or to calm him when he was unhappy. Although he could not any longer work well in England— for a dullness came over him, from the climate and old, vexatious associations—he still liked to have some foothold there, and Emily's letters refreshed his memories.

At first, he thought her a novelist manqué, then he realised that letter-writing is an art by itself, a different kind of skill, though, with perhaps a similar motive—and one at which Englishwomen have excelled.

As she wrote, the landscape, flowers, children, cats and dogs, sprang to life memorably. He knew her neighbours and her relation to them, and also knew people, who were dead now, whom she had loved. He called them by their Christian names when he wrote to her and re-evoked them for her, so that, being allowed at last to mention them, she felt that they became light and free again in her mind, and not an intolerable suppression, as they had been for years.

* * *

Coming to the village, on this hot morning, she was more agitated than she could ever remember being, and she began to blame Edmund for creating such an ordeal. She was angry with herself for acquiescing, when he had suggested that he, being at last in England for a week or two, should come to see her. "For an hour, or three at most. I want to look at the flowers in the *very* garden, and stroke the cat, and peep between the curtains at Mrs Waterlow going by."

'He knows too much about me, so where can we begin?' she wondered. She had confided such intimacies in him. At that distance, he was as safe as the confessional, with the added freedom from hearing any words said aloud. She had written to his mind only. He seemed to have no face, and certainly no voice. Although photographs had once passed between them, they had seemed meaningless.

She had been so safe with him. They could not have wounded one another, but now they might. In *ten* years, there had been no inadvertent hurts, of rivalry, jealousy, or neglect. It had not occurred to either to wonder if the other would sometimes cease to write; the letters would come, as surely as the sun.

"But will they now?" Emily was wondering.

She turned the familiar bend of the road and the sea lay glittering below—its wrinkled surface looking solid and without movement, like a great sheet of metal. Now and then a light breeze came off the water and rasped together the dried grasses on the banks; when it dropped, the late morning silence held, drugging the brain and slowing the limbs.

*   *   *

For years, Emily had looked into mirrors only to see if her hair were tidy or her petticoat showing below her dress. This morning, she tried to take herself by surprise, to see herself as a stranger might, but failed.

He would expect a younger woman from the photograph of some years back. Since that was taken, wings of white hair at her temples had given her a different appearance. The photograph would not, in any case, show how poor her complexion was, unevenly pitted, from an illness when she was a child. As a girl, she had looked at her reflection and thought 'No one will ever want to marry me' and no one had.

When she went back to the living-room, the cat was walking about, smelling lobster in the air; balked troubled by desire, he went restlessly about the little room, the pupils of his eyes two thin lines of suspicion and contempt. But the lobster was high up on the dresser, above the Rockingham cups, and covered with a piece of muslin.

Emily went over to the table and touched the knives and forks, shook the salt in the cellar nicely level, lifted a wine glass to the light. She poured out a glass of sherry and stood, well back from the window—looking out between holly-hocks at the lane.

Unless the train was late, he should be there. At any moment, the station taxi would come slowly along the lane and stop, with terrible inevitability, outside the cottage. She wondered how tall he was—how would he measure against the hollyhocks? Would he be obliged to stoop under the low oak beams?

The sherry heartened her a little—at least, her hands stopped shaking—and she filled her glass again. The wine was cooling in a bucket down the well and she thought that perhaps it was time to fetch it in, or it might be too cold to taste.

The well had pretty little ferns of a very bright green growing out of the bricks at its sides, and when she lifted the cover, the ice-cold air struck her. She was unused to drinking much, and the glasses of sherry had, first, steadied her; then, almost numbed her. With difficulty, she drew up the bucket; but her movements were clumsy and uncertain, and greenish slime came off the rope on to her clean dress. Her hair fell forward untidily. Far, far below, as if at the wrong end of a telescope, she saw her own tiny face looking back at her. As she was taking the bottle of wine from the bucket, she heard a crash inside the cottage.

She knew what must have happened, but she felt too muddled to act quickly. When she opened the door of the living-room she saw, as she expected, the cat and the lobster and the Rockingham cups spread in disorder about the floor.

She grabbed the cat first—though the damage was done now—and ran to the front door to throw him out into the garden; but, opening the door, was confronted by Edmund, whose arm was raised, just about to pull on the old iron bell. At the sight of the distraught woman with untidy hair and her eyes full of tears, he took a pace back.

"There's no lunch," she said quickly. "Nothing." The cat struggled against her shoulder, frantic for the remains of the lobster, and a long scratch slowly ripened across her cheek; then the cat bounded from her and sat down behind the hollyhocks to wash his paws.

"How do you do," Emily said. She took her hand away from his almost as soon as she touched him and put it up to her cheek, brushing blood across her face.

"Let us go in and bathe you," he suggested.

"Oh, no, please don't bother. It is nothing at all. But, yes, of course, come in. I'm afraid . . ." She was incoherent and he could not follow what she was saying.

At the sight of the lobster and the china on the floor, he understood a little. All the same, she seemed to him to be rather drunk.

"Such wonderful cups and saucers," he said, going down on his knees and filling his hands with fragments. "I don't know how you can bear it."

"It's nothing. It doesn't matter. It's the lobster that matters. There is nothing else in the house."

"Eggs?" he suggested.

"I don't get the eggs till Friday," she said wildly.

"Well, cheese."

"It's gone hard and sweaty. The weather's so . . ."

"Not that it isn't too hot to eat anything," he said quickly. "Hotter than Rome. And I was longing for an English drizzle."

"We had a little shower on Monday evening. Did you get that in London?"

"Monday? No, Sunday we had a few spots."

"It was Monday here, I remember. The gardens needed it, but it didn't do much good."

He looked round for somewhere to put the broken china. "No, I suppose not."

"It hardly penetrated. Do put that in the wastepaper-basket."

"This cup is fairly neatly broken in half, it could be riveted. I can take it back to London with me."

"I won't hear of it. But it is so kind . . . I suppose the cat may as well have the remains of this—though not straight away. He must be shown that I am cross with him. Oh, dear, and I fetched it last thing from the village so that it should be fresh. But that's not much use to you, as it's turned out."

She disappeared into the kitchen with her hands full of lobster shells.

He looked round the room and so much of it seemed familiar to him. A stout woman passing by in the lane and trying to see in through the window might be Mrs Waterlow herself, who came so amusingly into Emily's letters.

He hoped things were soon going to get better, for he had never seen anyone so distracted as Emily when he arrived. He had been prepared for shyness, and had thought he could deal with that, but her frenzied look, with the blood on her face and the bits of lobster in her hands, made him feel that he had done some damage which, like the china, was quite beyond his repairing.

She was a long time gone, but shouted from the kitchen that he must take a glass of sherry, as he was glad to do.

"May I bring some out to you?" he asked.

"No, no thank you. Just pour it out and I will come."

When she returned at last, he saw that she had washed her face and combed her hair. What the great stain all across her skirt was, he could not guess. She was carrying a little dish of sardines, all neatly wedged together as they had been lying in their tin.

"It is so dreadful," she began. "You will never forget being given a tin of sardines, but they will go better with the wine than the baked beans, which is the only other thing I can find."

"I am *very* fond of sardines," he said.

She put the dish on the table and then, for the first time, looked at him. He was of medium height after all, with broader shoulders than she had imagined. His hair was a surprise to her. From his photograph, she had imagined it white—he was, after all, ten years older than she—but instead, it was blond and bleached by the sun. 'And I always thought I was writing to a white-haired man,' she thought.

Her look lasted only a second or two and then she drank her sherry quickly, with her eyes cast down.

"I hope you forgive me for coming here," he said gravely. Only by seriousness could he hope to bring them back to the relationship in which they really stood. He approached her so fearfully, but she shied away.

"Of course," she said. "It is *so* nice. After all these years. But I am sure you must be starving. Will you sit here?"

How are we to continue? he wondered.

She was garrulous with small talk through lunch, pausing only to take up her wine-glass. Then, at the end, when she had handed him his coffee, she failed. There was no more to say, not a word more to be wrung out of the weather, or the restaurant in Rome they had found they had in common, or the annoyances of travel—the train that was late and the cabin that was stuffy. Worn-out, she still cast about for a subject to embark on. The silence was unendurable. If it continued, might he not suddenly say, "You are so different from all I had imagined", or their eyes might meet and they would see in one another's nakedness and total loss.

*   *   *

"I *did* say Wednesday," said Mrs Waterlow.

"No, Thursday," Emily insisted. If she could not bar the doorway with forbidding arms, she did so with malevolent thoughts. Gentle and patient neighbour she had always been and Mrs Waterlow, who had the sharp nose of the total abstainer and could smell alcohol on Emily's breath, was quite astonished

The front door of the cottage opened straight into the living-room and Edmund was exposed to Mrs Waterlow, sitting forward in his chair, staring into a coffee-cup.

"I'll just leave the poster for the Jumble Sale then," said

Mrs Waterlow. "We shall have to talk about the refreshments another time. I think, don't you, that half a pound of tea does fifty people. Mrs Harris will see to the slab cake. But if you're busy, I mustn't keep you. Though since I am here, I wonder if I could look up something in your Encyclopaedia. I won't interrupt. I promise."

"May I introduce Mr Fabry?" Emily said, for Mrs Waterlow was somehow or other in the room.

"Not Mr *Edmund* Fabry?"

Edmund, still holding his coffee cup and saucer, managed to stand up quickly and shake hands.

"The author? I could recognise you from your photo. Oh, my daughter will be so interested. I must write at once to tell her. I'm afraid I've never read any of your books."

Edmund found this, as he always found it, unanswerable. He gave an apologetic murmur, and smiled ingratiatingly.

"But I always read the reviews of them in the Sunday papers." Mrs Waterlow went on, "I'm afraid we're rather a booky family."

So far, she had said nothing to which he could find any reply. Emily stood helplessly beside him, saying nothing. She was not wringing her hands, but he thought that if they had not been clasped so tightly together, that was what would have happened.

"You've *really* kept Mr Fabry in the dark, Emily," said Mrs Waterlow.

Not so *you* to *me*; Edmund thought. He had met her many times before in Emily's letters, already knew that her family was 'booky' and had had her preposterous opinions on many things.

She was a woman of fifty-five, whose children had grown up and gone thankfully away. They left their mother almost permanently, it seemed to them, behind the tea-urn at the village hall—and a good watching-place it was. She had, as

Emily once put it, the over-alert look of a ventriloquist's dummy. Her head, cocked slightly, turned to and fro between Emily and Edmund. 'Dyed hair' she thought, glancing away from him. She was often wrong about people.

"Now, don't let me interrupt you. You get on with your coffee. I'll just sit quiet in my corner and bury myself in the Encyclopaedia."

"Would you like some coffee?" Emily asked. "I'm afraid it may be rather cold."

"If there *is* some going begging, nothing would be nicer. 'Shuva to Tom-Tom', that's the one I want." She pulled out the Encyclopaedia and rather ostentatiously pretended to wipe dust from her fingers.

She has presence of mind, Edmund decided, watching her turn the pages with speed, and authority. She has really thought of something to look up. He was sure that he could not have done so as quickly himself. He wondered what it was that she had hit upon. She had come to a page of photographs of Tapestry and began to study them intently. There appeared to be pages of close print on the subject. So clever, Edmund thought.

She knew that he was staring at her and looked up and smiled; her finger marking the place. "To settle an argument," she said. "I'm afraid we are a very argumentative family."

Edmund bowed.

A silence fell. He and Emily looked at one another, but she looked away first. She sat on the arm of a chair, as if she were waiting to spring up to see Mrs Waterlow out—as indeed she was.

The hot afternoon was a spell they had fallen under. A bluebottle zig-zagged about the room, hit the window-pane, then went suddenly out of the door. A petal dropped off a geranium on the window-sill—occasionally—but not often enough for Edmund—a page was turned, the thin paper rustling silkily over. Edmund drew his wrist out of his sleeve and glanced secretly at his watch, and Emily saw him do it. It was a long journey he had made to see her, and soon he must be returning.

Mrs Waterlow looked up again. She had an amused smile, as if they were a couple of shy children whom she had just introduced to one another. "Oh, dear, why the silence? I'm not listening, you know. You will make me feel that I am in the way."

You preposterous old trollop, Edmund thought viciously. He leant back, put his finger-tips together and said, looking across at Emily; "Did I tell you that cousin Joseph had a nasty accident? Out bicycling. *Both* of them, you know. Such a deprivation. No heir, either. But Constance very soon consoled herself. With one of the Army padres out there. They were discovered by Joseph's batman in the most unusual circumstances. The Orient's insidious influence, I suppose. So strangely exotic for Constance, though." He guessed—though he did not look—that Mrs Waterlow had flushed and, pretending not to be listening, was struggling hard *not* to flush.

"Cousin Constance's Thousand and One Nights," he said. "The padre had courage. Like engaging with a boa-constrictor, I'd have thought."

If only Emily had not looked so alarmed. He began to warm to his inventions, which grew more macabre and outrageous—and, as he did so, he could hear the pages turning quickly and at last the book was closed with a loud thump. "That's clinched *that* argument," said Mrs Waterlow. "Hubert is so often inaccurate, but won't have it that he can ever be wrong." She tried to sound unconcerned, but her face was set in lines of disapproval.

"You are triumphant, then?" Edmund asked and he stood up and held out his hand.

When she had gone, Emily closed the door and leant against it. She looked exhausted.

"Thank you," she said. "She would never have gone otherwise. And now it is nearly time for *you* to go."

"I am sorry about Cousin Joseph. I could think of no other way."

In Emily's letters, Mrs Waterlow had been funny; but she was not in real life and he wondered how Emily could suffer so much, before transforming it.

"My dear, if you are sorry I came, then I am sorry, too."

"Don't say anything. Don't talk of it," she begged him, standing with her hands pressed hard against the door behind her. She shrank from words, thinking of the scars they leave, which she would be left to tend when he had gone. If he spoke the truth, she could not bear it; if he tried to muffle it with tenderness, she would look upon it as pity. He had made such efforts, she knew; but he could never have protected her from herself.

He, facing her, turned his eyes for a moment towards the window; then he looked back at her. He said nothing; but she knew that he had seen the station-car drawing to a standstill beyond the hollyhocks.

"You have to go?" she asked.

He nodded.

Perhaps the worst has happened, she thought. I have fallen in love with him—the one thing from which I felt I was completely safe.

Before she moved aside from the door, she said quickly, as if the words were red-hot coals over which she must pick her way—"If you write to me again, will you leave out today, and let it be as if you had not moved out of Rome?"

"Perhaps I didn't," he said.

At the door, he took her hand and held it against his cheek for a second—a gesture both consoling and conciliatory.

When he had gone, she carried her grief decently upstairs

to her little bedroom and there allowed herself some tears. When they were dried and over, she sat down by the open window.

She had not noticed how clouds had been crowding into the sky. A wind had sprung up and bushes and branches were jigging and swaying.

The hollyhocks nodded together. A spot of rain as big as a halfpenny dropped on to the stone sill, others fell over leaves down below, and a sharp cool smell began to rise at once from the earth.

She put her head out of the window, her elbows on the outside sill. The soft rain, falling steadily now, calmed her. Down below in the garden the cat wove its way through a flower-bed. At the door, he began to cry piteously to be let in and she shut the window a little and went downstairs. It was dark in the living-room; the two windows were fringed with dripping leaves; there were shadows and silence.

While she was washing up, the cat, turning a figure-of-eight round her feet, brushed her legs with his wet fur. She began to talk to him, as she often did, for they were alone so much together. "If you were a dog," she said, "we could go for a nice walk in the rain."

As it was, she gave him his supper and took an apple for herself. Walking about, eating it, she tidied the room. The sound of the rain in the garden was very peaceful. She carried her writing-things to the table by the window and there, in the last of the light, dipped her goose-quill pen in the ink, and wrote, in her fine and flowing hand, her address, and then, "Dear Edmund."

A Troubled State of Mind

IN the old part of the town, between the castle and the cathedral, were some steep and cobbled streets whose pavements were broken open by the roots of plane trees. The tall and narrow houses stood back, beyond the walls of gardens and courtyards, but there were glimpses of them through wrought-iron gates. The quiet here was something that country people found unbelievable. Except for the times when the cathedral bells were ringing, the silence was broken only by the rooks in the castle trees or, as on this afternoon, by the sound of rain.

Lalage left the car in the garage at the foot of the hill and the two girls—Lalage herself and her step-daughter, Sophy—walked as quickly as they could towards home, carrying the smaller pieces of Sophy's luggage, Lalage, already hostess-like (Sophy thought), bowed over to one side with the weight of the bigger suitcase, and the other arm thrust out shoulder-high to right her balance.

The road narrowed gradually to less than a car's width and rain ran fast down the cobbles, swirling into drains. Reaching the gate in the wall, Sophy swung her skis off her back and turned the iron handle. The scraping, rusty sound of it was suddenly remembered and was as strange to her as anything else in a world where every familiar thing had moved into a pattern too fantastic ever—she was sure—to be dealt with or understood. She and Lalla, for instance, going in through this gate as they had done so often before; but

Sophy now at a loss to guess what might be waiting for her inside, in her own home.

Her father, Colonel Vellacott, had always loved Italy and everything Italian and had tried to make a Venetian court-yard in wet England. Its sadness was appalling, Sophy thought. The paving-stones were dark with rain and drops fell heavily from the vine and the magnolia, off statues and urns and, in a sudden gust of wind, rattled like bullets on the broad fig leaves by the wall. In the seats of some iron chairs puddles reflected the cloudy sky.

"John will be back for dinner," Lalage said, as they picked their way across the wet stones—"He had to go because he was in the chair."

Ah yes, 'John', of course, Sophy thought.

The front door opened and Miss Sully came out to take the case from Lalage, primly eager to wring all she could from the peculiar situation. "It is just like old times," she said to Sophy, "when Madam used to come to stay with you in the holidays and I used to listen to hear the gate so that I could run out with a welcome."

'Madam' had been a shock and a calculated one, Sophy thought. She smiled and shook hands. "In the old days, you always said we had grown. Not any more, I hope."

"Grown *up*, I should say."

"Isn't she brown?" said Lalla.

"As brown as a berry."

They went into the dark hall where the Italian influence continued in glass and marble, trailing leaves and a wrought-iron screen which served no purpose. Nothing visible had been altered since Sophy was here last, a year ago, but everything invisible had been. At Sophy's bedroom door, Miss Sully turned away, with promises of tea in five minutes and a fire in the drawing-room. Sophy, standing in the middle of the room, looking about her, but not at Lalla, asked: "How do you get on with *her*?"

"As I always did, trying to be as nice as pie, wearing myself out, really, but not getting anywhere. She is, as we always found her, a mystery woman."

"Kind . . ." Sophy began.

"Kindness itself. Thoughtful, considerate, efficient. But what lies underneath, who knows? Something does. She's learning Italian now."

"Perhaps that's what's underneath. Not enough goes on here for her. She's too intelligent to be a housekeeper, and too ambitious."

"Then why go on?"

Sophy could not now say "I think because she hoped to marry my father." She had sometimes thought it in the past and suddenly wondered if she had ever told Lalla. She felt that she must have done, for she had told her everything, though she no longer could.

"What was Switzerland *like*?" Lalla asked, "I mean really."

"It went on too long."

Sophy put her fingers to the locks of her suitcase, about to spring them open, and then could not be bothered, and straightened her back, thinking, She will wonder why, if I found it too long, I did not come back earlier, as I could have done, and should have done and would have done, if it had not been for *that*. It was always 'that' in her mind—the marriage of her father and her dearest friend. The other questions—Sophy's questions—that hovered between them were too unseemly to be spoken—for instance 'why?' and 'how?' and 'where did it begin?' The only question in the least possible Sophy was turning over in her mind and beginning to make a shape of it in words, when Lalla, before it could be spoken, answered it. Since early girlhood, they had often found their thoughts arriving at the same point without the promptings of speech.

"I am so happy, you know," Lalla said. "It is all so lovely.

in this house and now to have you in it with me at last!
Though," she added quickly, "it is you who have always
been here and I who has at last arrived."

"But, Lalla dear, you always seemed *part* of the house to
me. We never called the spare room anything but 'Lalla's
room'. When other people came to stay, it seemed wrong
to me that they should hang their clothes in your cupboard."

Then she suddenly bent down and unclicked her suitcase
after all, to have something to do with her trembling fingers,
and wondered, what is the spare room called now? I have
made another booby-trap for us, where there already were
too many.

"Did you notice," Lalage asked, as if she had not heard,
"how eagerly Miss Sully ran out to greet you? She has been
quite excited all the week."

"I can understand that." Sophy lifted the lid of the
suitcase and looked gloomily at her creased and folded
clothes. "She loves situations and she wanted to see how I
was facing this one."

"Yes, to see if you were jealous of me, hoping perhaps,
that life here from now on would be full of interesting little
scenes between us, something to sustain and nourish her
while she chops the parsley—which she does—doesn't she?
—with not just *kitchen* venom?"

"She will analyse everything we say and fit it into her
conception of our relationship."

"She has already tried to haunt me with your mother—
so beautiful she was and you are growing up to be her
image."

Sophy lifted her head from the unpacking and could not
help giving a quick look into the mirror before her. "How
absurd!" she said. "If she could throw up a woman so long
dead, how impatiently she must have waited for *me* to
throw *myself* up."

"She longs for incidents. I am sure she will hover to see who pours out the tea and whether, from habit, you will go to your old place at the table."

This was brave of Lalage and seemed to clear the air.

"It is a good thing," Sophy said, "that you and I have read so many novels. The hackneyed dangers we should be safe from."

"We shall be safe *together*," Lalla said. "Loving one another," she added, so quietly that she seemed to be talking to herself.

"Demurrings and deprecations will not escape notice either," said Sophy. "Saying '*you* do it, please,' or 'you go first'. We must beware of every one of those. I will be a straightforward daughter to you, I think. It may be ageing for you, but I think it will be safer than for us to try to be like sisters. I thought of that in Switzerland, and I decided that a daughter has privileges and a rôle to play, which a younger or inferior sister has not."

"As long as I am never called 'Mamma'."

Miss Sully, hovering at the foot of the stairs, heard laughter as the bedroom door opened and Lalage's voice saying with great gaiety "Who—a year ago—would have believed that we could come to this?"

They were on the stairs now, and Miss Sully hurried back to the kitchen for the hot scones. She wanted to watch the approach to the tea table.

This turned out to be disappointing. Sophy went straight to the drawing-room window and, with her back turned to the room, said; "Since last I saw you, Lalla, I've given up milk and sugar. What father used to call 'puppy-fat' turned out just to be fat."

"Then I must do the same," said Lalla and sat down before the tray and took up the tea-pot. "And every time John goes out, we will have those slimming meals I am always reading about at the hairdresser's—meagre things like tomato jellies and stuffed cucumbers and lettuce juice. Meanwhile, you could have a scone, couldn't you?''

Sophy turned from the window and sat down in a chair, opposite the one where she had always sat before.

"Only this time," she said.

Miss Sully, having very slowly put a log on the fire and rearranged the tongs, was now obliged to go. At the door, she heard Sophy say, "Just to celebrate the occasion."

By the time Colonel Vellacott returned from his meeting, a mode of behaviour was established between the two girls. It had often been tried out in their minds during their separation, suggested and explored with nervous tact in their letters to one another.

He found them by the drawing-room fire, Lalage winding wool from Sophy's outstretched hands. Kneeling on the rug, Sophy rocked from side to side, and swayed her arms, turning her wrists deftly as the wool slipped off them. So often, bemused and patient, she had held Lalla's wool for her: the knitting craze came and went, jerseys were seldom finished and, if they were, were sorry things. From past experience, neither had high hopes for this new skein.

"A charming sight," Colonel Vellacott said. They had settled down together already, he was relieved to see. It was like bringing a new dog into a house where another had reigned alone for a long time. The scene might have been prearranged—the girls were so tangled up in wool that they could not extricate themselves and the kisses he gave each on the top of her head were almost simultaneous, Lalla hardly first at all.

That's *that* over, he thought, and for no reason felt self-congratulatory. 'That' for him, was his embarrassment. Now, it was as easy as could be to talk about Switzerland and Sophy most brilliantly took the lead with her descriptions of the school and the lunacy of its inhabitants.

"Don't!" Lalage half-sobbed, gasping with laughter, and wiped her eyes on the ball of wool.

"Ah, you are going into fits," her husband said. He remembered all the holiday laughter in this house, Lalla's cries of "Don't" and her collapsed state, his teasing of them both and his mocking echoes of their girlish phrases. He had felt in those days wonderfully indulgent. "Bring Lalla back with you," he always told Sophy. "It is sad for you to be alone—and sad for her, too." Lalla—the poor orphan child —lived with an aunt, but was more often, in school holidays, at Ancaster, with Sophy.

"Now, Lalla!" he said, in a severe voice. He leant back in his chair and folded his arms with a show of excessive patience. "If you snort again, you must be sent away."

"Oh, please, I *ache*," she implored Sophy, holding the ball of wool tight to her ribs, her beautiful eyes glittering with tears.

"Oh, please, I *ache*, Sophy," said Colonel Vellacott.

"I am only telling you what happened," Sophy said, with what Lalla called her straight face.

"The experience seems to have been worth every penny," her father said.

"Yes, I am truly finished."

The end of the wool slipped from her fingers, she sank back on her heels and looked up at her father, at last returning his gaze, smiling with love and delight, but with a reserve of mischief, too, and that pleased him most of all, it was what gave reality to her warm-heartedness. If she were dissembling her gaiety and friendliness, she would not have dissembled *that*, he thought. It would not have occurred to her as a necessary ingredient of mirth.

*   *   *

Sophy kept up her spirits throughout dinner and then flagged. It was her long journey, the other two said and she agreed. "And you miss the clarity of that air," her father added.

But there were other exhaustions she could less easily endure and the chief was, she saw, that she had cast herself in a rôle that would take too much from her.

She remembered—and this was after she had said good-night and gone to her room—long ago and when her mother was alive, she herself perhaps five or six years old, being taken on a train journey, from Edinburgh, her mother's old home it may have been. Kneeling in her corner seat, breathing on the window, breathing and wiping, in stupefying boredom, she had begun suddenly to talk in baby talk, demanding, for no reason she could now recall, in a lispy, whiny voice that had never been her own, a "chocky bikky." Her mother, gently remonstrating, had made publicly clear that this odd voice was to be regarded as a game. "Icky chocky bikky," Sophy had insisted pouting. It was then that she had first realised her own power of mimicry; power it was and went to her head. She had *become* the nauseating infant she impersonated. Other people in the compartment took the lead from her mother and laughed. Sophy herself had pretended not to hear this and turned her back and breathed on the window again, but soon she could not help herself. "Pitty gee-gees", she said, pointing. When she had tired of talking, she let her eyelids droop and began to suck her thumb as she had scornfully watched other children doing. Her mother, who knew that things were going too far, but was never brisk with her in public, tried to distract her attention, but could not. The performance had been tiring, like playing Lady Macbeth with heart and soul and, in the end, Sophy had become sickened by her own creation, caught in its tentacles and quite unable to escape. Everyone else was tired, too; she knew that her mother was desperate and that glances were exchanged; but she seemed powerless to end the misery. It was too late to speak suddenly in her own voice. What voice was it, and what things did it say? She could remember putting her forehead to the cool window-pane and counting to herself 'One, two, then three and then I'll speak again as I used and they will all know the other voice has gone.' But her shyness was too great, she was too committed to the other character and had no way of breaking loose from it. Badgered, exhausted and embarrassed, she had at last burst into tears, taking refuge, as she wept, against her mother's arm. "Over-tired," the grown-ups said. "Such a long journey. She's stood up to it very well."

Lalla and her father had said goodnight and used the same words, though now the climate was to blame as well. They were no more true than when she was a child. The acting had exhausted her, and nothing else. She could have cried, as she had when a young girl, "Oh, my darling Mamma, why did you have to die?" The words were so loud in her head and her breast that she might have said them aloud. They returned with the aching familiarity of a long time ago, when she had lain in bed after lights-out at boarding-school, or on their first Christmas Eve alone, with her father trying to remember everything her mother had always done, so that Sophy should not be deprived of one sprig of holly or Christmas tree candle. In the end, unbelievably, the words had become a habit and lost their pain. Her life without her mother was different from before, but it was, after all, the same life. If Mamma had been here, she sometimes thought, accepting that she could not be.

This evening the phrase sprang at her with a sudden freshness, the first time for years. She sat down on the edge of her bed and her hands dropped into her lap, palms upwards in a gesture of hopeless inertia. 'If she were alive,' she thought, 'she would be downstairs with father, and Lalla here with me, as she ought to be. Or not under this roof at all. And I should be relieved of this tiring pretence, that won't end with the end of the train journey, as it did before. It will be there waiting for me in the morning and all the mornings after—having to be gay and unself-conscious—as if it were a perfectly normal thing for one's father to marry one's school-friend—fifty-three and eighteen and all plotted and planned with me safely out of the way in a foreign country,' she added, feeling self-pity. 'I must be gracious and hand over my home and my place in it and have, day in, day out, my constant companion chosen for me.'

Sometimes, at school, Lalla had stolen marches on her. She could remember well the case of the borrowed treasure and the broken promise, the forgotten appointment, the betrayed confidence. Many instances came to her mind from the dark place where they had long ago been thrust impatiently away.

'I must get away,' she thought, and her hands sprang to life and were clenched tight, drumming on her knees. 'I must run away from my own home, as soon as I have come back to it.' In Switzerland, she had longed for it so much, in that clear air her father had mentioned, faced for months at a time with the monotony of the snow, and the dark trees that never shed their leaves, as trees ought, she was sure. "Write to me about England," she had begged her father and Lalage. "Describe a nice drizzle, a beautiful muggy evening with the fallen leaves sticking to the pavements. *You* describe it for me, though; not I to you."

Instead, they had written to say that they were getting married. They had met several times in London, for both had been lonely, missing Sophy. In their loneliness they had flown together, and clung, and wished to remain so for ever. The loneliness had been much stressed—orphan and widower, as they constantly referred to themselves. Companionship (and Sophy was to share in this, too) and common interests (both liked going to plays, but seldom did so) were enlarged upon. Love itself was not once mentioned and Sophy was glad that it was not. She was to fly home for the wedding—very quiet, just the three of them and Lalage's aunt. But Sophy would not go. She was on her way up to a chalet for the winter sports and had made arrangements which she could not confuse. She knew that they were glad to have her stay in Switzerland and she was glad to do so, although she was sure that if she had not gone there in the first place, she could have prevented things from reaching such a pass.

Her bedroom, above her father's, overlooked the courtyard and when she heard footsteps out there, she went across to the window and looked out. It was almost dark. Lalage and her father were going for a walk in the rain. He opened the courtyard door into the street and as Lalage passed through it, put his hand on her shoulder.

'Ah, yes, and bedtime, too,' Sophy thought turning away. 'Beyond one's imagination, thank God. I hope I can hide my revulsion from her. I daresay there's nothing to stop her having a baby even. It is perfectly possible.'

Their footsteps and voices faded away down the street. The drizzle continued, and downstairs Miss Sully was singing 'Oh, what a Beautiful Morning.'

'I must get a job,' Sophy thought. 'Without a day's delay.'

*   *   *

"Sophy's job", was soon a great topic of conversation.

Colonel Vellacott was full of facetious suggestions. At every meal some new one came to mind, and Sophy grinned, and wondered if her face would crack in two, as her heart must.

"Oh, hush, I can't hear of it," Lalage would beg her husband, and stuff her fingers in her ears. "Sophy, please!

You will make me think you are running away from *me* and it will be as Miss Sully predicted.'' She kept her hands pressed to her cheekbones, ready to make herself deaf again, if necessary. Her bracelets slid down her thin arms to her elbows. Her eyes were full of pleading.

'Affected,' Sophy thought. 'She used not to be. Father loves it.'

"I always meant to get a job," she said. "I couldn't have just stayed here and looked after the house—which Miss Sully does much better anyhow." But this was dangerous ground and she stepped from it quickly. "I should have taken the Secretarial course with you, Lalla, if Father hadn't made me go to Switzerland first."

"*Made?*" said Colonel Vellacott.

"Persuaded, then."

"Your French was horrible."

"Well, 'made' me, then."

"You'd have loathed the Secretarial School," Lalla said complacently. "I hated every moment."

'And was glad to leave it and get married,' Sophy thought. 'So it was typing and shorthand that drove you to it. He hasn't after all, a spectacular enough amount of money to be married for. And love? If you love him, you show none of it. Perhaps I inhibit you and force you to keep it for when you are alone. In which case, the sooner I go, the better.'

She felt absurdly in the way, but also shut out that they should turn to secrecy because of her.

*   *   *

It was not easy to slip away from Lalage, her too-constant companion, but, one morning, she managed to, and set out, as if on an illicit errand, through wet alleyways towards the Market Place. It had rained for all of the fortnight she had been at home, but had this morning stopped. The clouds had lifted and broken open and bright light, though not yet quite sunshine, poured down over the puddles and dripping eaves. Slate roofs dried rapidly and pavements steamed. It was the end of April.

"We begin the second of May," said the Principal of the Secretarial School in Market Street. She underlined this date on the application form. "Your father will complete this for you." She thought it strange for the girl to come there on her own, making enquiries. Sophy stared at her hands, which were a dark plum colour, scarred from broken chilblains. Clumsy as they were, she used them affectedly, drawing attention to them with hooked fingers as she wrote, and then by twisting round an engagement ring of dull little diamonds.

"I know your father very well," Miss Priestley said. "Although I don't suppose he would be able to place *me*. I was a reporter once upon a time on the *Ancaster Herald* and used to cover some of the Court cases when he was on the bench. And my late fiancé was in his regiment in the war. He didn't come back," she added, in an affectedly casual voice she had learnt at the cinema.

"I'm so sorry," Sophy murmured.

"Yes, we had been engaged for eleven years. But you don't want to listen to all my sad affairs."

Although this was true, Sophy felt obliged to make a sound which she hoped suggested denial as well as a certain amount of discouragement. If only there were something amusing in this she thought. Something with which to decorate the plain statement when I tell them at lunch. But there was not: the bereaved Miss Priestley with her chilblains was saddening and unattractive and the office was stuffy and untidy, not a good example to the pupils.

The sun was shining when Sophy stood, dazed by its brightness, on the steps in Market Street. The Town Hall clock struck twelve. She hurried back home and was there before Lalla returned from the hairdresser's.

"Just *see* what they've done," was Lalla's piteous cry at luncheon. They had always done the same thing and Sophy only briefly glanced.

"Why don't you tell them?" asked Colonel Vellacott and seemed to have an edge of exasperation to his voice.

"I tell them and tell them. As smooth as smooth, I always say. Not a kink or a curl or I shall be so cross."

"It will settle down," Sophy said. "It always does."

They had just finished what Miss Sully called "chicken and all the trimmings."

"They've caught that man," Miss Sully said, as she lifted the dishes off the table. "They gave it out on the one o'clock news."

"What man?" asked Lalla, still fidgeting with her hair.

"The one that assaulted that little boy and then smothered him."

"Oh dear!" Lalage frowned.

"I shouldn't have mentioned it, only I thought you'd like to know. It isn't very nice at mealtimes, I'm afraid." She stacked the plates and carried them away.

"This is a very rum Baba," said Colonel Vellacott, as he always did when given this pudding, and Sophy felt the usual embarrassment, wondering—as she was also used to wondering—just how tedious her friend found this heavy jocularity. Then she remembered that her father was much more Lalage's responsibility. The old situation was reversed. It should be Lalla's task to try to prevent the inevitable phrases, to turn the conversations as deftly as she could as the stale quip rose ominously before them.

'And I shall enjoy seeing how she does it, as time goes on,' she thought. At present, Lalla was merely smiling her bright, usual smile, a guest's smile, vaguely willing.

"I met someone this morning who knows you, Father," Sophy suddenly told him, deciding that as any kind of approach to her embarrassment would lead to it, this would do as well as any. "In fact, I did not so much meet her as go to see her."

Colonel Vellacott waited—with the calm of a man who has nothing to fear—for the mystery to unfold, but Lalla stopped eating, put her fork down on her plate and glanced anxiously at Sophy, who went on: "Though she says you would never be able to place *her*. *Can* you place someone called Miss Priestley, who has a secretarial school—no, college, so sorry—in Market Street?"

"No. She is right. I can't."

"Is she from your past?" Lalla asked. "Poor Miss Priestley! I am glad that I am in your present."

"No, she simply wrote down in shorthand things you said in Court," Sophy explained. "And her fiancé was in the regiment and was killed, but I don't think she blamed you for it."

"It was generous of her. Especially as I survived. I should have thought she would have resented that."

"Why did you go to see her?" Lalla asked, taking up her fork again.

"She is going to teach me to be a secretary."

"Oh no! Then I shall come too, I won't be left here on my own. May I go, too, John?"

"You know that we agreed not to be sisters," Sophy told her. "You have to learn to be my Mamma and stay at home while I go off to school."

"I shall be lonely."

"Mothers are. Though perhaps they get used to it, and even rather like it in the end."

"Why did you go about the business in so odd a way?" her father asked. "There was no necessity to be secretive. If you wanted to do it at all, you should have said so."

"I said, and said."

"We thought you were joking."

"Yes, I knew you thought that."

"And I might have been consulted, I should have thought.
I could have done much better for you than this Miss
Whatshername, of whom I certainly have never heard."

"Then why did you do nothing?"

"Now, Sophy, don't try to be cool with me. You are only
just home from Switzerland and there was all the time in
the world to make arrangements."

"I never like to do things at a leisurely pace," Sophy
said, looking calmly at him. "One may as well get on with
life." As you did, her voice implied.

"But we know nothing of this Miss Thingummy. She
seems a strange end to your education."

"It is what I want, Father."

Lalla, murmuring 'coffee', left the room.

"I was bringing it," said Miss Sully, who was never
caught out. The tray was in her hands.

Instead of going ahead to the drawing-room, Lalla ran
upstairs murmuring 'handkerchief'.

In the dining-room Colonel Vellacott and his daughter
were arguing. "Unlike you, Sophy," Miss Sully heard.

"I've put the coffee in the drawing-room," she said, then
hurried forward to rearrange the fire. But there was nothing
for her to listen to but the sound of their chairs being
pushed back. "Madam will be down directly," she added.

This was unanswerable and unanswered. Sophy crossed
the hall to the drawing-room and without sitting down,
carelessly poured out her father's coffee and her own. She
took hers over to the window-seat and began to sip it,
lifting the cup only a little from its brimming saucer. She
supposed that Lalla was upstairs, waiting for them to finish
their quarrel.

*   *   *

Displeased and austere Colonel Vellacott remained for
days, wearing what Sophy called his Doge's face. With

Lalage, too, and in private, he was reserved. Rebellion was in the air—a youthful contagion that he intended should not spread. Don't *you* go running to some Miss Thingummy, or even worse, his mood seemed to warn her.

That Sophy's action was hardly drastic he constantly reminded himself, but her way of taking it had been cold and secretive. For her to earn her own living was nothing other than he intended and desired, but it seemed to him that there was no desperate need and that for a month or two she might have helped him out with Lalla. 'Helped me out' was his own phrase. He had seen what he called 'Bride's despondency' in Lalage's eyes, in spite of her bright smiles and her laughter. He did not know how to cheer her up; his time was so much given over to public work and there was no theatre here in Ancaster. She was lonely and suffering reaction from the sudden adventure of their courtship and wedding. He could not hide his anxiety that the house was dull and silent and—with all his Italian décor long ago perfected—too completed. She had simply taken over what was there and had had nothing to contribute. Although he was pleased with what he had done, he began to wonder if it was what a bride would hope for. "One day, we will have a change," he had promised, but could not bring himself to move one fern or sconce. She had insisted—not knowing what was good for her—that nothing should be touched and that she loved it exactly as it was.

Sophy's home-coming had raised her spirits and he himself had felt freer and happier and less anxious. He looked forward to entering the house when he returned from his meetings. People who have had the best of both worlds are the crossest of all when the best in one is lost, and he knew this and scolded himself, but the Doge's face remained and, inhibited by his new habit of sternness, he found himself unable to make love to Lalage. The marriage, Miss Sully thought, was crumbling even more quickly than she had predicted.

*   *   *

At Miss Priestley's, Sophy was by far the eldest girl and the slowest one at learning, too. Miserably, she bowed her head over the abominable hooks and dots of her shorthand, or touch-typed rows of percentage signs or fractions where should have been 'Dear Sirs, We beg to confirm receipt of your esteemed order.'

The other girls had left school at sixteen and seemed as quick as birds with their taking down and reading back, always put their carbon paper in the right way round and never typed addresses on upside-down envelopes.

The class-rooms were on the first floor of the old house, a building now given over to offices. The boards were bare and the long tables were ribbed and splintered and ink-stained. Miss Priestley felt the cold and even in May the windows were kept shut, so that the air was chalk-laden and smelt of lead pencils and glue and india-rubber and girls. The windows faced south, over the top branches of budding lilac trees. Below was a tangled garden into which Sophy found herself more and more inclined to stare. At twelve and four, the heavy notes of the Town Hall clock descended on the roof tops in the most gracious—Sophy thought— signal of release. She was the first to have her books closed, knowing before the chimes began that they were imminent; she could feel the air growing tense and the clock gathering itself to strike, and her face would put on its bright, good-bye look, turned expectantly towards Miss Priestley for dismissal.

Then, being free, she was suddenly loth to go home to Lalla's 'I knew you'd hate it!' The other girls clustered together and showed one another their work, but Sophy took down her jacket from its peg. She knew that the others exchanged looks when she left them and when she called out 'goodbye' only one or two answered her, and then in a surprised tone as if it were strange of her to address them.

Sometimes, instead of going home to tea, she would buy an evening paper and read it in a little café in Market Street. The idea of punishment being in the air, it suited her to think of her teacup on the tray at home, unfilled. There, in the Oak Beams Tea Shop, she met Graham Dennis again. He was working in a solicitor's office nearby and had so grown up that she had not recognised him.

*   *   *

The Dennis's parties were famous in Ancaster, and Sophy had been going to them for as long as she could remember. Mrs Dennis always described herself as putting herself out for her young people and was not content with Christmas and birthday parties. There were Hallowe'en parties and garden parties, and parties at the New Year and on Guy Fawkes' Day. Her husband could find no escape. If there were not children bobbing for apples in the hall, they were playing charades in several rooms, or hunting for treasure all over the house. "I shall rope Herbert in," Mrs Dennis told her friends, who, rather aggrieved because she put themselves so much to shame, wondered how she could manage it. Herbert had been roped in to let off fireworks or be Father Christmas. Lately, as Denise and Graham were no longer children, he was roped in to make claret cup or dance with an odd girl out.

Sophy remembered even the first parties, when she was a little girl. After the exquisite orderliness of her own home, the great, shabby, untidy house with its lighted windows and its noise infected her with delicious excitement.

Mrs Dennis was always kindness itself. "You are only young once," she often told her children and their friends and made sure that, as well as youth, they had as many other delights lavished on them as she could find time and money to bestow. At the back of her mind, she knew that the two most important parties of all would come at the end: even in nursery days, watching the little ones departing with their balloons and presents, she felt that she was only rehearsing for the culmination of it all—Denise's wedding and Graham's twenty-first birthday. Now, both were looming in the same year and 'loom' was her own word for their approach. She was confident that she would surpass herself—the Dennis wedding would be talked about for years; but, for the last time of many, Denise would say, as she drove away: "Thank you for doing it all." Beyond, lay a blank future for her mother. But first would come Graham's twenty-first birthday and any champagne left over from that would come in later for the wedding. Only one thing perplexed her, as they went over the list of invitations. Lalage, when staying with Sophy, as she so often was, had always been invited too. For years and years, she had attended the Dennis parties.

"We couldn't leave her out now," Mrs Dennis said.

"And how possibly ask her?" Graham said. "Husbands and wives go to parties together. You'd have to ask that old man."

"He is only your father's age," Mrs Dennis said, but she knew that that was what Graham meant. It was an awkward situation. She realised that she and Herbert were only at the parties themselves in order to see that the food and drink were plentiful and available. Herbert knew his place and preferring it, made off to his study as soon as he was able, and Mrs Dennis was always in and out of the kitchen.

"How sad to leave her out, after all these years, poor girl," she said.

*   *   *

Lalage felt both sad and embarrassed when Sophy's invitation came. Her husband, watching her show of unconcern, realised for the first time the consequences of their romance. The marriage, surviving important hazards, seemed now as likely as not to founder upon trivial matters, on this invitation, for instance, and others that would follow. Lalage had been ardent and generous in her love, to come first in someone's life exalted her and, radiant and incredulous, she had given herself in gratitude. Yet, at the sight of an invitation to a party, she appeared to falter, she glanced away and was confused and could not hide her feeling that she had placed herself in a special position with her contemporaries, was being markedly pushed by them into the ranks of the middle-aged.

Sophy, her father realised, was no longer making things easier, but worsening them. The sooner she could go away and leave them, the better for them all. He could perfectly see this now and wondered how he could hasten what he had so lately tried to prevent.

"As you seem so sure about your typing and shorthand," he said one day, with a great show of tolerance, "and are really settled to it, I am quite willing for you to do the thing properly, to go up to London and train at some reputable place."

But Sophy had not settled to her shorthand and typing; every day she fell back, as the other girls progressed; and now she no longer wanted to go away from Ancaster, having at the twenty-first birthday party, fallen in love with Graham Dennis.

Graham and Sophy had rediscovered one another, as young people do who have lived in the same neighbourhood for years and then been separated by school, so that, meeting in the holidays, they seem almost total strangers. Violent changes of height and voice and manner were bewildering and shyness descended. Now, with all the changes made—as they thought—quite grown-up and likely to remain the same for ever, they could sum one another up, and come to a conclusion. Sophy and Graham concluded that they were in love, that they must always have loved, though first immaturity and then separation had hindered their acceptance of the fact.

To Colonel Vellacott, Graham's National Service had not made the man of him it should. Nonchalant and without ambition, he had spent the two years cheerfully peeling potatoes or drinking in the Naafi. Promotion had seemed to him quite as undesirable as it was unlikely. To Colonel Vellacott's questions, on their first meeting after some years, he gave unsatisfactory answers. Nor did Colonel Vellacott like his clothes—his dirty cord trousers and suède shoes and vivid pullovers. Particularly he disliked—and in a cathedral city it was out of place, as Graham himself was—the car he drove. It was an old London taxi painted yellow, with window-boxes and lace curtains. Once, Graham had had written across the back "Do not laugh, Madam, your daughter may be inside." In love, and serious at last, he had painted this over.

Even so, that *his* daughter should be inside annoyed Colonel Vellacott considerably.

"Lots of young men have cars like it," Sophy told him. "It isn't smart to have a new one. The older and funnier the better."

"Not in a place like this."

"We can't *help* living in a place like this. And I think it's amusing. You were young once yourself, remember."

Lalage who could not easily escape these much dreaded discussions, turned aside.

*   *   *

Sophy and Lalla found their so gallantly planned relationship beginning to wear threadbare. It was difficult to keep up, especially as it was so unproductive of incredulity in others—its primary aim. Their affection for one another was too easily taken for granted and few of their friends or acquaintances seemed to find it at all remarkable. Their laughter about the hackneyed jealousies that might have threatened them was joined in by their guests, who—so infectious was the gaiety—did not realise how much of relief it contained.

Sophy was the first to find the ordeal going on too long. It had become a mere routine of good behaviour, with no congratulation in it for herself. Miss Sully thought, observing the minute omens, that soon the situation would have more piquancy. Lalla seemed dull and puzzled, with nothing to do but mend her clothes, change her library books and water all the ferns—too often, for they began to droop and rot away.

One morning, when Colonel Vellacott was in Court and Sophy at her Typing School, Lalage, feeling more restless than ever, wandered into the kitchen, where Miss Sully was making stuffing for green peppers. Lalla sat on a corner of the table and watched, picking up bits of parsley and chewing them, holding pepper-seeds on the tip of her tongue until it tingled.

Miss Sully, mixing raisins and rice, was talking of the days when she was companion to an old lady whose footman had interfered with one of the gardener's boys. She brought in many a Freudian phrase along with those of the cheapest newspapers and her voice dropped to its cathedral hush as it did when she talked of sex. One side of her neck was a bright red. Deftly her fingers worked and when she took up a large knife and began to chop some mushrooms, she abandoned herself almost obscenely to the job. "What's for pudding?" Lalla asked, like a little girl, as soon as there was quiet again. It had never occurred to her that she might order meals herself. She had once timidly put forward a suggestion that Colonel Vellacott would like jugged hare, but had been told that hare was out of season.

"Well, what *shall* we have?" Miss Sully asked suddenly indulgent. The names of puddings at once went from Lalla's head, although Miss Sully had such a repertoire of them—there was Cabinet Pudding and High Church Pudding and Guardsman's Pudding and even Railway Pudding—they were mostly sponge mixtures, differing with a dash of spice or jam, or a handful of candied peel. Lalla could never remember which was which.

"What about rice pudding?" she asked. "I haven't had that since I was at school."

"Well, we can't very well have rice two courses running, can we?" Miss Sully asked, laughing gently and pointing at the dish of peppers, now ready for the oven. "And you will have to give me plenty of warning for rice pudding, because the grain must soak at least an hour, you know."

Lalage hadn't known.

"Is there anything I can do?" she asked, jumping down from the table. It was only eleven o'clock.

"Well, now, you could run the ribbon through the hem of Miss Sophy's petticoat. I know she'll be wanting it this evening. Then I can get on with some scones for tea." ("Without you under my feet," she seemed to imply.) By the time she had told Lalla where to find the petticoat and then the ribbon and the bodkin, she thought that she could have done the job herself.

"The shiny side of the ribbon facing you, mind," she warned her, thinking, "Really, she's as useless as a little doll."

When Lalla had finished that small task, she carried the petticoat to Sophy's room and laid it carefully on the bed, hoping she would be touched and grateful when she discovered it there. And I would do anything for her, she thought, if there were anything else to do.

She went over to the window and looked down into the courtyard—so still and full of heat and the scent of honeysuckle this sunny morning. On the wall below her, was the starry jasmine that framed her own bedroom window. She leaned out, resting her elbows on the rough stone sill, feeling insecurely attached to space and time—the seconds would never tick on till luncheon, or the silence be broken, or the sun ever again go in.

It was the room behind her that overcame, at last, her sense of unreality—though she had turned her back upon it, she felt it awaiting her attention—Sophy's room, where Sophy shut the door on all that she pretended downstairs and where she was confronted by her own thoughts, which she kept imprisoned in this place. They were almost palpably imprisoned, Lalla suddenly felt, and she spun round quickly from the window as if to catch them unawares.

The room was menacing to her now and laden with treachery, its air heavy with secrets. The clock ticked slyly and a curtain lifted slowly and sank back full of warning. It was an alien territory and one where Lalla knew she had no right to be. Even the way the towels hung by the basin expressed hostility, she thought, and so did the truculent angle of the looking-glass. It did not seem too fanciful to imagine mute things infected by Sophy's own antagonism.

A letter addressed to Graham lay on the writing-table, the envelope unsealed and the pages sticking out from it as if as a reminder that they were to be added to, or something else enclosed.

In terror, Lalla thought, I could find out if I cared to, just where I stand with her and why, for weeks, she has shrugged me aside in that bright, cold way.

She recoiled and then, almost immediately, stepped quickly forward and drew the pages from the envelope, very careful to make no sound, lest Miss Sully, far below in the kitchen, would prick up her ears and sense the treachery.

'It is the worst thing people can do to one another,' she told herself, 'and I knew nothing about myself, when I believed that I could not.'

The first lines—Sophy's lament at Graham's absence for five whole days—Lalla passed over. She was looking only for her own name and, sure that she would find it, turned to the second page.

"Father, of course, will disapprove and say that I should not go, for he gets more stuffy and morose each day. Anyone young is what he can't bear nowadays, and all that we two do is vulgar and absurd. I wish that Lalla would try to be a wife to him and not a romping schoolgirl still. I should think he would like to be quiet for a while and serious, and so should I. To see him all the time exposed to her high spirits—that gather *me* in, but exclude him—and in any case they are far beyond his powers—is quite painful. He is less and less in the house, and when he is, is so sour and gruff. But he can't—so far—be gruff with *her*, so is with me instead. Where can it end? But all the same, I'll brave his wrath and tell him that I'll go away with you."

There was no more. Very gently, Lalla folded the pages and put them inside the envelope. Then she tiptoed from the room. Her heart beat so loudly that she thought it would betray her. Her hands were icy-cold, and hurt, as if they had touched poison.

*   *   *

She tried to eat luncheon, but failed. The sight of the dish of peppers reminded her of how short a time ago she had been sitting in the kitchen, bored and restless, but still innocent and loving.

Perhaps it is a baby already, Sophy thought, when Lalla, too sick to stay, had left the room. She now had her father to herself and in a nonchalant voice said: "Graham and I think of going to France in August, as soon as Denise's wedding is over!"

"You couldn't choose a worse month," said Colonel Vellacott and threw down his napkin and stood up. "I'm worried about Lalla. I think I'll go up to her." Sophy sat alone. Her eyebrows were raised and she looked down at her plate with an air of surprise and curiosity.

* * *

Afterwards she went to her bedroom. The petticoat threaded with its scarlet ribbon lay on the bed, and she wondered if Lalla had done it. She could imagine her trying to while away her mornings with one trivial task after another, spending as long upon them as she could. She pictured her standing in this sunny room, with the petticoat over her arm, feeling lonely and out-of-place. Then a fearful intuition sprang upon Sophy and she swung round and looked for the letter she had so carelessly left on the table. It lay there, just as she expected, and with a trembling hand she picked it up and stared at it. 'I have been read' it seemed to say.

* * *

Miss Sully could now watch things worsening daily. The laughter had worn off: it was strange to her that it had lasted so long.

Lalla recovered from her sickness, but was dispirited. Her attitude towards her husband changed, was appealing and conciliatory and over-anxious. With Sophy she was reserved. They had drawn a long way apart and the distance was clouded with suspicions and mistrust.

Colonel Vellacott, as the letter had stated, was less and less in the house, and when she was alone, Lalla paced up and down, clasping her hands tight to her breast, and then the other words of the letter echoed over and over in her mind, with burning emphasis—"Where can it end? Where can it end?"

"You are run down," her husband told her. He was wonderfully solicitous, yet bored. She seemed unreal to him, but he would do his best for her. This summer he was feeling his age; marriage had drawn too much attention to it, and so much youth in the house underlined it. Once, he had thought it would have the opposite effect.

"You need a holiday, poor Lalla. And you shall have one. In September I should be able to get away for a couple of weeks. How would you like to go to Florence?"

Yes, she would like to go to Florence and she smiled and nodded; but she thought, 'I am not really used to him *here*, and now I must try to get used to him in a foreign country.'

She tried hard to be more wifely to him, but when she made attempts at serious discussion, he smiled so fondly, so indulgently, that she was aggravated. Sophy watched her attempts with grim understanding. 'I know what *this* is all about,' she thought.

So they were all going abroad—Lalla and her husband sedately to Florence, and Sophy and Graham, full of secrecy and excitement to France. There was a great difference, Lalla thought.

*   *   *

"I neglect you shamefully," said Colonel Vellacott. "I promise I will mend my ways after our holiday. I will come off some of my committees."

"But couldn't I go with you?" Lalla asked. "I should be so interested to hear you speak. Just this once?"

"You would be bored to death and, in any case, I'm afraid tonight's meeting is in camera."

To her own distress, her eyes filled with tears. She was most dreadfully sorry for herself and grieved that no one else was.

She knew that the tears were a pity and that he would think her more childish than ever. "Where will it end?" she wondered, as he patted her cheek, saying "goodbye".

Sophy was out with Graham, Miss Sully listening to a Murder play on the wireless in her sitting-room. 'I could teach myself Italian, perhaps,' Lalla thought, and she went to the study and looked along the shelves, but, though there were many books written in Italian, she could find none to teach the language to her. One was expected to know it already.

'In Florence, they will all gabble away and leave me out of it,' she thought, growing sorrier and sorrier for herself. 'It really is too bad.' Now, they were to be joined in Italy by Major and Mrs Mallett, old friends of the Colonel's, a pleasant elderly couple, who still regarded the Colonel as of a younger generation.

'They are only going because he would be so bored with just me,' Lalla thought, crossly. 'Oh, I have been complaisant for too long'; she decided. 'I have tried hard and given in and got nowhere.'

She thought that, instead of meekly waiting up for him she would go up to bed, without telling Miss Sully even. She would turn out the lights and if she were not asleep when he came home, she would pretend to be.

A long drawn-out scream came from Miss Sully's wireless-set as Lalla crossed the hall and went softly upstairs.

*   *   *

When she awoke it was dark and she was still alone. She got out of bed and went to the window. Lamplight shone over leaves in the street beyond the wall and fell over the courtyard. The statues and urns looked blanched. In the centre was an ornamental stand for plants. Its wrought-iron lilies threw slanting shadows across the paving-stones; she could even see the shadows of the fuchsia blossoms—real flowers, these—swinging upon the ground.

It was a romantic place in this light, and she knelt by the window looking down at it, quite awake now and refreshed by her sleep. Then she saw that Sophy and Graham found the place romantic too. She had not noticed them at first, under the dark wall, clasped close together, as still as the tree beyond them. But before Lalla could turn away, she saw them move—they swayed lightly, like the fuchsia blossoms, as if rocked by the same faint air, of which they were so heedless.

She went back to bed and lay down and drew the covers over her, her eyes wide open to the darkness. 'Defend me from envy, God', she prayed. But the poison of it gathered in her against her will and when it had filled her and she was overflowing with despair, tears broke in her like waves. Even Miss Sully, coming upstairs when the play was over, could hear her.

The True Primitive

LILY had not considered culture—as a word or anything else
—until she fell in love. As soon as that happened it, culture,
descended on her. It was as if all the books Mr Ransome had
ever read were thrown at her one after the other—Voltaire,
Tolstoi, Balzac—the sharp names came at her, brutal
spondees, brutally pronounced. She thought, though, that
she hated Dostoievski most of all. "Yes, Dad," Mr Ransome's
two sons continually said, agreeing to rate Zola higher than
Dickens if he wished them to, promising to remember
what he had told them about Michelangelo. Painters
names were also part of the attack, but Lily thought they
sounded gentler. She had felt curiosity about someone
called Leonardo when first she heard him mentioned and
had wondered if he were Harry's cousin. When she asked
Harry he laughed and referred her to his father, which
meant three-quarters of an hour wasted, sitting in the
kitchen listening, and then it was too late for them to go for
their walk. Trembling with frustrated desire, she had learnt
her lesson; she asked no more questions and sat sullenly
quiet whenever the enemy names began again.

Only winter courting seemed to be allowed: then, with
the Thames Valley giving off impenetrable vapours or
taking in, day after day, torrents of rain until the river rose
and spread over the fields, Harry was free to take her out;
except, of course, for his two evenings at the Art School.
They held hands coming back in the bus from the cinema,

kissed beneath dripping trees in the muddy lane, choked and whispered in the fog.

"Silly notion, venturing out tonight," Mr Ransome would tell them. "You've no right, letting her catch her death, Harry."

"I think it's easing up now," Lily would say. "Just the clearing-up shower. And a spot or two of rain doesn't do anyone any harm."

Mr Ransome, with a daunting-looking book open in front of him, would be hurriedly unfolding his spectacles.

"We ought to be going," Lily whispered.

"Man is a political animal," boomed Mr Ransome, wanting to throw as many words at them as he could before they escaped, but Lily had gone, was through the scullery and already standing in the wet garden and Harry sent an apologetic smile back at his father and followed her.

"Good Lord," said Lily. "Once he gets going."

"He's a wonderful old man," Harry said.

"You're both afraid of him, I think—you and Godfrey."

"We *respect* him," Harry said sententiously. "He's been a good father and since Mother died he has no one to read to in the evenings. He misses that."

'She did the best thing, dying,' Lily thought.

Mr Ransome was a lock-keeper. He and his sons lived in a red-brick cottage at the side of the lock. On hot summer afternoons, the garden was what people going through in their boats called a riot of colour. The primary colours assaulted the eye—salvias, geraniums, lobelias, calceolarias were made all the more dazzling by everything being white-washed that Mr Ransome could lay his brush on—flower-tubs, step-edges, the boulders round flower-beds, the swinging chains round the little lawns. In winter-time, it seemed that it could not really have been so bright.

Now, when all the locks down the river were closed, the cottage was lost in a cauldron of steam and the sad sound of the weir came drearily through the fog. Mr Ransome wondered how Harry and Lily could prefer the sodden lanes to a nice fire and a book to read beside it. He read so much about great passions, of men and women crossing continents because of love, and enduring hardship and peril, not just the discomforts of a dark, wet night—but he could not see Harry and Lily go out without feeling utter exasperation at their fecklessness.

"It will be lovely when the summer comes," Lily sometimes said; but Harry knew that it would not be, if by 'lovely' she meant they would have long evenings together in the golden meadows or walking along the towing-path. "He does like us to get out with our sketching, Godfrey and me," he said.

"I don't mind. We can go miles away. You can sketch with one hand and I'll sit beside you and hold the other."

"We couldn't very well do that, you see, because Dad likes to come out with us."

"I can't think why you bother with it when you've got such a nice job."

Harry knew why he bothered. His father, self-taught painter, had once had a picture hung in a local exhibition— an oil-painting, moreover. "I jib at nothing," he had explained. The bright, varnished scene hung in the parlour now. "It was not for sale," he said, when no one bought it. Jibbing at nothing, he had used a great deal of paint and had, in some way, caught the hard, venomous colours of his own garden. 'The Towing Path of A Sunday' was inscribed carefully on the frame. The white chains stood out thickly, like icing piped on the canvas; the chestnut-trees had pink cones of blossom stuck about them and dropped down sharp ovals of shadow on the emerald grass. "If I had of had tuition," Mr Ramsay so often said. He would see to it, he added, that his sons should not look back and have to say the same. In their earliest days they had been given paint-boxes and sketching-blocks; he had taken them to London to the National Gallery and shown them the Virgin of the Rocks and, standing in front of it, lectured them on Leonardo. They had not known which was most painful—their embarrassment or their shame at their own disloyalty in suffering it. Young as they were at the time, they realised that he was much stared at—the thin, fierce man with his square beard and so old-fashioned clothes—but they could not help feeling that he deserved it, booming away as he did in the echoing gallery. They even began to think that he expected to be noticed and took pleasure from it.

Harry and Godfrey, articled in respectable offices in the nearby town, were not quite yet a disappointment to him; for many great men mature late, their father reminded them, reach their height after middle age: Voltaire, for one. They went on with their art classes at evening school and were painstaking enough in their desire to please; but, some-times, looking at them and then at their feeble paintings, Mr Ransome could not help thinking that passion was missing from them.

'They are not on fire,' he mourned. 'As I have been.'

Then Harry met Lily and seemed, to his father, to be less on fire than ever. "But it will come," he encouraged his sons. It must come. What had been in him so powerful a desire, so bitterly a failed attempt, could not be wasted, must be passed on, and in greater strength, too, if things were to turn out as he considered just.

Lily, impinging on his plan with her sly, mincing manner, her pout and her impatient sighs, was the eternal female enemy. He had built a bastion, a treasure-house for his sons, with all the great names they had heard from the cradle, the learning he had struggled for to make their inheritance. It had come too easily, he realised now, and

Harry would rather spend an evening talking inanities, lowering his mind to Lily's level. His attitude towards her was vexing, suggesting that he was willing, eager to learn something from her and even that she might be able to teach it: suppliant, receptive he was with her; yet it was surely for him to instruct, who knew so much, and dominate, being a man, and to concede, whatsoever he felt inclined to concede; not beg for favours.

Mr Ransome thought of his own happy married life—the woman, so gentle and conciliatory listening to him as he read. Into those readings he had put the expression of his pleasure at being able to share with her the best he had discovered. She had sat and sewed and, when she raised her eyes to look for her scissors, she would also glance across at him and he, conscious of her doing so would pause to meet this glance, knowing that it would be full of humble gratitude. She had never been able to comprehend half of what he had offered her, she had muddled the great names and once dozed off after a few pages of Stendhal; but something, he thought, must have seeped into her, something of the lofty music of prose, as she listened, evening after evening of her married life. Now he missed her and so much of the sound of his own voice that had gone with her.

How different was Lily. The moment he began to read aloud, or even to quote something, down came her eyelids to half-mast. An invisible curtain dropped over her and behind it she was without any response, as if heavily drugged. He would have liked to have stuck pins in her to see if she would cry out: instead, he assaulted her—indecently, she thought, and that was why she would not listen—with Cicero and Goethe, Ibsen and Nietzsche and a French poet, one of his specials, called Bawdyleer. Having removed herself, as it were, she would then glance at the clock, wind a curl round her finger and suddenly loosen it to spring back against her cheek. Distracted by this, Harry

would murmur, "Yes, Dad, I remember you telling us."
So Mr Ransome had lost them both. 'Come here,' Lily
seemed to be enticing his son. 'Come behind my invisible
curtain and we can think of other things and play with my
hair and be alone together.'

Sometimes, but very rarely, Mr Ransome would manage
to catch her unawares and force one of the names on her
before she had time to bring down the curtain. Then her
manner was rude and retaliatory instead of vague. "And
who, pray, is Dosty what's-is-name when he's at home?"
She knew that Mr Ransome was her enemy and felt not only
malice in his attitude towards her, but something she might
have defined as obscenity if she had known the meaning
of the word.

He—for he was at heart puritanical—had once or twice
delighted to indulge in a bout of broad-mindedness. She
should learn that he and some of the great thinkers of the
world could face the truth unflinchingly and even some of
the words the truth must be described in. To the pure, he
said, all things are pure: he watched Lily's look of prim
annoyance, implying that to her they obviously were not.
He was defeated, however, by the silence that fell—Lily's
and his son's. His remark, made to seem blatant by being
isolated and ignored, repeated itself in his own head and he
felt his cheeks and brow darkening. He did not want to
appear to have any impurity in his own mind and quickly
bent down and rearranged the coals on the fire.

The spring was beginning; the puddles along the rutted
lanes were blue, reflecting the bright sky, and lilac-trees in
cottage-gardens bore buds as small as grape-pips. Although
the darkness fell later, the interval of daylight after tea was
of no use to Lily, for Mr Ransome had his two sons out,
white-washing and weeding and trimming. "We shall have
no time to do it once the season has begun," he said.

"But what about us?" Lily asked Harry.

"I can't help but give him a hand of an evening. It wouldn't be right to leave it all to Godfrey."

"It sounds as if the summer's going to be just as bad as the winter."

All along, Harry had known it would be worse.

In the summer, the lock was always full, boats jostled together, smart women in motor launches stared through their dark glasses at men in rowing-boats wearing braces and knotted handkerchiefs on their heads: in the narrowness of the lock they were all resentful of their proximity to one another, and were glad, when the water had finished rising or falling, to see the gates opening slowly. The locks were an ordeal to be negotiated, not made easier by the passers-by on the tow-path who stopped to watch them lying exposed below and hoped that they would ram their craft into the gates, or take the paint off one of the white launches.

Steamers came through at intervals and then the lock was a well of noise with someone thumping at the piano in the saloon and cheery messages thrown from deck to towing-path; glasses of beer were held up to tantalise and the funny man of the party, wearing a yachting cap, sang 'A life on the ocean wave is better than going to sea.'

The pretty stretch of river with its willows hanging down to the water and the brilliance of the lock garden brought artists, with folding stools and easels, who took up much of Mr Ransome's time. Such an odd character they thought him, forgetting—as, of all people, the English should not— that characters are encouraged at the cost of their families' destruction. He showed them his own painting of the same scene and they were enraptured, they called him a true primitive and talked of the Douanier Rousseau.

On summer evenings, after days of advising these amateur artists, talking about himself, bringing in a great deal about Leonardo, Mr Ransome behaved as if he had been drinking too much. He boasted, belaboured his son

with words and then, from too much excitement, sur-
rendered to self-pity. It suddenly seemed to him that he had
wasted his life: he had seen this on the face of one stranger
after another. 'You!' they had been thinking, 'a man who
has all the great Masters at his finger-tips and can summon
from memory one thundering phrase after another, who
would expect to find you in such a backwater, living so
humbly?'

"You two, my sons, shall make up for me," he told them.
"Then I have not lived in vain." "I am the teacher of
athletes," he intoned. "He that by me spreads a wider
breast than my own proves the width of my own. He
most knows my style who learns under it to destroy the
teacher."

"Yes, father," said his sons.

"Walt Whitman," he added, giving credit where credit
was due.

Lily, who had given up working in a shop to become a
laundress, now had Saturday afternoons free. The full
significance of this she told Harry when they were lingering
over, postponing from minute to minute, their farewell
embrace in the dark lane near her home. To draw apart was
so painful to them that, as soon as they attempted it, they
suffered too much and flew together again for comfort.

"It must be gone eleven," she said. "Dad's tongue
will curdle the milk. But guess what, though. Did you
realise?"

"Realise what?" he mumbled, and lifted her hair from
her shoulders and kissed underneath it, along the back of
her neck, with busy little nibbling kisses. In a curious and
contradictory way, she felt that he was so intent on her that
she no longer existed.

"Why, Saturday afternoons, of course," she said. "You'll
be free: now I'll be free as well." She could not help
noticing that the kissing stopped at once.

"Well, you do know week-ends in the season I have to give Dad a hand," Harry said.

"It isn't the season yet. We'll have a fortnight before that. I can meet you any time after dinner. Sooner the better," she whispered and raised herself on tiptoe and put her warm mouth against his. He was unhappy and she became angry.

"Say about tea-time," he suggested.

"Why not earlier?"

She knew, although of course she could not see, that he was blushing.

"Ever since we were little, Dad's liked us to be together on Saturday afternoons."

"What for, pray?"

"Just to have a quiet time together. It's a family custom."
Now she could feel him blushing.

"If you ask me, he's round the bend," she said loudly. "And even if you don't ask me, he is."

She pushed Harry away and began to walk down the lane towards her home. He followed her. "And so are you," she added. She did not turn her head as she spoke, but the words came back to him clearly. "No wonder that girl Vera Webster gave up going out with Godfrey. She could see the way the wind was blowing. 'Dad likes this and Dad likes that.' I'm sick and tired of Dad and one of these days I'll tell him so. 'You and your Bawdyleer', I'll say, 'you boring old . . .'" her voice rose and trembled, " 'codger' " she cried. "And you, too," she had reached her gate, threw it open and hurried up the path.

"Saturday tea-time then?" he called after her anxiously.

"Saturday nothing," she shouted back, and she lifted the latch and went in boldly to face her father's sarcasm.

"You're in early this morning," he said. "The milkman hasn't been yet."

The next day her beautiful anger had dissolved. She had

enjoyed it while she indulged in it, but now her words haunted and alarmed her. Perhaps they had meant the end of Harry's love for her and, so, of all her hopes. Her future life with him dissolved—a whole council-house full of day-dreams; trousseau, wedding-presents, pots and pans, dainty supper-dishes, baby-clothes; cradle, even a kitten asleep on a cushion. She imagined him going to work and then on to his evening class, his head tilted proudly back, the stain of anger on his cheeks. The day after would be Saturday and if it turned out that he had taken her at her furious word, she could not endure to go on living.

"Not going out with Harry?" her mother asked her, when Lily began to wash her hair at the kitchen sink on Saturday afternoon.

"I think love's sweet song has run into a few discords," her father said. "*Very* hoity-toity words coming up the path the night before last."

Lily poured a jug of water over her head and so her tears were hidden.

By four o'clock her hair was quite dry. Harry had not come. She was restless and felt herself watched by her mother and father. Soon she decided that there was, after all, nothing to stop her walking along the towing-path for a breath of fresh air. It was a public way and there was no one who could stop her. It would be a sorry thing if, just because of Harry Ransome, she could never walk along the river bank again.

It was a bright and blowy evening. She met no one. At every bend in the lane, she expected to see Harry come hastening, full of apologies, towards her. Then she came to the river and still no one was in sight. The water was high, after the winter's rain, and flowed fast, covered with bubbles, bearing away scum and twigs and last year's leaves. The sound and look of it completed her depression.

With her head turned towards the river and not in the

direction of the cottage, she walked along the lock-side. She went on beyond it a little way and then turned and sauntered back. The kitchen window was dark, but from the parlour a light fell faintly through the wooden shutters which had been drawn across the outside of the window. This seemed quite strange to Lily, for it would not be dark for some hours to come and in all the months she had known Harry she had never seen anyone go into the parlour except to fetch a book. She remembered Harry's shame and reluctance when she had tried to make plans for this afternoon and an unreasonable suspicion overtook her that he was in that shuttered room making love to someone, that he had known beforehand that he would be doing so, and knowing, had gone on kissing Lily; though he had had, she admitted, the decency to blush. She stepped quietly on to the little plot of grass and hesitated, glancing round her. There was no one in sight and not a sound except for the river. She went softly across to the window and listened there; but there was a shameful silence from within. Her heart beating with great violence unnerved her and only the extreme tension of her jealousy enabled her to lay her hand on the shutter and move it gently towards her.

The light in the room was not so very bright; but standing upright in a strange stiff pose with hand on hip and one knee slightly bent, she could see Mr Ransome facing her not two yards away, his beard jutting forward and his expression fixed. A rosy glow from an oil-stove close beside him fell over his completely naked body.

Their eyes met, his widened with surprise, Lily's with horror. Then she slammed back the shutter and leant against it for a moment, sick and trembling. Through the narrow slit between the shutters she had not seen the two sons, sitting unwillingly but dutifully behind their easels. Terror, in any case, had quite put the thought of Harry out of her mind. She was afraid that Mr Ransome would come leaping out of the house after her and chase her down the towing-path, naked and mad as he was, shouting Balzac and Voltaire after her. She summoned all her strength and turned and ran across the lawn, as fast as she could go, away from the cottages and her legs were as heavy as lead, as if she were running in a nightmare.

The Rose, The Mauve,
The White

In the morning, Charles went down the garden to practise calling for three cheers. When he came to the place farthest of all from the house and near to the lake, he paused among clumps of rhubarb and mounds of lawn-clippings, and glanced about him. His voice had broken years before, but was still uncertain in volume; sometimes it wavered, and lost its way and he could never predict if it would follow his intention or not. If his voice was to come out in a great bellow or perhaps frenziedly high-pitched, people would turn towards him in surprise, even astonishment, but how, if it sank too low would he claim anyone's attention after the boisterous confusions of Auld Lang Syne? He could hardly be held responsible for it, he felt, and had often wished that he might climb to the top of a mountain and there, alone, make its acquaintance and come to terms with it. As he could not, this morning in the garden at home, he put on what he hoped was an expression of exultant gaiety, snatched off his spectacles and, waving them in the air, cried out: "And now three cheers for Mrs Frensham-Bowater." He was about to begin 'Hip, hip hooray', when a bush nearby was filled with laughter; all the branches were disturbed with mirth. Then there were two splashes as his little sisters leapt into the lake for safety. "And now three cheers for Charles," they called, as they swam as fast as they could away from the bank.

If he went after them, he could only stand at the edge of the water and shake his fist or make some other ineffectual protest, so he put his spectacles on again and walked slowly back to the house. It was a set-back to the day, with Natalie arriving that afternoon and likely to hear at once from the twins how foolishly he had behaved.

"Mother, could you make them be quiet?" he asked desperately, finding her at work in the rose-garden. When he told her the story, she threw back her head and laughed for what seemed to him to be about five minutes. "Oh, poor old Charles. I wish I'd been in hiding, too." He had known he would have to bear this or something like it, but was obliged to pay the price; and at long last she said: "I will see to it that their lips are sealed; their cunning chops shut up."

"But are you sure you can?"

"I think I know how to manage my own children. See how obedient you yourself have grown. I cross my heart they shall not breathe a word of it in front of Natalie."

He thanked her coldly and walked away. In spite of his gratitude, he thought: 'She is so dreadfully chummy and slangy. I wish she wouldn't be. And why say just "Natalie" when there are two girls coming? I think she tries to be "knowing" as well,' he decided.

Two girls were coming. His sister, Katie, was picking sweet-peas for the room these school-friends were to share with her.

"You are supposed to cut those with scissors," Charles said. The ones she couldn't strip off, she was breaking with her teeth. "What time are they coming?"

"In the station-taxi at half-past three."

"Shall I come with you to meet them?"

"No, of course not. Why should you?"

Katie was sixteen and a year younger than Charles. It is a very feminine age and she wanted her friends to herself.

At school they slept in the same bedroom, as they would here. They were used to closing the door upon a bower of secrets and intrigue and diary-writing; knew how to keep their jokes to themselves and their conversations as incomprehensible as possible to other people. When Charles's friends came to stay, Katie did not encroach on them, and now she had no intention of letting him spoil that delightful drive back from the station: she could not imagine what her friends would think of her if she did.

So after luncheon she went down alone in the big, musty-smelling taxi. The platform of the country station was quite deserted: a porter was whistling in the office, keeping out of the hot sun. She walked up and down, reading the notices of Estate Agents posted along the fence and all the advertisements of auction-sales. She imagined the train coming nearer to her with every passing second; yet it seemed unbelievable that it would really soon materialise out of the distance, bringing Frances and Natalie.

They would have the compartment to themselves at this time of the day on the branch line and she felt a little wistful thinking that they were together and having fun and she was all alone, waiting for them. They would be trying out dance-steps, swaying and staggering as the train rocked; dropping at last, weak with laughter, full-length on the seats. Then, having been here to stay with Katie on other occasions, as they came near to the end of their journey they would begin to point out landmarks and haul down their luggage from the rack—carefully, because in the suitcases were the dresses for this evening's dance.

The signal fell with a sharp clatter making Katie jump. 'Now where shall I be standing when the train stops?' she wondered, feeling self-conscious suddenly and full of responsibility. 'Not here, right on top of the Gents' lavatory of all places. Perhaps by the entrance.' Nonchalantly, she strolled away.

The porter came out of the office, still whistling, and stared up the line. Smoke, bowing and nodding like a plume on a horse's head, came round a bend in the distance and Katie, watching it, felt sick and anxious. 'They won't enjoy themselves at all,' she thought. 'I wish I hadn't asked them. They will find it dreadfully dull at home and the dance is bound to be a failure. It will be babyish with awful things like "The Dashing White Sergeant" and "The Gay Gordons". They will think Charles is a bore and the twins a bloody nuisance.'

But the moment they stepped out of the train all her constraint vanished. They caught her up into the midst of their laughter. "You can't think what happened," they said. "You'll never believe what happened at Paddington." The ridiculous story never did quite come clear, they were so incoherent with giggling. Katie smiled in a grown-up way. She was just out of it for the moment, but would soon be in the swim again.

As they drove up the station-slope towards the village, they were full of anticipation and excitement. "And where is Charles?" asked Natalie, smoothing her dark hair.

*   *   *

Tea was such great fun, their mother, Myra Pollard, told herself: though one moment she felt rejuvenated; the next minute, as old as the world. She had a habit of talking to herself, as to another person who was deeply interested in all her reactions: and the gist of these conversations was often apparent on her face.

'They keep one young oneself—all these young people,' she thought as she was pouring out the tea. Yet the next second, her cheek resting on her hand as she watched them putting away great swags and wadges and gobbets of starch, she sighed; for she had not felt as they all felt, eager and full of nonsense, for years and years. To them, though they were polite, she was of no account, the tea pourer-out, the starch-provider, simply. It was people of her own generation who said that Charles and she were like brother and sister— not those of Charles's generation, to whom the idea would have seemed absurd.

Frances and Natalie were as considerate as could be and even strove to be a little woman-to-womanly with her. "Did you ever find your bracelet, Mrs Pollard? Do you remember you'd lost it when we were here last time? At a . . . a dance, wasn't it?" Natalie faltered. Of course, Katie's mother went to dances, too. Indeed, why not? Grotesque though they must be. She was glad that her own parents were more sedate and did not try to ape the young.

"I wish *we* could go to a ball," said Lucy, one of the twins.

"Your time will come," their mother said. She laid her hand to the side of the silver tea-pot as if to warm and comfort herself.

"Oh, do you remember that boy, Sandy, in the elimination dance?" Katie suddenly exploded.

Frances, who was all beaky and spectacly, Mrs Pollard thought, exploded with her.

"The one who was wearing a kilt?" Natalie asked, with more composure. She wondered if Charles was thinking that she must be older than the other girls and indeed she was, by two and a half months.

"Will Mrs Frensham-Bowater be there?" Lucy asked.

Her sly glance, with eyelids half-lowered, was for Caroline's—her twin's—benefit.

"Of course, Mrs Frensham-Bowater always organises the dance," their mother said briskly, and changed the subject.

Charles was grateful to her for keeping her promise; but all the same he had had an irritating afternoon. The twins, baulked in one direction, found other ways of exasperating him. When he came out of the house with his gun under

his arm, they had clapped their hands over their ears and
fled shrieking to the house. "Charles is pointing his gun at
us," they shouted. "Don't be bloody silly," he shouted
back. "Charles swore," they cried.

'What an unholy gap between Katie and me and those
little perishers,' he thought. 'Whatever did mother and
father imagine they were up to? What can the neighbours
have thought of them—at their time of life?' He shied
away from the idea of sexual love between the middle-aged;
though it was ludicrous, evidence of it was constantly to be
seen.

"Did you shoot anything?" his mother asked him.

"There wasn't anything to shoot." He had known there
wouldn't be and had only walked about in the woods with
his gun for something to do until the taxi came.

"And the girl next door?" Frances asked. "I have forgotten her name. Will she be going to the dance tonight?"

"Oh, Deirdre," said Caroline to Lucy.

"Yes, Deirdre," Lucy said, staring across the table at
Charles.

"No, she has gone to school in Switzerland," said Katie.

"Poor Charles!" the twins said softly.

"Why not try to be your age?" he asked them in a voice
which would, he hoped, sound intimidating to them, but
nonchalant to everybody else.

"Have you had nice holidays?" Mrs Pollard asked,
looking from Frances to Natalie, then thinking that she was
being far too hostessy and middle-aged, she said without
waiting for their answer; "I do adore your sweater,
Natalie."

"Jesus bids us shine, with a pure, clear light," Caroline
began to sing, as she spread honey on her bread.

"Not at the table," said her mother.

*   *   *

"What shall we do now?" Katie asked after tea. She was beginning to feel her responsibility again. There was no doubt that everything was very different from school; there were Frances and Natalie drawn very close together from sharing the same situation; and she, apart, in the predicament of hostess. It was now that she began to see her home through their eyes—the purple brick house looked heavy and ugly now that the sun had gone behind a cloud; the south wall was covered by a magnolia tree; there were one or two big, cream flowers among the dark leaves: doves were walking about on the slate roof; some of the windows reflected the blue sky and moving clouds. To Katie, it was like being shown a photograph which she did not immediately recognise—unevocative, as were the photographs of their mothers in the dormitory at school—they seldom glanced at them from the beginning of term to the end.

They sat down on the grass at the edge of the orchard and began to search for four-léaf clovers. Their conversation consisted mostly of derogatory remarks about themselves—they were hopeless at dancing, each one said; could never think what to say to their partners; and they had all washed their hair that morning and now could do simply nothing with it.

"So lucky having red hair, Katie. How I envy you."

"But it's horrible. I hate it."

"It's so striking. Isn't it, Frances?"

"Well, yours is, too, in a different way. It's this awful mousiness of mine I can't abide."

"You can't call it mousy: it's chestnut."

It was just a game they played and when they had finished with their hair they began on the shape of their hands. There was never any unkindness in anything they said. They were exploring themselves more than each other.

The twins wandered about the garden, shaking milk in jars to make butter: every few minutes they stopped to compare the curd they had collected. They had been doing this tirelessly for days, but were near the time when that game would seem dull and done with and they would never play it again. This evening, they marched about the lawn, chanting a meaningless song.

The older girls were discussing whether they would rather be deaf or blind. Frances lay on her stomach watching the children and wondering if they were not lucky to be so free of care and without the great ordeal of the dance ahead of them.

"Deaf any day," said Katie.

"Oh, no!" said Natalie. "Only think how cut off you'd be from other people; and no one is ever as nice to the deaf or has much patience with them. Everyone is kinder to the blind."

"But imagine never seeing any of this ever again," said Frances. Tears came up painfully in Katie's eyes. "This garden, that lovely magnolia tree, sunsets. Never to be able to read 'Jane Eyre' again."

"You could read it in Braille," Katie said.

"It wouldn't be the same. You know it wouldn't be. Oh, it would be appalling ... I can't contemplate it ... I really can't."

Anyone who reminded them that the choice might not arise would have been deeply resented.

"I suppose we had better go in and iron our frocks," Katie said. No one had found a four-leaf clover.

"Where is Charles?" Natalie asked.

"The Lord knows," said Katie.

Frances was silent as they went towards the house. She could feel the dance coming nearer to her.

*　　　*　　　*

"The house is full of girls," Charles told his father. George Pollard left the car in the drive and went indoors. "And steam," he said.

Natalie, Frances and Katie had been in the bathroom for
nearly an hour and could hardly see one another across the
room. Bath-salts, hoarded from Christmas, scented the steam
and now, still wearing their shower-caps, they were standing
on damp towels and shaking their Christmas talcum powder
over their stomachs and shoulders.

"Will you do my back and under my arms?" asked Katie,
handing to Frances the tin of Rose Geranium. "And then
I will do yours."

"What a lovely smell. It's so much nicer than mine,"
said Frances, dredging Katie as thoroughly as if she were a
fillet of fish being prepared for the frying-pan.

"Don't be too long, girls!" Mrs Pollard called, tapping
at the door. She tried to make her voice sound gay and
indulgent. "The twins are waiting to come in and it's
rather past their bedtime." She wondered crossly if Katie's
friends were allowed to monopolise bathrooms like that in
their own homes. Katie was plainly showing off and would
have to be taken aside and told so.

"Just coming," they shouted.

At last they opened the door and thundered along the
passage to their bedroom where they began to make the
kind of untidiness they had left behind them in the bathroom.

Yvette, the French mother's-help, whose unenviable
task it now was to supervise the twins' going to bed, flung
open the bathroom window and kicked all the wet towels to
one side. 'They will be clean, certainly,' she was thinking.
'But they will not be chic.' She had seen before the net
frocks, the strings of coral, the shining faces.

She rinsed the dregs of mauve crystals from the bath and
called out to the twins. The worst part of her day was about
to begin.

*   *   *

"This is the best part of the day," George said. He shut the bedroom door and took his drink over to the window. Myra was sitting at her dressing-table. She had taken off her ear-rings to give her ears a little rest and was gently massaging the reddened lobes. She said: "It doesn't seem a year since that other dance, when we quarrelled about letting Katie go to it."

"She was too young. And still is."

"There were girls of thirteen there."

"Well, that's no affair of mine, thank God."

"I wonder if Ronnie what's-his-name will be sober. For the M.C. of a young people's dance I consider he was pretty high last time. He always has drunk unmercifully."

"What the devil's this?" George asked. He had gone into his dressing-room and now came back with his safety-razor in his hand.

"Oh, the girls must have borrowed it."

"Very hospitable guests they are, to be sure. They manage to make me feel quite at home."

"Don't fuss. You were young yourself once."

She dotted lipstick over her cheekbones and he watched her through the looking-glass, arrested by the strange sight. The incredulous expression made her smile, eyebrows raised, she was ready to tease. He tilted her face back towards him and kissed her quickly on the mouth.

"You look absurd," he said.

As soon as she was released, she leant to the mirror again and began to smooth the dots of colour over her cheeks until they were merged into the most delicate flush. "A clever girl," he said, finishing his drink.

*   *   *

The girls were still not dressed when a boy called Benedict Nightingale arrived in his father's car—and dinner-jacket, George decided. 'Katie's first beau,' he told himself, 'come calling for her.' He felt quite irritable as he took the boy into the drawing-room.

"They won't be long," he said, without conviction.

"Don't be too long, girls," Myra called again in her low, controlled and unexasperated voice. She stopped to tap on their bedroom door before she went downstairs; then, knowing that Charles would be having trouble with his tie, she went in to his rescue.

"What about a drink?" George asked Benedict reluctantly.

"No thank you, sir."

"Cigarette?"

"No thank you, sir."

"I don't know what they can be doing all this time. Now what the hell's happening up there?"

The twins were trying to get into Katie's bedroom to pry into adolescent secrets, and the girls, still in their petticoats, held the door against them. From the other side of it Lucy and Caroline banged with their fists and kicked until dragged away at last by Yvette.

"Now we shall be late," said Katie.

They lifted their frocks and dropped them over their heads, their talcumed armpits showed white as they raised their elbows to hook themselves at the back. Frances tied Natalie's sash, Natalie fastened Katie's bracelet.

"Is this all right? Does it hang down? You're sure? Am I done up?" they asked.

"Oh, yes, yes, yes, I mean no," they all answered at once, not one of them attending.

"*This* is what *I'm* allowed," said Katie, smudging on lipstick, stretching her mouth as she had seen her mother do. "So pale, I'm wasting my time."

Natalie twisted her bracelet, shook back her hair: she hummed; did a glissade across the clothes-strewn floor, her skirts floating about her. She was away, gone, in Charles's arms already. She held her scented arm to her face and breathed deeply and smiled.

Frances stood uncertainly in the middle of the room. 'I am the one who will be asked to dance last of all,' she thought, cold with the certainty of her failure. 'Katie and Natalie will go flying away and I shall be left there on my own, knowing nobody. The time will go slowly and I shall wish that I were dead.' She turned to the long looking-glass and smoothed her frock. "I hate my bosoms," she suddenly said. "They are too wide apart."

"Nonsense, that's how they're supposed to be," Katie said, as brisk as any Nannie.

*   *   *

"Give those girls a shout, Charles," George said and helped himself to another drink.

But they were coming downstairs. They had left the room with its beds covered with clothes, its floor strewn with tissue-paper. They descended; the rose, the mauve, the white. Like a bunch of sweet-peas they looked, George thought.

"What a pretty frock, Frances," Myra said, beginning with the worst. 'Poor pet,' she thought, and Frances guessed the thought, smiling primly and saying thank you.

"And such a lovely colour, Natalie," Myra went on.

"But is it, though?" Natalie asked anxiously. "And don't my shoes clash terribly?" "I think I look quite bleak in it, and it is last year's, really."

Myra had scarcely wanted to go into all that. "Now, Katie," she began to say, as soon as she could. "I don't think your friends know Benedict. And when you have introduced them we must be on our way. Your father and I have to go out to dinner after we've taken you to the dance. So who's to go with whom?"

That was what Frances had wondered. The worst part of

being a guest was not being told enough about arrangements. One was left in a shifting haze of conjecture.

Benedict had come to attention as the girls came in and now he stepped forward and said with admirable firmness: "I will take Katie in my car." Then he was forced to add: "I would have room for someone else in the back."

'That's me,' thought Frances.

"Good! Now don't crush your dresses, girls," said Myra. "Gather them up—so—from the back of the skirt. Have you got everything?"

"Of course, mother," said Katie. 'We aren't children,' she thought.

*   *   *

Four hours later, Charles let go of Natalie's hand and took a pace forward from the circle of 'Auld Lang Syne'. "Three Cheers for Mrs Frensham-Bowater," he shouted. "Hip, hip, hooray!"

Myra, standing in the entrance hall with the other parents, tried to look unconcerned. She knew that Charles had been nervous all along of doing that little duty and she was thankful that it was safely over. And that meant that the dance was over, too.

With the first bars of "God Save The Queen", they all became rigid, pained-looking, arms to their sides and heads erect; but the moment it was over, the laughter and excitement enlived their faces again. They began to drift reluctantly towards the hall.

"How pretty the girls are," the mothers said to one another. "Goodness, how they grow up. That isn't Madge's girl, surely, in the yellow organza? They change from day to day at this age."

"Was it lovely?" Myra asked Katie.

"So lovely! Oh and someone spilt fruit-cup all down poor Natalie's front."

"Oh, no!" said Myra.

"She doesn't care though."

"But her mother. . . . I feel so responsible."

"Oh, her mother's awfully understanding. She won't give a damn." ('Unlike you,' Katie's voice seemed to imply.) "It was last year's, anyway."

Benedict was hovering at Katie's shoulder.

"Charles had torn the hem already, anyway," Katie said.

"But how on earth?"

"They won a prize in the River Dance."

Myra had not the faintest idea what a River Dance was and said so.

"The boys have to run across some chalk lines carrying their partners and he tore her skirt when he picked her up. She's no light weight, I can assure you."

"I hope it hasn't been rowdy," Myra said, but this remark was far too silly to receive an answer.

Frances had attached herself to Charles and Natalie, so that she would not seem to leave the floor alone; but she knew that Mrs Pollard had seen her standing there by the door, without a partner, and for the last waltz of all things. To be seen by her hostess in such a predicament underlined her failure.

"Did you enjoy it, Frances?" Myra asked. And wasn't that the only way to put her question, Frances thought, the one she was so very anxious to know—"Did you dance much?"

"We had better go back as we came," Myra said. "Have you all got everything? Well then, you go on, Benedict dear, with Frances and Katie, and we will follow."

'I wish she wouldn't say "dear" to boys,' Katie thought. 'And she doesn't trust us, I suppose, to come on after. I hope that Benedict hasn't noticed that she doesn't trust him: he will think it is his driving, or worse, that she is thoroughly evil-minded. Goodness knows what she got up to in her young days to have such dreadful ideas in her head.'

*   *   *

The untidy room was waiting for them. Five hours earlier, they had not looked beyond the dance or imagined a time after it.

"Well, I don't think that poor boy, Roland, will thank you much for asking him in your party," Frances said. "He was wondering how he would ever get away from me."

She thought, as many grown-up women think, that by saying a thing herself she prevented people from thinking it. She had also read a great many nostalgic novels about girls of long ago spending hours in the cloakroom at dances and in her usual spirit of defiance she had refused to go there at all, had stuck the humiliation out and even when she might have taken her chance with the others in the Paul Jones had stuck that out, too.

"He told me he thought you danced very well," Katie said.

This made matters worse for Frances. So it wasn't just the dancing, but something very much more important— her personality, or lack of it; her plainness—what she was burdened with for the rest of her life, in fact.

Natalie seemed loth to take off her frock, stained and torn though it now was. She floated about the room, spreading the skirt about her as she hummed and swayed and shook her hair. She would not be back on earth again until morning.

"Here is your safety-pin, Katie," said Frances.

"And here, with many thanks, your necklace safe and sound."

The trinkets they had borrowed from one another were handed back; they unhooked one-another; examined their stockings for ladders. Katie took a pair of socks out of her brassière.

One by one, they got into bed. Natalie sat up writing her diary and Katie thought hers could wait till morning. Benedict's amusing sayings would be quite safe till then and by tomorrow the cloud that had been over the evening might have dispersed. The next day, when they were swimming in the lake, or cleaning out the rabbits or making walnut-fudge, surely Frances would be re-established among them, not cut off by her lack of success as she now was, taking the edge off Benedict's remembered wit, making Katie's heart ache just when it was beginning to behave as she had always believed a heart should.

Turning in Benedict's arms as they danced she had sometimes caught Frances's eyes as she stood there alone or with some other forlorn and unclaimed girl. Katie had felt treachery in the smile she had been bound to give—the most difficult of smiles, for it had to contain so much, the assurance that the dance was only a dance and nothing very much to miss, a suggestion of regret at her—Katie's—foolishness in taking part in it and surprise that she of all people had been chosen. 'It is soon over,' she tried to signal to Frances. 'You are yourself. I love you. I will soon come back.'

And Frances had received the smiles and nodded. 'There are other things in the world,' she tried to believe.

"Shall we have a picnic tomorrow?" Katie asked. She snuggled down into bed and stared up at the ceiling.

"Let's have one day at a time," said Natalie. She had filled in the space in her diary and now locked the book up with a little key that hung on a chain round her neck.

"Do put out the light before the moths come in," said Frances.

They could hear Katie's parents talking quietly in the next room. Frances thought; 'I expect she is saying, "Poor Frances." I'm afraid she didn't get many dances; but I am sure that Katie did what she could for her. It would really have been kinder not to have invited her.' The unbroken murmuring continued on the other side of the wall and Frances longed for it to stop. She thought: 'She is for ever working things out in her mind, and cruelly lets people guess what they are. It would be no worse if she said them out loud.' She had prayed that before Myra came to fetch them from the dance it would all be over; "God Save The Queen safely" sung and her own shame at last behind her. As the last waltz began, she had longed for someone to claim her—any spotty, clammy-handed boy would do. Benedict and Katie had hovered by her, Benedict impatient to be away, but Katie reluctant to leave her friend alone at such a crucial moment. "Please *go*," Frances had told them and just as they danced away, Myra had appeared in the doorway, looking tired but watchful, her eyes everywhere— Katie accounted for, Charles, Natalie, then a little encouraging smile and nod to Frances herself, trying to shrink out of sight on the perimeter of the gaiety. 'As I expected,' her eyes said.

Gradually, the murmurings from the other room petered out and the house became silent. Then, in Charles's room across the landing, Natalie heard a shoe drop with a thud on the floor and presently another. 'Sitting on the edge of the bed, dreaming,' she thought. She lay awake, smiling in the darkness and stroking her smooth arms long after the other two had fallen asleep.

Summer Schools

SITTING outside on the sill, the cat watched Melanie through the window. The shallow arc between the tips of his ears, his baleful stare, and his hunched-up body blown feathery by the wind, gave him the look of a barn-owl. Sometimes, a strong gust nearly knocked him off balance and bent his whiskers crooked. Catching Melanie's eye, he opened his mouth wide in his furious, striped face, showed his fangs and let out a piteous mew instead of a roar.

Melanie put a finger in her book and padded across the room in her stockinged feet. When she opened the french windows, the gale swept into the room and the fire began to smoke. Now that he was allowed to come in, the cat began a show caprice; half in, he arched his back and rubbed against the step, purring loudly. Some leaves blew across the floor.

"Either in or out, you fool," Melanie said impatiently. Still holding the door, she put her foot under the cat's belly and half-pushed, half-lifted him into the room.

The french windows had warped, like all the other wooden parts of the house. There were altogether too many causes for irritation, Melanie thought. When she had managed to slam the door shut, she stood there for a moment, looking out at the garden, until she had felt the full abhorrence of the scene. Her revulsion was so complete as to be almost unbelievable; the sensation became ecstatic.

On the veranda, a piece of newspaper had wrapped itself,

113

quivering frenziedly, round a post. A macrocarpa hedge tossed about in the wind; the giant hydrangea by the gate was full of bus-tickets, for here was the terminus, the very end of the esplanade. The butt and end, Melanie thought, of all the long-drawn-out tedium of the English holiday resort. Across the road a broken bank covered with spiky grass hid most of the sands, but she could imagine them clearly, brown and ribbed, littered with bits of cuttle-fish and mussel-shells. The sea—far out—was staved with white.

Melanie waited as a bowed-over, mufflered man, exercising a dog, then a duffel-coated woman with a brace of poodles on leads completed the scene. Satisfied, she turned back to the fire. It was all as bad as could be and on a bright day it was hardly better, for the hard glitter of the sun seemed unable to lift the spirits. It was usually windy.

The creaking sound of the rain, its fitful and exasperated drumming on the window, she listened to carefully. In one place at the end of the veranda, it dropped more heavily and steadily: she could hear it as if the noise were in her own breast. The cat—Ursula's—rubbed its cold fur against her legs and she pushed him away crossly, but he always returned.

"A day for indoors," Ursula said gaily. She carried in the tea-tray, and set down a covered dish on the hearth with the smug triumph of one giving a great treat.

I am to be won over with buttered scones, Melanie thought sulkily. The sulky expression was one that her face, with its heavy brows and full mouth, fell into easily. "One of Miss Rogers's nasty looks," her pupils called it, finding it not alarming, but depressing. Ursula, two years younger, was plumper, brighter, more alert. Neither was beautiful.

"Oh, sod that cat of yours," Melanie said. He was now mewing at the french windows to be let out. Melanie's swearing was something new since their father had died— an act of desperation, such as a child might make. Father would turn in his grave, Ursula often said. Let him turn,

said Melanie. "Who will look after him while you're
away?" she asked, nodding at the cat. Ursula put him outside again and came back to pour out the tea. "How do you
mean, look after him? Surely you don't mind. I'll order the
fish. You'll only have to cook it and give it to him."

"I shan't be here."

The idea had suddenly occurred, born of vindictiveness
and envy. For Pamela had no right to invite Ursula to stay
there on her own. Melanie was only two years their senior;
they had all been at the same school. Apart from all that,
the two sisters always spent their holidays together; in fact,
had never been separated. To Melanie, the invitation
seemed staggering insolent, and Ursula's decision to accept
it could hardly be believed. She had read out the letter at
breakfast one morning and Melanie, on her way out of the
room to fetch more milk, had simply said, "How extraordinary," her light, scornful voice dismissing the subject.
Only a sense of time passing and middle-age approaching
had given Ursula the courage (or effrontery) to renew the
subject. For the first time that either she or Melanie could
remember, her energy and enthusiasm overcame the
smothering effect of her sister's lethargy.

She means to go, Melanie told herself. Her sensation of
impotence was poison to her. She had a bitter taste in her
mouth, and chafed her hands as if they were frozen. If
Ursula were truly going, though, Melanie determined that
the departure should be made as difficult as possible. Long
before she could set out for the station she should be worn out
with the obstacles she had had to overcome.

"You can't expect me to stay here on my own just in
order to look after your cat."

And lest Ursula should ask where she was going before
she had had time to make her plans, she got up quickly and
went upstairs.

*   *   *

The cat was to stay in kennels and Ursula grieved about it. Her grief Melanie brushed aside as absurd, although she was at the same time inclined to allow Ursula a sense of guilt. "A dog one can at least take with one," she told her. She had decided that the cat reflected something of Ursula's own nature—too feminine (although it was a tom); it might be driven, though not led, and the refusal to co-operate mixed, as it was, with cowardice resulted in slyness.

The weather had not improved. They could remember the holidays beginning in this way so often, with everything —rain, flowers, bushes—aslant in the wind. It will be pretty miserable at Pamela's, Melanie thought. She could imagine that house and its surroundings—a parade of new shops nearby, a tennis club, enormous suburban pubs at the corners of roads. She was for ever adding something derogatory to the list. "Dentists' houses always depress me," she said. "I don't think I could stay in one—with all that going on under the same roof."

What awaited herself was much vaguer.

"It will be like being at school—though having to run to the bell instead of ringing it," Ursula said, when she had picked up the prospectus for the Summer Lecture Course. "A pity you can't just go to the discussions and not stay there. Breakfast 8.15," she read. "Oh, Lord. The Victorian Novel. Trollope. 9.30."

Melanie, in silence, held out her hand for the prospectus and Ursula gave it to her. She did not see it again.

"Will you want Mother's fur?" she asked, when she began to pack. "I just thought . . . evenings, you know, it might be useful . . ."

"I shall have evenings, too," Melanie reminded her.

Their mother could not have guessed what a matter of contention her ermine wrap would turn out to be when she was dead.

*   *   *

"How is Melanie?" Pamela asked.

"Oh, she's well. She's gone on a little holiday, too."

"I'm so glad. I should have liked to have asked her to come with you," Pamela lied. "But there's only this single bed."

Ursula went over to the window. The spare room was at the back of the house and looked across some recreation grounds—a wooden pavilion, a bowling-green; and tennis courts—just as Melanie had said there would be.

That evening, there was the pub.

All afternoon the front-door bell had rung, and Pamela and Ursula, sitting in the drawing-room upstairs could hear the crackle of Miss Potter's starched overall as she crossed the hall to answer it. Patients murmured nervously when they entered, but shouted cheerful good-byes as they left, going full tilt down the gravelled drive and slamming the gate after them.

"I'm sorry about the bell," Pamela said. "At first, I thought it would send me out of my mind, but now it's no worse than a clock striking."

Ursula thought it extraordinary that she had changed so much since their schooldays. It was difficult to find anything to talk about. The books they had once so passionately discussed were at the very bottom of the glass-fronted case, beneath text-books on dentistry and Book Club editions, and Ursula, finding Katherine Mansfield's Journal covered with dust, felt estranged. Perhaps Pamela had become a good cook instead, she thought, for there were plenty of books on that.

Melanie would have scorned the room, with its radiogram and cocktail cabinet and the matching sofa and chairs. The ash-trays were painted with bright sayings in foreign languages; there were piles of fashion magazines that later —much later, Ursula guessed—would be put in the waiting-room downstairs. The parchment lamp-shades were stuck over with wine labels and the lamps were made out of chianti bottles. The motif of drinking was prevalent, from a rueful yet humorous viewpoint. When Pamela opened the cigarette-box it played "The More we are Together", and Ursula wondered if the clock would call "Prosit" when it struck six.

"That's the last patient," Pamela said. "Mike will come up panting for a drink."

Her full-skirt, printed with a jumble of luggage-labels, flew out wide as she made a dash to the cocktail cabinet. She was as eager to be ready with everything as if she were opening a pub.

Panic now mingled with the feeling of estrangement, as Ursula listened to the footsteps on the stairs. "Hello, there, Ursula," said Mike as he threw open the door. "And how are you? Long time, no see, indeed."

"Not since our wedding," Pamela reminded him.

"Well, what will you be after taking?" Mike asked. He slapped his hands together, ready for action, took up a bottle and held it to the light.

'I suppose he feels uneasy because I am a school-mistress,' Ursula thought; 'And perhaps also—lest I shall think Pam married beneath her.'

Pamela put out the glasses and some amusing bottle-openers and corkscrews. Ursula remembered staying with her as a girl, had a clear picture of the gloomy dining-room: a dusty, cut-glass decanter, containing the dregs of some dark, unidentified liquid had stood in the centre of the great sideboard, its position never shifting an inch to the right or left. From that imprisoning house and those oppressive parents, Mike had rescued his betrothed and, though she had shed Katherine Mansfield somewhere on the way, she seemed as gay as could be that she had escaped.

Now she kissed her husband, took her drink and went

downstairs—to turn the waiting-room back into a dining-room, she said. Mike's uneasiness increased. He was clearly longing for her to return.

"You must be a brave man," Ursula said suddenly. "I remember Pam's mother and father and how nervous I was when I stayed there. Even when we were quite well on in our teens, we were made to lie down after luncheon, in a darkened room for ages and ages. 'And no reading, dears,' her mother always said as we went upstairs. At home, we never rested—or only when we were little children, but I pretended that we did, in case Pam's mother should think badly of mine. They seemed so very stern. To snatch away their only daughter must have needed courage."

For the first time, he looked directly at her. In his eyes was a timid expression. He may have been conscious of this and anxious to hide it, for almost immediately he glanced away.

"I girded on my armour," he said, "and rode up to the portcullis and demanded her. That was all there was to it."

She smiled, thinking, 'So this room is the end of a fairy tale.'

"Astonishing good health, my dear," Mike said, lifting his glass.

* * *

Melanie took her coffee and, summoning all her courage, went to sit down beside Mrs Rybeck, who gave her a staving-off smile, a slight shake of her head as she knitted, her lips moving silently. When she came to the end of the row, she apologised, and jotted down on her knitting-pattern, whatever it was she had been counting.

"What a stimulating evening," Melanie said.

"Have you not heard George Barnes lecture before?" Mrs Rybeck was obviously going to be condescending again, but

Melanie was determined to endure it. Then—what she had hoped—Professor Rybeck came in. She felt breathless and self-conscious as he approached.

"Darling!" he murmured, touching his wife's hair, then bowed to Melanie.

"Miss Rogers," his wife reminded him quickly. "At Saint Winifred's, you know, where Ethel's girls were."

"Yes, of course I know Miss Rogers," he said.

His dark hair receded from a forehead that seemed always moist, as were his dark and mournful eyes. As soon as they heard his voice—low, catarrhal and with such gentle inflections—some of the women, who had been sitting in a group by the window, got up and came over to him.

"Professor Rybeck," one said. "We are beside ourselves with excitement about your lecture tomorrow."

"Miss Rogers was just saying that she thought highly of George's talk this evening," said Mrs Rybeck.

"Ah, George!" her husband said softly. "I think George likes to think he has us all by the ears. Young men do. But we mustn't let him sharpen his wits on us till we ourselves are blunt. None the less, he knows his Thackeray."

Melanie considered herself less esteemed for having mentioned him.

"How I love 'Middlemarch'," some woman said. "I think it is my favourite novel."

"Then I only hope I do it justice tomorrow," Professor Rybeck said. Although he seemed full of confidence, he smiled humbly. Nothing was too much trouble.

*   *   *

Pamela had insisted that the three of them should squeeze into the front of the car and Ursula, squashed up in the middle, sat with rounded shoulders and her legs tucked to one side. She was worried about the creases in her skirt. The wireless was on very loud and both Pamela and Mike joined

in the Prize Song from Die Meistersinger. Ursula was glad
when they reached The Swan.

The car-park was full. This pub was where everybody
went, Pamela explained; "at the moment," she added. In
the garden, the striped umbrellas above the tables had been
furled; the baskets of geraniums over the porch were
swinging in the wind.

"Astonishingly horrid evening," Mike said, when some
of his acquaintances greeted him. "This is Pam's friend,
Ursula. Ursie, this is Jock"—or Jean or Eve or Bill. Ursula
lost track. They all knew one another and Mike and Pam
seemed popular. "Don't look now, the worst has happened," someone had said in a loud voice when Mike opened
the door of the Saloon Bar.

Ursula was made much of. From time to time, most of
them were obliged to bring out some dull relation or duty-
guest. ("Not really one of us"), and it was a mark of
friendliness to do one's best to help with other people's
problems—even the most tiresome of old crones would be
attended to; and Ursula, although plump and prematurely
grey, was only too ready to smile and join in the fun.

"You're one of us, I can see," someone complimented her.

"Cheers!" said Ursula before she drank. Melanie would
have shivered with distaste.

"We are all going on to Hilly's," Pam called to Mike
across the bar at closing-time.

This moving-on was the occasion for a little change round
of passengers and, instead of being squeezed in between
Pamela and Mike, Ursula was taken across the car-park by a
man called Guy.

"Daddy will give you a scarf for your head," he promised,
opening the door of his open car. The scarf tucked inside his
shirt was yellow, patterned with horses and when he took it
off and tied it round Ursula's head, the silk was warm to her
cheeks.

They drove very fast along the darkening roads and were the first to arrive.

"Poor frozen girl," said Guy when he had swung the car round on the gravelled sweep in front of the house and brought it up within an inch of the grass verge. With the driving off his mind, he could turn his attention to Ursula and he took one of her goosefleshy arms between his hands and began to chafe it. "What we need is a drink," he said. "Where the hell have they all got to?"

She guessed that to drive fast and to arrive first was something he had to do and, for his sake and to help on the amiability of the evening, she was glad that he had managed it.

"You're sure it's the right house?" she asked.

"Dead sure, my darling."

She had never been called 'darling' by a man and, however meaningless the endearment, it added something to her self-esteem, as their arriving first had added something to his.

She untied the scarf and gave it back to him. He had flicked on his cigarette lighter and was looking for something in the dash-pocket. For a moment, while the small glow lasted, she could study his face. It was like a ventriloquist's dummy's—small, alert, yet blank; the features gave the appearance of having been neatly painted.

He found the packet of cigarettes; then he put the scarf round his neck and tied it carefully. "Someone's coming," he said. "They must have double-crossed us and had one somewhere on the way."

"You drove fastest, that's all," she said, playing her part in the game.

"Sorry if it alarmed you, sweetheart." He leaned over and kissed her quickly, just before the first of the cars came round the curve of the drive.

*   *   *

'That's the first evening gone,' Ursula thought, when later, she lay in bed, rather muzzily going over what had happened. She could remember the drawing-room at Hilly's. She had sat on a cushion on the floor and music from a gramophone above her had spilled over her head, so that she had seen people's mouths opening and shutting but had not been able to hear the matching conversations. In many ways the room—though it was larger—had seemed like Pamela's, with pub-signs instead of bottle-labels on the lampshades. Her sense of time had soon left her and her sense of place grew vaguer, but some details irritated her because she could not evade them—particularly a warming-pan hanging by the fireplace in which she confronted her distorted reflection.

There had seemed no reason why the evening should ever end and no way of setting going all the complications of departure. Although she was tired, she had neither wanted to leave or to stay. She was living a tiny life within herself, sitting there on the cushion; sipping and smiling and glancing about her. Mike had come across the room to her. She turned to tilt back her head to look up into his face but at once felt giddy and had to be content with staring at his knees, at the pin stripes curving baggily, a thin stripe, then a wider, more feathery one. She began to count them, but Mike had come to take her home to bye-byes he said, stretching out a hand. If I can only do this, I can do anything, Ursula thought, trying to rise and keep her balance. I was silly to sit so low down in the first place, she decided. "I think my foot has gone to sleep," she explained and smiled confidingly at his knees. His grip on her arm was strong; although appearing to be extending a hand in gallantry, he was really taking her weight and steadying her, too. She had realised this, even at the time and later, lying safe in bed at last, she felt wonderfully grateful for his kindness, and did not at all mind sharing such a secret with him.

Pamela had put a large jug of water by her bed. An hour earlier, it had seemed unnecessary, but now water was all she wanted in the world. She sat up and drank, with a steady, relentless rhythm, as animals drink. Then she slid back into the warm bedclothes and tried to reconstruct in her mind that drive with Guy and became, in doing so, two people, the story teller and the listener; belittling his endearments, only to reassure herself about them. The sports car, the young man (he was not very old, she told herself), the summer darkness, in spite of its being so windy, were all things that other young girls she had known had taken for granted, at Oxford and elsewhere, and she herself had been denied. They seemed all the more miraculous for having been done without for so long.

Of recent years she had often tried to escape the memory of two maiden-ladies who had lived near her home when she and Melanie were girls. So sharp-tongued and cross-looking, they had seemed then as old as could be, yet may have been no more than in their fifties, she now thought. Frumpish and eccentric, at war with one another as well as all their neighbours, they were to be seen tramping the lanes, single-file and in silence, with their dogs. To the girls, they were the most appalling and unenviable creatures, smelling of vinegar, Melanie had said. The recollection of them so long after they were dead disturbed Ursula and depressed her, for she could see how she and Melanie had taken a turning in their direction, yet scarcely anything as definite as this, for there had been no action, no decision; simply, the road they had been on had always, it seemed, been bending in that direction. In no time at all, would they not be copies of those other old ladies? The Misses Rogers, the neighbours would think of them, feeling pity and nervousness. The elder Miss Rogers would be alarmingly abrupt, with her sarcastic voice and old-fashioned swear-words. They won't be afraid of me, Ursula decided; but had

no comfort from the thought. People would think her
bullied and would be sorry. She, the plumper one, with her
cat and timid smiles, would give biscuits to children when
Melanie's back was turned. Inseparable, yet alien to one
another, they would become. Forewarned as she was, she
felt herself drifting towards that fate and was afraid when
she woke at night and thought of it.

Her first drowsiness had worn off and her thirst kept her
wakeful. She lay and wondered about the details of
Pamela's escape from her parents' sad house and all that
had threatened her there—watchfulness, suspicion, envy
and capricious humours; much of the kind of thing she
herself suffered from Melanie. Pamela's life now was bright
and silly, and perhaps she had run away from the best part
of herself; but there was nothing in the future to menace
her as Ursula was menaced by her own picture of the
elderly Misses Rogers.

*   *   *

"But *surely*," insisted the strained and domineering
voice. The woman gripped the back of the chair in front of
her and stared up at Professor Rybeck on the platform.

At the end of his lecture, he had asked for questions or
discussions. To begin with, everyone had seemed too
stunned with admiration to make an effort; there were
flutterings and murmurings, but for some time no one stood
up. Calmly, he waited, sitting there smiling, eyes half-
closed and his head cocked a little as if he were listening
to secret music, or applause. His arms were crossed over his
chest and his legs were crossed too, and one foot swayed
back and forth rhythmically.

The minute Mr Brundle stood up, other people wanted to.
He was an elderly, earnest man, who had been doggedly on
the track of culture since his youth. His vanity hid from him
the half-stifled yawns he evoked, the glassy look of those

who, though caught, refused to listen and also his way of
melting away to one victim any group of people he approached. Even Professor Rybeck looked restless, as Mr
Brundle began now to pound away at his theory. Then
others, in disagreement or exasperation, began to jump to
their feet, or made sharp comments, interrupting; even
shot their arms into the air, like schoolchildren. World
Peace they might have been arguing about, not George
Eliot's Dorothea Casaubon.

"Please, please," said Professor Rybeck, in his melodious
protesting voice. "Now, Mrs Thomas, let us hear you."

"But *surely*," Mrs Thomas said again.

"Wouldn't it be time to say?" asked Mrs Wetherby—
She sounded diffident and had blushed; she had never
spoken in the presence of so many people before, but wanted
badly to make her mark on the Professor. She was too shy
to stand upright and leaned forward, lifting her bottom a
couple of inches from the chair. Doing so, she dropped her
notebook and pencil, her stole slipped off and when she bent
down to pick it up she also snatched at some large, tortoise-
shell pins that had fallen out of her hair. By the time she
had done all this, her chance was gone and she had made her
mark in the wrong way. The one and only clergyman in the
room had sprung to his feet and, knowing all the tricks
needed to command, had snatched off his spectacles and
held them high in the air while, for some reason no one was
clear about, he denounced Samuel Butler.

"I think, Comrade . . . Professor, I should say," Mr
Brundle interrupted. "If we might return but briefly to the
subject. . . ."

Melanie closed her eyes and thought how insufferable
people became about what has cost them too much to possess
—education, money, or even good health.

Lightly come or not at all, is what I like, she told
herself crossly and, when she opened her eyes, glanced up at

Professor Rybeck, who smiled with such placid condescension as the ding-dong argument went on between clergyman and atheist (for literature—Victorian or otherwise—had been discarded) and then she looked for Mrs Rybeck and found her sitting at the end of the second row, still knitting. She gave, somehow, an impression of not being one of the audience, seemed apart from them, preoccupied with her own thoughts, lending her presence only, like a baby-sitter or the invigilator at an examination—well accustomed to the admiration her husband had from other women of her own age, she made it clear that she was one with him in all he did and thought; their agreement, she implied, had come about many years ago and needed no more discussion, and if the women cared to ask her any of the questions he had no time to answer, then she could give the authorised replies. With all this settled, her placidity, like his, was almost startling to other people, their smiling lips (not eyes), their capacity for waiting for others to finish speaking (and it was far removed from the act of listening), is often to be found in the mothers of large families. Yet she was childless. She had only the Professor, and the socks she knitted were for him. She is more goddessy than motherly, Melanie thought.

"We are summoned to the banqueting-hall," said the Professor, raising his hand in the air, as a bell began to ring. This was the warning that lunch would be ready in ten minutes, the Secretary had told them all when they arrived, and "warning" was a word she had chosen well. The smell of minced beef and cabbage came along passages towards them. To Melanie it was unnoticeable, part of daily life, like other tedious affairs; one disposed of the food, as of any other small annoyance, there were jugs of water to wash it down and slices of bread cut hours before that one could crumble as one listened to one's neighbour.

One of Melanie's neighbours was an elementary school-teacher to whom she tried not to be patronising. On her other side was a Belgian woman whose vivacity was intolerable. She was like a bad caricature of a foreigner, primly sporty and full of gay phrases. "Mon Dieu, we have had it, chums," she said, lifting the water-jug and finding it empty. The machine-gun rattle of consonants vibrated in Melanie's head long after she was alone. "Oh, là, là!" the woman sometimes cried, as if she were a cheeky French maid in an old-fashioned farce.

"You think 'Meedlemahtch' is a good book," she asked Melanie. They all discussed novels at mealtimes too; for they were what they had in common. Melanie was startled, for Professor Rybeck had spent most of the morning explaining its greatness. "It is one of the great English novels," she said.

"As great as Charles Morgan, you think? In the same class?"

Melanie looked suspicious and would not answer.

"It is such a funny book. I read it last night and laughed so much."

"And will read 'War and Peace' between tea and dinner, I suppose," the elementary school-teacher murmured. "Oh dear, how disgusting!" She pushed a very pale, boiled caterpillar to the side of her plate. "If that happened to one of our little darlings at school dinner, the mother would write at once to her M.P."

At Melanie's school, the girls would have hidden the creature under a fork in order not to spoil anyone else's appetite, but she did not say so.

"A *funny* book?" she repeated, turning back to the Belgian woman.

"Yes, I like it so much when she thinks that the really delightful marriage must be that where your husband was a sort of father, and could teach you Hebrew if you wished it. Oh, là, là! For heaven's sake."

"Then she did read a page or two," said the women on Melanie's other side.

A dreadful sadness and sense of loss had settled over Melanie when she herself had read those words. They had not seemed absurd to her; she had felt tears pressing at the back of her eyes. So often, she had longed for protection and compassion, to be instructed and concentrated upon; as if she were a girl again, yet with a new excitement in the air.

As they made their way towards the door, when lunch was over, she could see Professor Rybeck standing there talking to one or two of his admirers. Long before she drew near to him, Melanie found another direction to glance in. What she intended for unconcern, he took for deliberate hostility and wondered at what point of his lecture he had managed to offend her so.

In a purposeless way, she wandered into the garden, The Georgian house—a boys' preparatory-school in the term-time—stood amongst dark rhododendron bushes and silver birches. Paths led in many directions through the shrub-beries, yet all converged upon the lake—a depressing stretch of water, as bleary as an old looking-glass, shadowed by trees and broken by clumps of reeds.

The pain of loneliness was a worse burden to her here than it had ever been at home and she knew—her behaviour as she was leaving the dining-room had reminded her—that the fault was in herself.

"Don't think that I will make excuses to speak to you," she had wanted to imply. "I am not so easily dazzled as these other women." But I wanted him to speak to me, she thought, and perhaps I only feared that he would not.

She sat down on the bank above the water and thought about the Professor. She could even imagine his lustrous eyes turned upon her, as he listened.

"I give false impressions," she struggled to explain to him. "In my heart . . . I am . . ."

"I know what you are," he said gently. "I knew at once."

The relief would be enormous. She was sure of that. She could live the rest of her life on the memory of that moment.

"But he is a fraud," the other, destructive voice in her insisted, the voice that had ruined so much for her. "He is not a fraud," she said firmly; her lips moved; she needed to be so definite with herself. "Perhaps he cannot find the balance between integrity and priggishness."

"Is that all?" asked the other voice.

The dialogue faded out and she sighed, thinking: I wish I hadn't come. I feel so much worse here than I do at home.

Coming round the lake's edge towards her was the atrocious little Mr Brundle. She pretended not to have seen him and got to her feet and went off in the other direction.

By the afternoon post came a letter from Ursula, saying how dull she was and that Melanie had been so right about it all—and that comforted her a little.

*   *   *

Ursula was polishing a glass on a cloth printed with a chart of vintage years for champagne. Although she was drunk, she wondered at the usefulness of this as a reference. It would be strange to go home again to a black telephone, white sheets and drying-up cloths on which there was nothing at all to read, not a recipe for a cocktail or a cheerful slogan.

On the draining-board two white tablets fizzed, as they rose and fell in a glass of water. The noise seemed very loud to her and she was glad when the tablets dissolved and there was silence.

"There you are," Guy said, handing the glass to her. The water still spat and sparkled and she drank it slowly, gasping between sips.

"Pamela will wonder where I am," she said. She put

the glass on the draining-board and sat down with a bump
on one of the kitchen chairs. She had insisted on washing
the two glasses before she went home, and had devoted
herself to doing so with single-mindedness; but Guy had
been right, and she gave in. Everything she had to do had
become difficult—going home, climbing the stairs, undressing. I shall just have to sit on this chair and let time
pass, she decided. It will pass, she promised herself, and it
mends all in the end.

"Where did we go after that Club?" she suddenly asked
frowning.

"Nowhere," said Guy. "On our way back to Pamela's
we stopped here for a drink. That's all."

"Ah, yes!"

She remembered the outside of this bungalow and a
wooden gate with the name Hereiam. It had been quite
dark when they walked up the stony path to the front door.
Now, it seemed the middle of the night. "I think you gave
me too much whisky," she said, with a faint, reproachful
smile.

"As a matter of fact, I gave you none. It was ginger-ale
you were drinking."

She considered this and then lifted her eyes to look at
him and asked anxiously: "Then had I had . . . was I . . . ?"

"You were very sweet."

She accepted this gravely. He put his hands under her
arms and brought her to her feet and she rested the side of
her face against his waistcoat and stayed very still, as if she
were counting his heart-beats. These, like the fizzing drink,
also sounded much too loud.

"I didn't wash the other glass," she said.

"Mrs Lamb can do it in the morning."

She went from one tremulous attempt at defence to
another, wanting to blow her nose, or light a cigarette or
put something tidy. In the sitting-room, earlier, when he

had sat down beside her on the sofa, she had sprung up and gone rapidly across the room to look for an ash-tray. "Who is this?" she had asked, picking up a framed photograph and holding it at arm's length, as if to ward him off. "Girl friend," he said briefly, drinking his whisky and watching her manœuvres with amusement.

"Haven't you ever wanted to get married?" she had asked.

"Sometimes. Have you?"

"Oh, sometimes . . . I daresay," she answered vaguely.

Now, in the kitchen, he had caught her at last, she was clasped in his arms and feeling odd, she told him.

"I know. There's some coffee nearly ready in the other room. That will do untold good."

What a dreadful man he is, really, in spite of his tenderness, she thought. So hollow and vulgar that I don't know what Melanie would say.

She was startled for a moment, wondering if she had murmured this aloud; for, suddenly, his heartbeat had become noisier—from anger, she was afraid.

"You are very kind," she said appeasingly. "I am not really used to drinking as much as people do here—not used to drinking at all."

"What *are* you used to?"

"Just being rather dull, you know—my sister and I."

His way of lifting her chin up and kissing her was too accomplished and she was reminded of the way in which he drove the car. She was sure that there was something here she should resent. Perhaps he was patronising her; for the kiss had come too soon after her remark about the dullness of her life. I can bring *some* excitement into it, he may have thought.

Without releasing her, he managed to stretch an arm and put out the light. "I can't bear to see you frowning," he explained. "Why frown anyway?"

"That coffee . . . but then I mustn't stay for it, after all. Pamela will be wondering . . ."

"Pam will understand."

"Oh, I hope not."

She frowned more than ever and shut her eyes tightly although the room was completely dark.

*　　*　　*

Melanie sat on the edge of the bed, coughing. She was wondering if she had suddenly got T.B. and kept looking anxiously at her handkerchief.

The sun was shining, though not into her room. From the window, she could see Professor Rybeck sitting underneath the Wellingtonia with an assortment of his worshippers. From his gestures, Melanie could tell that it was he who was talking, and talking continuously. The hand rose and fell and made languid spirals as he unfolded his theme, or else cut the air decisively into slices. Mrs Rybeck was, of course, knitting. By her very presence, sitting a little apart from her husband, like a woman minding a stall on a fairground, she attracted passers-by. Melanie watched the Belgian woman now approaching, to say her few words about the knitting, then having paid her fee, to pass on to listen to the Professor.

Desperately, Melanie wished to be down there listening, too; but she had no knowledge of how to join them. Crossing the grass, she would attract too much attention. Ah, *she* cannot keep away, people would think, turning to watch her. She must be in love with the Professor after all, like the other women; but perhaps more secretly, more devouringly.

She had stopped coughing and forgotten tuberculosis for the moment, as she tried to work out some more casual way than crossing the lawn. She might emerge less noticeably from the shrubbery behind the Wellingtonia, if only she could be there in the first place.

She took a clean handkerchief from a drawer and smoothed her hair before the looking-glass; and then a bell rang for tea and, when she went back to the window, the group under the tree was breaking up. Mrs Rybeck was rolling up her knitting and they were all laughing.

I shall see him at tea, Melanie thought. She could picture him bowing to her, coldly, and with the suggestion that it was she who disliked him rather than he who disliked her. I could never put things right now, she decided.

She wondered what Ursula would be doing at this minute. Perhaps sitting in Pamela's little back garden having tea, while, at the front of the house, the patients came and went. She had said that she would be glad to be at home again, for Pamela had changed and they had nothing left in common. And coming here hasn't been a success, either, Melanie thought, as she went downstairs to tea. She blamed Ursula very much for having made things so dull for them both. There must be ways of showing her how mistaken she had been, ways of preventing anything of the kind happening again.

"Miss Rogers," said the Professor with unusual gaiety. They had almost collided at the drawing-room door. "Have you been out enjoying the sun?"

She blushed and was so angry that she should that she said quite curtly, "No, I was writing letters in my room."

He stood quickly aside to let her pass and she did so without a glance at him.

*   *   *

Their holiday was over. On her way back from the station, Ursula called at the kennels for the cat and Melanie, watching her come up the garden path, could see the creature clawing frantically at her shoulder, trying to hoist himself out of her grasp. The taxi-driver followed with the suitcase.

Melanie had intended to be the last home and had even caught a later train than was convenient, in order not to have to be waiting there for her sister. After all her planning, she was angry to have found the house empty.

"Have you been home long?" Ursula asked rather breathlessly. She put the cat down and looked round. Obviously Melanie had not, for her suitcase still stood in the hall and not a letter had been opened.

"Only a minute or two," said Melanie.

"That cat's in a huff with me. Trying to punish me for going away, I suppose. He's quite plump though. He looks well, doesn't he? Oh, it's so lovely to be home."

She went to the hall-table and shuffled the letters, then threw them on one side. Melanie had said nothing.

"Aren't *you* glad to be home?" Ursula asked her.

"No, I don't think so."

"Well I'm glad you had a good time. It was a change for you."

"Yes."

"And now let's have some tea."

She went into the kitchen and, still wearing her hat, began to get out the cups and saucers. "They didn't leave any bread," she called out. "Oh, yes, it's all right, I've found it." She began to sing, then stopped to chatter to the cat, then sang again.

Melanie had been in the house over an hour and had done nothing.

"I'm so glad you had a good time," Ursula said again, when they were having tea.

"I'm sorry you didn't."

"It was a mistake going there, trying to renew an old friendship. You'd have hated the house."

"You'd have liked *mine*. Grey stone, Georgian, trees and a lake."

"Romantic," Ursula said and did not notice that

Melanie locked her hands together in rather a theatrical gesture.

"Pam seems complacent. She's scored over me, having a husband. Perhaps that's why she invited me."

"What did you do all the time?"

"Just nothing. Shopped in the morning—every morning —the housewife's round—butcher, baker, candlestick maker. 'I'm afraid the piece of skirt was rather gristly, Mr Bones.' That sort of thing. She would fetch half a pound of butter one day and go back for another half-pound the next morning—just for the fun of it. One day, she said, 'I think we'll have some hock for supper.' I thought she was talking about wine, but it turned out to be some bacon—not very nice. Not very nice of me to talk like this, either."

However dull it had been, she seemed quite excited as she described it; her cheeks were bright and her hands restless.

"We went to the cinema once, to see a Western," she added. "Mike is very fond of Westerns."

"How dreadful for you."

Ursula nodded.

"Well, that's their life," she said, "I was glad all the time that you were not there. Darling puss, so now you've forgiven me."

To show his forgiveness, the cat jumped on to her lap and began dough-punching, his extended claws catching the threads of her skirt.

"Tell me about *you*," Ursula said. She poured out some more tea to sip while Melanie had her turn; but to her surprise Melanie frowned and looked away.

"Is something the matter?"

"I can't talk about it yet, or get used to not being there. This still seems unreal to me. You must give me time."

She got up, knocked over the cream jug and went out of the room. Ursula mopped up the milk with her napkin and then leant back and closed her eyes. Her moment's consternation at Melanie's behaviour had passed; she even forgot it. The cat relaxed, too, and, curled up against her, slept.

Melanie was a long time unpacking and did nothing towards getting supper. She went for a walk along the sea road and watched the sunset on the water. The tide was out and the wet sands were covered with a pink light. She dramatised her solitary walk and was in a worse turmoil when she reached home.

"Your cough is bad," Ursula said when they had finished supper.

"Is it?" Melanie said absent-mindedly.

"Something has happened, hasn't it?" Ursula asked her, and then looked down quickly, as if she were confused.

"The end of the world," said Melanie.

"You've fallen in love?" Ursula lifted her head and stared at her.

"To have to go back to school next week and face those bloody children—and go on facing them, for ever and for ever—or other ones exactly like them . . . the idea suddenly appals me."

Her bitterness was so true, and Ursula could hear her own doom in her sister's words. She had never allowed herself to have thoughts of that kind.

"But can't you . . . can't he?" she began.

"We can't meet again. We never shall. So it *is* the end of the world, you see," said Melanie. The scene gave her both relief and anguish. Her true parting with Professor Rybeck (he had looked up from *The Times* and nodded as she crossed the hall) was obliterated for ever. She could more easily bear the agonised account she now gave to Ursula and she would bear it—their noble resolve, their last illicit embrace.

"He's married, you mean?" Ursula asked bluntly.

"Yes, married."

Mrs Rybeck, insensitively knitting at the execution of

their hopes, appeared as an evil creature, tenacious and sinister.

"But to say good-bye for ever . . ." Ursula protested. "We only have one life . . . would it be wicked, after all?"

"What could there be . . . clandestine meetings and sordid arrangements?"

Ursula looked ashamed.

"I should ruin his career," said Melanie.

"Yes, I see. You could write to one another, though."

"Write!" Melanie repeated in a voice as light as air. "I think I will go to bed now. I feel exhausted."

"Yes, do, and I will bring you a hot drink." As Melanie began to go upstairs, Ursula said, "I am very sorry, you know."

While she was waiting for the milk to rise in the pan, she tried to rearrange her thoughts, especially to exclude (now that there was so much nobility in the house) her own squalid—though hazily recollected—escapade. Hers was a more optimistic nature than Melanie's and she was confident of soon putting such memories out of her mind.

When she took the hot milk upstairs, her sister was sitting up in bed reading a volume of Keats' letters. "He gave it to me as I came away," she explained, laying the book on the bedside table, where it was always to remain.

We have got this to live with now, Ursula thought, and it will be with us for ever, I can see—the reason and the excuse for everything. It will even grow; there will be more and more of it, as time goes on. When we are those two elderly Miss Rogers we are growing into it will still be there. "Miss Melanie, who has such a sharp tongue," people will say. "Poor thing . . . a tragic love-affair a long way back." I shall forget there was a time when we did not have it with us.

Melanie drank her milk and put out the light; then she lay down calmly and closed her eyes and prepared herself for her dreams. Until they came, she imagined walking by the lake, as she had done, that afternoon, only a few days ago; but instead of Mr Brundle coming into the scene, Professor Rybeck appeared. He walked towards her swiftly, as if by assignation. Then they sat down and looked at the tarnished water—and she added a few swans for them to watch. After a long delicious silence, she began to speak. Yet words were not really necessary. She had hardly begun the attempt; her lips shaped the beginning of a sentence— "I am . . ." and then he took her hand and held it to his cheek. "I know what you are," he said. "I knew at the very beginning."

Although they had parted for ever, she realised that she was now at peace—She felt ennobled and enriched, and saw herself thus, reflected from her sister's eyes, and she was conscious of Ursula's solemn wonder and assured by it.

Perhaps a Family Failing

OF course, Mrs Cotterell cried. Watery-eyed, on the arm of the bridegroom's father, she smiled in a bewildered way to left and right, coming down the aisle. Outside, on the church steps, she quickly dashed the tears away as she faced the camera, still arm-in-arm with Mr Midwinter, a man she detested.

He turned towards her and gave a great meaningless laugh just as the camera clicked and Mrs Cotterell had his ginny breath blown full in her face. Even in church he had to smell like that, she thought, and the grim words, "Like father, like son", disturbed her mind once more.

Below them, at the kerb's edge, Geoff was already helping his bride into the car. The solemnity of the service had not touched him. In the vestry, he had been as jaunty as ever, made his wife blush and was hushed by his mother, a frail, pensive creature, who had much, Mrs Cotterell thought, to be frail and pensive about.

It was Saturday morning and the bridal car moved off slowly amongst the other traffic. Mrs Cotterell watched until the white-ribboned motor disappeared.

The bridesmaids, one pink, one apple-green, were getting into the next car. Lissport was a busy place on Saturdays and to many of the women it was part of the morning's shopping-outing to be able to stand for a minute or two to watch a bride coming out of the church. Feeling nervous and self-conscious, Mrs Cotterell, who had often herself stood and watched and criticised, crossed the pavement to the car. She was anxious to be home and wondered if everything was all right there. She had come away in a flurry of confused directions, leaving two of her neighbours slicing beetroot and sticking blanched almonds into the trifles. She was relieved that the reception was her own affair, that she could be sure that there would be no drunkenness, no rowdy behaviour and suggestive speeches, as there had been at Geoff's sister's wedding last year. One glass of port to drink a toast to the bride and bridegroom she had agreed to. For the rest she hoped that by now her kindly neighbours had mixed the orange cordial.

*　　　*　　　*

Mrs Cotterell cried again, much harder, when Beryl came downstairs in her going-away suit, and kissed her and thanked her (as if her mother were a hostess, not her own flesh and blood, Mrs Cotterell thought sorrowfully) and with composure got into Geoff's little car, to which Mr Midwinter had tied an empty sardine-tin.

Then everyone else turned to Mrs Cotterell and thanked her and praised the food and Beryl's looks and dress. It had all gone off all right, they said, making a great hazard of it. "You'll miss her," the women told her. "I know what it's like," some added.

The bridesmaids took off their flower wreaths and put on their coats. Geoff's brothers, Les and Ron, were taking them out for the evening. "Not long till opening-time," they said.

Mrs Cotterell went back into the house, to survey the wedding-presents, and the broken wedding-cake, with the trellis work icing she had done so lovingly, crumbled all over the table. Beryl's bouquet was stuck in a vase, waiting to be taken tomorrow to poor Grandma in hospital.

In the kitchen, the faithful neighbours were still hard at work, washing up the piles of plates stained with beetroot and mustard and tomato sauce.

"She's gone," Mrs Cotterell whispered into her crumpled handkerchief as her husband came in and put his arm round her.

*   *   *

"Soon be opening-time," Geoff said, driving along the busy road to Seaferry. He had long ago stopped the car, taken the sardine-tin off the back axle and thrown it over a hedge. "Silly old fool, Dad," he had said fondly. "Won't ever act his age."

Beryl thought so, too, but decided not to reopen that old discussion at such a time. For weeks, she had thought and talked and dreamt of the wedding, studied the advice to brides in women's magazines, on make-up, etiquette and Geoff's marital rights—which he must, she learnt, not be allowed to anticipate. "Stop it, Geoff!" she had often said firmly. "I happen to want you to respect me, thank you very much." Unfortunately for her, Geoff was not the respectful kind, although, in his easy-going way he consented to the celibacy—one of her girlish whims—and had even allowed the gratifying of his desires to be postponed from Easter until early summer, because she had suddenly decided she wanted sweet peas in the bridesmaids' bouquets.

To the women's magazines Beryl now felt she owed everything; she had had faith in their advice and seen it justified. I expect Geoff's getting excited, she thought. She was really quite excited herself.

"Now where are you going?" she asked, as he swerved suddenly off the road. It was perfectly plain that he was going into a public house, whose front door he had seen flung open just as he was about to pass it by.

"Well, here it is," he said. "The White Horse. The very first pub to have the privilege of serving a drink to Mr and Mrs Geoffrey Midwinter."

This pleased her, although she wanted to get to the hotel as quickly as she could, to unpack her trousseau, before it creased too badly.

It was a dull little bar, smelling frowsty. The landlord was glumly watchful, as if they might suddenly get out of hand, or steal one of his cracked ashtrays.

Geoff, however, was in high spirits, and raised his pint pot and winked at his wife. "Well, here's in anticipation," he said. She looked demurely at her gin and orange, but she smiled. She loved him dearly. She was quite convinced of this, for she had filled in a questionnaire on the subject of love in one of her magazines, and had scored eighteen out of twenty, with a rating of "You and Cleopatra share the honours." Only his obsession with public houses worried her, but she was sure that—once she had him away from the influence of his father and brothers—she would be able to break the habit.

*   *   *

At six o'clock Mr Midwinter took his thirst and his derogatory opinions about the wedding down to the saloon bar of The Starter's Orders. His rueful face, as he described the jugs of orangeade, convulsed his friends. "Poor Geoff, what's he thinking of, marrying into a lot like that?" asked the barmaid.

"Won't make no difference to Geoff," said his father. "Geoff's like his Dad. Not given to asking anybody's by-your-leave when he feels like a pint."

Mrs Midwinter had stayed at home alone. It had not occurred to her husband that she might be feeling flat after the day's excitement. She would not have remarked on it herself, knowing the problem was insoluble. He could not

have taken her to a cinema, because Saturday evening was
sacred to drinking, and although she would have liked to
go with him for a glass of stout, she knew why she
could not. He always drank in the Men Only bar at The
Starter's Orders. "Well, you don't want me drinking with
a lot of prostitutes, do you?" he often asked, and left her
no choice, as was his habit.

*   *   *

Beryl had never stayed in an hotel before, and she was
full of admiration at the commanding tone Geoff adopted as
they entered the hall of The Seaferry Arms.

"Just one before we go up?" he inquired, looking towards
the bar.

"Later, dear," she said firmly. "Let's unpack and tidy
ourselves first; then we can have a drink before dinner."
The word "dinner" depressed him. It threatened to waste a
great deal of Saturday evening drinking time.

From their bedroom window they could see a bleak
stretch of promenade, grey and gritty. The few people
down there either fought their way against the gale, with
their heads bowed and coats clutched to their breasts, or
seemed tumbled along with the wind at their heels. The sun,
having shone on the bride, had long ago gone in and it
seemed inconceivable that it would ever come out again.

"No strolling along the prom tonight," said Geoff.

"Isn't it a shame? It's the only thing that's gone wrong."

Beryl began to hang up and spread about the filmy, lacy,
ribboned lingerie with which she had for long planned to
tease and entice her husband.

"The time you take," he said. He had soon tipped everything out of his own case into a drawer. "What's this?" he
asked, picking up something of mauve chiffon.

"My nightgown," she said primly.

"What ever for?"

"Don't be common." She always affected disapproval when he teased her.

"What about a little anticipation here and now?" he suggested.

"Oh, don't be so silly. It's broad daylight."

"Right. Well, I'm just going to spy out the lie of the land. Back in a minute," he said.

She was quite content to potter about the bedroom, laying traps for his seduction; but when she was ready at last, she realised that he had been away a long time. She stood by the window, wondering what to do, knowing that it was time for them to go in to dinner. After a while, she decided that she would have to find him and, feeling nervous and self-conscious, she went along the quiet landing and down the stairs. Her common sense took her towards the sound of voices and laughter and, as soon as she opened the door of the bar, she was given a wonderful welcome from all the new friends Geoff had suddenly made.

*   *   *

"It seems ever so flat, doesn't it?" Mrs Cotterell said. All of the washing-up was done, but she was too tired to make a start on packing up the presents.

"It's the reaction," her husband said solemnly.

Voices from a play on the wireless mingled with their own, but were ignored. Mrs Cotterell had her feet in a bowl of hot water. New shoes had given her agony. Beryl, better informed, had practised wearing hers about the house for days before.

"Haven't done my corns any good," Mrs Cotterell mourned. Her feet ached and throbbed, and so did her heart.

"It all went off well, though, didn't it?" she asked, as she had asked him a dozen times before.

"Thanks to you," he said dutifully. He was clearing out

the budgerigar's cage and the bird was sitting on his bald head, blinking and chattering.

Mrs Cotterell stared at her husband. She suddenly saw him as a completely absurd figure, and she trembled with anger and self-pity. Something ought to have been done for her on such an evening, she thought, some effort should have been made to console and reward her. Instead, she was left to soak her feet and listen to a lot of North Country accents on the radio. She stretched out her hand and switched them off.

"What ever's wrong, Mother?"

"I can't stand any more of that 'By goom' and 'Nowt' and 'Eee, lad'. It reminds me of that nasty cousin Rose of yours."

"But we always listen to the play on a Saturday."

"This Saturday isn't like other Saturdays." She snatched her handkerchief out of her cuff and dabbed her eyes.

Mr Cotterell leaned forward and patted her knee and the budgerigar flew from his head and perched on her shoulder.

"That's right, Joey, You go to Mother. She wants a bit of cheering-up."

"I'm not his mother, if you don't mind, and I don't want cheering-up from a bird."

"One thing I know is you're overtired. I've seen it coming. You wouldn't care to put on your coat and stroll down to the Public for a glass of port, would you?"

"Don't be ridiculous," she said.

*　　*　　*

After dinner, they drank their coffee, all alone in the dreary lounge of The Seaferry Arms, and then Beryl went to bed. She had secret things to do to her hair and her face. "I'll just pour you out another cup," she said. "Then, when you've drunk it, you can come up."

"Right," he said solemnly, nodding his head.

"Don't be long, darling."

When she had gone, he sat and stared at the cupful of black coffee and then got up and made his way back to the bar.

All of his before-dinner cronies had left and a completely different set of people stood round the bar. He ordered some beer and looked about him.

"Turned chilly," said the man next to him.

"Yes. Disappointing," he agreed. To make friends was the easiest thing in the world. In no time, he was at the heart of it all again.

*   *   *

At ten o'clock, Beryl, provocative in chiffon, as the magazines would have described her, burst into tears of rage. She could hear the laughter—so much louder now, towards closing-time—downstairs in the bar and knew that the sound of it had drawn Geoff back. She was powerless—so transparently tricked out to tempt him—to do anything but lie and wait until, at bar's emptying, he should remember her and stumble upstairs to bed.

*   *   *

It was not the first happy evening Geoff had spent in the bar of The Seaferry Arms. He had called there with the team, after cricket-matches in the nearby villages. Seaferry was only twenty miles from home. Those summer evenings had all merged into one another, as drinking evenings should—and this one was merging with them. 'I'm glad I came,' he thought, rocking slightly as he stood by the bar with two of his new friends. He couldn't remember having met nicer people. They were a very gay married couple. The wife had a miniature poodle who had already wetted three times on the carpet. "She can't help it, can you, Angel?" her mistress protested. "She's quite neurotic; aren't you, precious thing?"

Doris—as Geoff had been told to call her—was a heavy
jolly woman. The bones of her stays showed through her
frock, her necklace of jet beads was powdered with
cigarette ash. She clutched a large, shiny handbag and had
snatched from it a pound note, which she began to wave in
the air, trying to catch the barmaid's eye. "I say, Miss!
What's her name, Ted? Oh, yes. I say, Maisie! Same again,
there's a dear girl."

It was nearly closing-time, and a frenzied reordering was
going on. The street door was pushed open and a man and
woman with a murderous-looking bull terrier came in.
"You stay there," the man said to the woman and the dog,
and he left them and began to force his way towards the
bar.

"Miss! Maisie!" Doris called frantically. Her poodle,
venturing between people's legs, made another puddle under
a table and approached the bull terrier.

"I say, Doris, call Zoë back," said her husband. "And put
that money away. I told you I'll get these."

"I insist. They're on me."

"Could you call your dog back?" the owner of the bull
terrier asked them. "We don't want any trouble."

"Come, Zoë, pet!" Doris called. "He wouldn't hurt her,
though. She's a bitch. Maisie! Oh, there's a dear. Same
again, love. Large ones."

Suddenly, a dreadful commotion broke out. Doris was
nearly knocked off her stool as Zoë came flying back to her
for protection, with the bull terrier at her throat. She
screamed and knocked over somebody's gin.

Geoff, who had been standing by the bar in a pleasurable
haze, watching the barmaid, was, in spite of his feeling of
unreality, the first to spring to life and pounce upon the
bull terrier and grab his collar. The dog bit his hand, but he
was too drunk to feel much pain. Before anyone could snatch
Zoë out of danger, the barmaid lifted the jug of water and

meaning to pour it over the bull terrier, flung it instead
over Geoff. The shock made him loosen his grip and the
fight began again. A second time he grabbed at the collar
and had his hand bitten once more; but now—belatedly,
everyone else thought—the two dog-owners came to his
help. Zoë, with every likelihood of being even more
neurotic in the future, was put, shivering, in her mistress's
arms, the bull terrier was secured to his lead in disgrace,
and Maisie called Time.

After some recriminations between themselves, the dog-
owners thanked and congratulated Geoff. "Couldn't get
near them," they said. "The bar was so crowded. Couldn't
make head or tail of what was going on."

"Sorry you got so wet," said Doris.

The bull terrier's owner felt rather ashamed of himself
when he saw how pale Geoff was. "You all right?" he
asked. "You look a bit shaken up."

Geoff examined his hand. There was very little blood, but
he was beginning to be aware of the pain and felt giddy. He
shook his head, but could not answer. Something dripped
from his hair onto his forehead, and when he dabbed it with
his handkerchief, he was astonished to see water and not
blood.

"You got far to go?" the man asked him. "Where's your
home?"

"Lissport."

"That's our way, too, if you want a lift." Whether Geoff
had a car or not, the man thought he was in no condition to
drive it; although, whether from shock or alcohol or both,
it was difficult to decide.

"I'd *like* a lift," Geoff murmured drowsily. "Many
thanks."

"No, any thanks are due to *you*."

*   *   *

"Doesn't it seem strange without Geoff?" Mrs Midwinter asked her husband. He was back from The Starter's Orders, had taken off his collar and tie and was staring gloomily at the dying fire.

"Les and Ron home yet?" he asked.

"No, they won't be till half-past twelve. They've gone to the dance at the Town Hall."

"Half-past twelve! It's scandalous the way they carry on. Drinking themselves silly, I've no doubt at all. Getting decent girls into trouble."

"It's only a dance, Dad."

"*And* their last one. I'm not having it. Coming home drunk on a Sunday morning and lying in bed till all hours to get over it. When was either of them last at Chapel? Will you tell me that?"

Mrs Midwinter sighed and folded up her knitting.

"I can't picture why Geoff turned from Chapel like that." Mr Midwinter seemed utterly depressed about his sons, as he often was at this time on a Saturday night.

"Well, he was courting . . ."

"First time I've been in a church was today, and I was not impressed."

"I thought it was lovely, and you looked your part just as if you did it every day."

"I wasn't worried about *my* part. Sort of thing like that makes no demands on *me*. What I didn't like was the service, to which I took exception, and that namby-pamby parson's voice. To me, the whole thing was—insincere."

Mrs Midwinter held up her hand to silence him. "There's a car stopping outside. It can't be the boys yet."

From the street, they both heard Geoff's voice shouting good-bye, then a car door was slammed, and the iron gate opened with a whining sound.

"Dad, it's Geoff!" Mrs Midwinter whispered. "There must have been an accident. Something's happened to Beryl."

"Well, he sounded cheerful enough about it."

They could hear Geoff coming unsteadily up the garden-path. When Mrs Midwinter threw open the door, he stood blinking at the sudden light, and swaying.

"Geoff! What ever's wrong?"

"I've got wet, Mum, and I've hurt my hand," Geoff said.

Good-Bye, Good-Bye

ON his last evening in England he broke two promises—one, that he would dine with his brother, and another, older promise made to a woman whom he loved. When he and Catherine had tried, years before, to put an end to this impermissible love for one another the best they could decide was to give it no nourishment and let it wither if it would. "No messages," she had said when they parted, "no letters." His letters had always incapacitated her: on days when she received them, she moved slowly at her work, possessed by his words, deaf to any others, from husband or children or friends. "I don't want to know how you are getting on," she told him, "or to think of you in any particular place. You might die: you might marry. I never want to know. I want you to stop, here, for ever." (*Then, there,* an autumn night, a railway station.) As his train moved off he saw that her face had a look of utter perplexity, as if the meaning of her future were beyond her comprehension. The look had stayed in his mind and was in his imagination this evening as he walked from the bus stop in the village and out on the sea-road towards the house.

This house, which she rented each summer for the children's holidays, was where they had sometimes been together. The recklessness, the deceit which, in London, they suppressed, they had indulged here, as if a different sort of behaviour were allowed at the seaside. Returning to her husband, who had no part in those holidays, she would at once feel so mortified and so uneasily ashamed, that their few meetings were humiliating to them both and full of recriminations and despair; and it was after such a summer that they had parted—for ever, both had believed.

The road under the sea-wall was sheltered. Inland, sheep cropped the salt-marshes where he and Catherine had walked in the evening when the children were in bed. When it was dark, they would kiss and say good-bye, then kiss again. He would walk back to the village along this sea-road and she would tiptoe into the house, so that the children's nurse would not be wakened or discover how late she had stayed out.

Memories agitated him as he walked along the road. The landscape seemed to have awaited him, to have kept itself unchanged to pain him now with a great sense of strangeness. He had no hopes for this visit, no vestige of confidence in it, knew that it was mistakenly made and fraught with all perils—her anger, her grief, her embarrassment. In him, love could not be reawakened, for it had not slept. He did not know what risk faced her; how she had dealt with her sadness, or laid him away in his absence. He was compelled to find out, to discover if he were quick or dead in her mind, and to see if the look—the perplexed expression—had hardened on her face, or vanished. But as he came round a bend in the road and saw the chimneys of the house and the beginning of the garden, he was so appalled by his venture that he walked more slowly and longed to turn back. He thought: 'She will be changed, look different, wear new clothes I have never seen, the children will be older, and, oh God,' he prayed, his heart swerving at the sudden idea, 'let there be no more! Let her not have had more children! Let her not have filled her life that way!'

He stopped in the road and listened for children's voices in the garden but in the still evening the bleating of sheep was the only sound. High up on the orchard trees red apples shone in the sun. An old net sagged across the tennis-lawn. The gabled, hideous house with its verandas and balconies came into view. At the open windows, faded curtains flapped over the newly-cleaned tennis-shoes bleaching on sills and sandy swim-suits and towels hung out to dry. The house, which looked as if it had been burst asunder, and left with all its doors ajar, had a vacant—though only lately vacant— appearance.

In the conservatory-porch a tabby cat was sleeping on a shelf among flower-pots and tennis racquets. A book lying open had all its pages arched up in the sun and a bunch of wild flowers were dying on a ledge. He pressed the bell and away at the back of the house heard it ringing. The heat under the dusty panes made him feel faint and he stepped back from it, away from the door. As he did so, a girl leaned from an upstairs window and called down to him. "Do you want mother?"

Hit by the irony of the words, the shock of seeing Catherine's eyes looking down at him, he could not answer her at once. Her daughter did not wait for his reply. "She's on the beach. They're all there. I'm just going, too. One moment!" She moved from sight, he heard her running downstairs, then she came to the door.

"You are Sarah?" he said.

"Yes."

'Oh, Catherine's eyes, those eyes!' he thought. 'The miracle, but the enormity, that they should come again; clearer, more beautiful'—he would not think it. "You don't remember me. I am Peter Lord."

"I remember the name. I remember *you* now. I had only forgotten. You came here once and helped us with a picnic on the beach; lit a fire, do you remember that? It's what they are all doing at this moment. I was waiting for a friend." She hesitated, looked towards the gate. "But they didn't come."

' "They" because she will not say "he",' Peter thought. 'The embarrassments of the English language!' She was bright with some disappointment.

"Shall we go down together and find them?" she asked; then, in the patronising tone young people use when they try to carry on conversations with their elders on equal terms, she asked: "Let me see, you went abroad, didn't you? Wasn't it South America?"

"South Africa."

"I always get those two muddled. And now you have come back home again?"

"For a short time. I am off in the morning."

"Oh, what a pity; but mother *will* be pleased that you came to say good-bye."

They crossed the road and climbed the bank to the top of the sea-wall. There they paused. The tide was out and the wet sand far down the beach reflected a pink light from the sun, which was going down in an explosive, Turneresque brilliance above the sand-hillocks. Farther along, they could see figures busily bringing driftwood to a fire and two children at the sea's edge were digging in the sand.

Seeing Peter and Sarah on the skyline, one of the group waved, then turned away again.

"He thinks you are my friend," Sarah said. She wore Catherine's anxious look. "That's Chris. Do you remember Chris? He is fifteen—nearly two years younger than me."

"Yes, I remember him." Peter was feeling tired now, rather puffed by keeping up with her across a stretch of hot white sand in which his feet sank at every step. This sand, seldom washed by the sea, was full of dried seaweed and bits of old newspapers. Clumps of spiky reed grew in it and sea-poppies and thistles.

"Who are all those other children?" he asked. He stopped and took off his shoes and socks, rolled his trousers above his ankles. 'A fine sight,' he thought crossly. 'Completely ridiculous.'

"Our friends," said Sarah, turning and waiting for him. He could see Catherine. She was apart from the others and was bending over a picnic-basket. When Sarah called to her, she turned and, still kneeling in the sand, looked up towards them, her arm shading her eyes. The incredulous look was on her face as if it had never left it and at the sight of the agitation she could not hide from her children and their friends, he realised the full cruelty of his treachery. She took his hand, and recovered enough to hide shock beneath a show of superficial surprise, glossing over the grotesque situation with an hostessy condescension.

"Are you on leave?" Her voice indicated his rôle of old friend of the family.

"No, my father died. I had to come over in a hurry."

"I am sorry. Graham will be sad when he hears that."

'So I am to be her husband's comrade, too!' he thought.

As if she were in her drawing-room she invited him to sit down, but before he could do so, the younger children had run up from the sea and stood on either side of their mother, staring in curiosity at him and awaiting an explanation.

They were all variations of her, her four sons and daughters and these two, a boy and a girl, with their unguarded, childish gaze, were more like her than the other two whose defined features were brightly masked to preserve the secrets of adolescence.

"Lucy, this is Mr Lord. He gave you your Fairy-Tale book that you love so much."

"Yes, I do."

"And this is Ricky."

"What did you give *me*?" the boy asked.

"I'm sure I don't know. Perhaps you were to share the book."

"No, it is only mine," Lucy said certainly.

"He gave you lots of things," said Catherine.

"More than me?"

"No, Lucy, I am sure not."

"I think *I* only had the book."

"This isn't a nice conversation. You should think of other things than what you are given. Go and help Chris to find some firewood. You can't enjoy the fire and the supper if you do nothing to help."

The children wandered off, but back to the edge of the sea. They left a vacuum. She had tried to fill it with what he disliked and had always thought of as 'fussing with the children'—the children whom he had half-loved, for having her likeness, and half-resented, for not being his, for taking her attention from him and forbidding their life together.

"They've grown," he said.

"Yes, of course."

She put her hand deep in the sand, burying it in coolness. He watched her, remembering how once long ago she had done that and he had made a tunnel with his own hand and clasped hers and they had sat in silence, their fingers entwined beneath the sand. Such far-off lovers' games seemed utterly sad now, utterly forlorn, dead, their meaning brushed away like dust.

"Why did you come?" she whispered, her eyes fixed on the young ones building their fire; but fearing his answer, she caught her breath and called to her son. "Chris, darling, bring the others over to meet Mr Lord."

They came over, polite and estranged, willing to be kind. Chris hadn't remembered, but now he did. He introduced his friends, the same bright, polite boys and girls as himself. The boys called him "Sir," the girls smiled warmly and encouragingly. 'You are quite welcome, don't feel out of it—the fun, the lovely evening—just because you are old,' their smiles said.

They diminished Catherine. They were all taller. She seemed to Peter now to be set apart as 'mother', their voices were protective to her, undemanding. (Once they had clamoured for her attention, claimed every second. "Look at me, mummy! Look at me!") They had set her firmly in her present rôle and, instinctively, they made her part quite clear to Peter.

They returned to the fire. Chris was peeling sticks and sharpening the ends so that they could hold sausages over the fire to cook.

"What about the children?" Sarah asked. "How long are you staying, Mother?"

This was Catherine's dilemma which she had been pondering as she sat there with her hand buried in the sand.

"They can stay up," she said. "We will all stay. It will be a special treat for the little ones and they can sleep late in the morning. You others shall have a party on your own another night."

She looked away from Sarah and her voice was gentle, for she knew that *this* could not be Sarah's special night, that the girl was desperate with disappointment. 'This evening is nothing,' Catherine tried to imply. 'There will be so many others for you.'

"We always like it better if you are here," Sarah said. "I was wondering about the children." She dreaded that her mother should feel old or left out, and she often was alone on these long holidays. Peter's presence lightened the load of responsibility she felt towards her. For an hour or two, Catherine had someone of her own and Sarah could let go of her, could turn back to her own secrets, aloof, in love.

'Has she a confidante among the other girls?' Catherine wondered. Remembering her own girlhood she did not hope to be confided in herself; the very last, she knew—even if first to know, before Sarah sometimes, yet still the last of all to be told.

If she had taken Lucy and Ricky home to bed, Peter would have gone with her. Then they would be alone and nothing could prevent him from talking to her. To stay where she was not much wanted and to endure an evening of social exchanges before the children—painful though it must be—would be less menacing than that.

She turned to the picnic-basket, put a loaf of bread on a board and began to cut it into slices. "You haven't changed much," she said. "Are you happy in South Africa and is the work interesting? How is your brother?"

"I had no intention of coming here, but suddenly, this morning, it seemed so unreasonable, so falsely dramatic— our promise."

"No, sensible."

"I'm sorry I gave no warning."

"You could have telephoned," she said lightly, her back turned to him.

"You would have said 'No'."

She wrapped the slices of bread in a napkin and put them back in the hamper. 'Being needlessly busy,' he thought. 'Fussing with the children, anything to exclude me.'

"You *would* have said 'No', wouldn't you?"

"Yes, of course."

"You haven't changed either," he said at last, dutifully.

She was smoothing her hair, thinking, 'I don't know what I look like.' She wished that she could glance in a mirror, or that she had done so before she had left the house.

In her brown hair, some strands, coarser than the others, were silver. Fine lines crossed her forehead, and deeper ones curved from the corners of her eyes.

"Graham all right?" he asked.

"Yes, very well. Very busy. He gets tired."

'And bloody cross, I bet,' Peter thought. He imagined the tetchy, pompous little man, returning from the city, brief-case full of documents and stomach full of bile.

"And is he as rich as ever?" he asked.

"I've noticed no difference," Catherine said angrily. "Have *you* prospered? You always had such money-troubles."

"Father's dying should help."

He had always refused to see Graham as anything but a monstrous begetter of money and children, and showed himself up in contrast—the bachelor beyond the gates, without home or family, whose schemes came to nothing as his love-making came to nothing, neither bearing fruit. His insistence on her wealth was partly from a feeling that she had shared too much with her husband and he could not bear her to share any more, not even anxieties about money.

"They are nice children," he said, looking on the sunnier side of her marriage. "A great credit to you."

"Thank you." Her eyes filled with tears and at that moment Sarah, standing by the fire, turned and looked curiously at her, then at Peter.

The fire was burning high and the young people moved about it continually as if performing some ceremony. As the sun went down, shadows fell across the beach from the sea-wall, cooling the sand quickly. Catherine spread out a rug for Peter to sit on and then sat down herself on a corner of it, as far from him as she could.

"Come by the fire," Chris shouted to her.

"It is too smoky for her," said Sarah.

"Not on the other side."

"It blows about."

Catherine had not asked her the one question she had dreaded—"He didn't come then?"—and so in turn she would protect her mother. She, Sarah, no longer prayed for him to come, for her thoughts of him were angry now. Absorbed in this anger, she asked only that no one should speak of him. Waiting for him and the gradual loss of hope had been destructive, and a corrosive indignation worked on her love; it became non-love, then nothing.

"Is that Ronnie coming?" Chris asked, mopping his eyes with a handkerchief, waving away smoke.

A figure in the dusk appeared on the sea-wall, then a dog followed and flew down through the sand, crashed over the stretch of loose shingle to the wet, runnelled sands where the children worked, murmuring and intent, over their digging. Lucy cried out as the dog bounded towards her and a man's voice—nothing like Ronnie's—called the dog back.

Sarah was glad that she had not moved forward to wave or made any mistake. Standing quite still by the fire, she had kept her patience; but all the carefully-tended hatred had vanished in those few seconds, love had come hurrying back with hope and forgiving. 'It is worse for her now,' Catherine thought, and she felt hostility towards men. 'As it is worse for me.'

The man and the dog disappeared. Lucy and Ricky, disturbed into realisation of the darkness falling, began to trail up from the sea. The water between the hard ribs of sand felt cold to their bare feet and they came up to the bonfire and stood watching it, at the fringe of their elders and betters who laughed and danced and waved their speared sausages in the air to cool.

"Let them cook their own," said Catherine, and Chris handed the little ones two sticks and fixed on the sausages for them. They stood by the fire holding the sticks waveringly over the flames. Once, Ricky's nervousness broke into a laugh, his serious expression disintegrated into excited pleasure. "It will never cook like that," Chris said. "Keep it to the hot part of the fire." He sighed affectedly and murmured, "Pesky kids" to one of the girls, who said haughtily: "*I* think they're sweet."

"They're all yours, then," said lordly Chris.

"I never had anything like this when I was young." Peter said. "I didn't even know any girls."

The children had their feast and Catherine and Peter sat and watched them; even, Catherine thought, in Peter's case, sat in judgment on them—'as if he were their father and jealous of their youth, saying "*I* didn't have this or do that when *I* was a boy; but was made to do such and such, and go without etcetera, and be grateful for nothing. And look at me. . . ." If he were their father, that is how he would be, if he had not come back to me this evening, I should never have thought such a thing of him. How I loved you, my darling, darling. The passion of tears, the groping bewilderment of being without you, the rhythm of long boredom and abrupt grief, that I endured because of you; then my prayers, my prayers especially that Sarah shall have a happier time, and a more fortunate love.'

The children brought them sausages wrapped in bread. The young girls were attentive to Catherine. "I *adore* your jersey," one said, and Catherine would not conceal her pleasure. "But it's so old. It's Chris's, really."

"Then you shouldn't let him have it back," the girl said. "*He* couldn't look so nice in it."

"All right!" said Chris. "You may cook your own sausages now. Didn't you know that the whole family wear my old cast-offs?"

"Not I," said Sarah.

"Not I," said Lucy.

Peter had glanced at the jersey in annoyance. He was beginning, Catherine knew, to harden against Chris, identifying him with his father, comparing himself and his own lost opportunitites with the boy and the life lying before him. When Chris brought sausages, said "For you, sir," he refused to eat.

"Then coffee," Catherine suggested, beginning to unscrew a flask.

"Oh, dear, it is so cold," Lucy cried, and she flung herself against Catherine's thighs, burrowing under her arm.

"Steady, my love, I can't pour out," Catherine said, and she held the flask and the cup high out of reach and for the first time looked truly at Peter and laughed.

"Come to me, then," he said, and he lifted Lucy away and held her to him. She lolled against him, her salty, sticky hair touching his cheek. "That isn't good for you," he said, taking the half-eaten sausage, which was pink inside, uncooked, and throwing it away across the sand.

"Fishes will eat it," Ricky said. "When the tide comes up."

"Coffee!" Catherine called out and they came over to fetch it, then went back to gather round the dying fire. The girls began to sing, one of their school songs, which the boys did not know and Chris said: "What a filthy row."

"Did you read that fairy book to me when I was in bed?" Lucy asked Peter drowsily.

"I don't know."

"Yes, you did,"

"Do you remember then?"

"No, Mummy told me."

Then Catherine had talked of him! He had often wanted to talk to someone about *her*, to say her name. In Africa, he had nicknamed a little native girl—his servant's child—'Catherine', for the sake of saying the name occasionally. "Good morning, Catherine" or "What a pretty frock, Catherine!" The child could not understand English. He might, he had sometimes thought, have said anything, out loud, bold and clear. "I cannot forget you, Catherine, and my life is useless without you."

Lucy had crawled inside his jacket for warmth, he rubbed her cold, sandy legs, held her bare feet, and once kissed her forehead. Catherine sipped her coffee, looking away from this display of tenderness, thinking: 'A barren evening.

Nothing said; nothing felt, but pain. The wheel starting to creak again, starting to revolve in agony.'

"If any . . . regrets . . . have arisen from my visit," Peter said, trying to speak obscurely, above Lucy's head in two senses, "I couldn't blame myself more or detest my own egotism."

"There is no need to say anything," she said hurriedly. "No need at all. I would rather you didn't."

"Are you . . .?"

"No," she interrupted him, afraid of what Lucy might hear. 'Am I what?' she wondered. 'I am in love with you still. In love, certainly. And there isn't a way out and never will be now.'

Her eyes might say this without Lucy knowing, and she turned to him so that before he went away he could be a witness to her constancy; but their situation was changed now; the observant eyes of the children were on them, Sarah's, the other girls, and Chris, brusque and guarded, goodness knew what thoughts *he* had about her.

"I shall soon have to go," Peter said and as he glanced at his watch, Lucy pushed herself closer to him, almost asleep.

Singing together now, the girls and boys were beginning to pack up—one of the girls turned cartwheels, and Sarah suddenly spun round, her bell-like skirt flying out.

"Are you staying at the pub?" Catherine asked.

"No, I am catching the last bus, then the last train."

"The last train," Lucy murmured cosily, as if there were no such thing save in a story he was telling her.

Catherine shivered.

"Are you sure you won't write to me?" Peter asked her, as quietly as he could. "Or let me write to you?"

"Quite sure."

"She will," said Lucy. "She writes to Sarah and Chris every day when they are at school."

"Then there wouldn't be time for me," said Peter.

Catherine packed the basket wishing that she might pack up the evening, too, and all that it had brought to the light, but it lay untidily about them. The children ran to and fro, clearing up, exhilarated by the darkness and the sound of the sea, the tide coming up across the sands, one wave unrolling under the spray of the next. The boys took the baskets and the girls looked the beach over, as if it were a room in some home of their own which they wished to leave tidy until they returned.

'Who will remember the evening?' Catherine wondered. 'Perhaps only he and I, and Sarah.' Little Ricky had attached himself to the others as they left the beach. He walked beside Sarah, clinging to her skirt. Peter had Lucy on his back, his shoes dangling by their laces round his neck as he walked unsteadily on the cold, loose sand.

"We live only once," he said.

"Of course," said Lucy, awake now and laughing. She wriggled her sandy feet, trying to force them into the pockets of his jacket.

"Lucy, sit still or walk," her mother said sharply.

A little surprised, she sat still for a bit and then, when she could see the house, the lights going on as the others went indoors, she slipped down and ran away from Peter, down the bank and across the lane.

Catherine and Peter sat down just below the sea-wall and put on their shoes.

"Will you forgive me?" he asked.

"I might have done the same."

"There is far too much to say for us to begin talking."

"And no time," she said. She fastened her sandals, then looked up at the sky, as if she were scanning it anxiously for some weather-sign, but he knew that she was waiting for tears to recede, her head high, breath held. If he kissed her, she would fail, would break, weep, betray herself to the children. 'To have thought of her so long, imagined, dreamed, called that child "Catherine" for her sake, started at the sight of her name printed in a book, pretended her voice to myself, called her in my sleep, and now sit close to her and it is almost over.' He stood up and took her hand, helping her to her feet.

In the lane the children were trying one another's bicycles, the lamp light swung over the road and hedges. Lucy was crying and Sarah attempted to comfort her, but impatiently. "The same old story," she told her mother. "Stayed up too late."

"Yes, she did."

"I didn't undo my sand-castle," Lucy roared.

"Hush, dear. It doesn't matter."

"I like to undo it. You know I like to undo it and now the sea will get it."

"It doesn't matter."

"Don't *say* it doesn't matter."

"Peter, do borrow Chris's bicycle. You can leave it at the pub and he can fetch it tomorrow."

"I like the walk."

'I am not leaving her like that,' he thought, 'not bicycling off up the road with a mob of adolescents.'

"Good-bye, and thank you for the picnic," the children began to say, coming one after another to shake hands with Catherine.

"You should have *reminded* me," shrieked Lucy, at the end of her tether.

"Oh, Christ . . ." said Chris.

"Chris, I won't have that," said Catherine.

"Good-bye, and thank you so much."

"I hope you will come again."

"Good-bye, good-bye," Chris shouted.

They swung on to their bicycles and began to ride away, turning often to wave.

"Good-bye, Fanny! Good-bye, Sue!" Chris shouted.

The voices came back, as the lights bobbed along the lane. "Good-bye, Sarah! Good-bye, Chris!"

Sarah called once, then she shook hands with Peter and turned towards the house, gathering up Ricky, who was swinging on the gate as if hypnotised, too tired to make the next step.

"Good-bye, Catherine, or I shall miss the bus."

"Yes. Good-bye, Peter."

"Take care of yourself. And *you* take care of her," he said to Chris with bright jocularity, as he began to walk away down the road.

"What, my dear old mum?" Chris said, and flung his arm across her shoulder so that she staggered slightly. Then, hearing a faint cry in the distance he rushed from her into the middle of the road and shouted again, his hands cupped to his mouth. "Good-bye, Good-bye."

Poor Girl

Miss Chasty's first pupil was a flirtatious little boy. At seven years, he was alarmingly precocious, and sometimes she thought that he despised his childhood, regarding it as a waiting time which he used only as a rehearsal for adult life. He was already more sophisticated than his young governess and disturbed her with his air of dalliance, the mockery with which he set about his lessons, the preposterous conversations he led her into, guiding her skilfully away from work, confusing her with bizarre conjectures and irreverent ideas, so that she would clasp her hands tightly under the plush table-cloth and pray that his father would not choose such a moment to observe her teaching, coming in abruptly as he sometimes did and signalling to her to continue the lesson.

At those times, his son's eyes were especially lively, fixed cruelly upon his governess as he listened, smiling faintly, to her faltering voice, measuring her timidity. He would answer her questions correctly, but significantly, as if he knew that by his aptitude he rescued her from dismissal. There were many governesses waiting employment, he implied—and this was so at the beginning of the century. He underlined her good fortune at having a pupil who could so easily learn, could display the results of her teaching to such an advantage for the benefit of the rather sombre, pompous figure seated at the window. When his father, apparently satisfied, had left them without a word, the boy's

169

manner changed. He seemed fatigued and too absent-minded to reply to any more questions.

"Hilary!" she would say sharply. "Are you attending to me?" Her sharpness and her foolishness amused him, coming as he knew they did from the tension of the last ten minutes.

"Why, my dear girl, of course."

"You must address me by my name."

"Certainly, dear Florence."

"Miss Chasty."

His lips might shape the words, which he was too weary to say.

Sometimes, when she was correcting his sums, he would come round the table to stand beside her, leaning against her heavily, looking closely at her face, not at his book, breathing steadily down his nose so that tendrils of hair wavered on her neck and against her cheeks. His stillness, his concentration on her and his too heavy leaning, worried her. She felt something experimental in his attitude, as if he were not leaning against her at all, but against someone in the future. "He is only a baby," she reminded herself, but she would try to shift from him, feeling a vague distaste. She would blush, as if he were a grown man, and her heart could be heard beating quickly. He was aware of this and would take up the corrected book and move back to his place.

Once he proposed to her and she had the feeling that it was a proposal-rehearsal and that he was making use of her, as an actor might ask her to hear his lines.

"You must go on with your work" she said.

"I can shade in a map and talk as well."

"Then talk sensibly."

"You think I am too young, I daresay; but you could wait for me to grow up, I can do that quickly enough."

"You are far from grown-up at the moment."

"You only say these things because you think that governesses ought to. I suppose you don't know how governesses go on, because you have never been one until now, and you were too poor to have one of your own when you were young."

"That is impertinent, Hilary."

"You once told me your father couldn't afford one."

"Which is a different way of putting it."

"I shouldn't have thought they cost much." He had a way of just making a remark, of breathing it so gently that it was scarcely said, and might conveniently be ignored.

He was a dandified boy. His smooth hair was like a silk cap, combed straight from the crown to a level line above his topaz eyes. His sailor-suits were spotless. The usual boldness changed to an agonised fussiness if his serge sleeve brushed against chalk or if he should slip on the grassy terrace and stain his clothes with green. On their afternoon walks he took no risks and Florence, who had younger brothers, urged him in vain to climb a tree or jump across puddles. At first, she thought him intimidated by his mother or nurse; but soon she realised that his mother entirely indulged him and the nurse had her thoughts all bent upon the new baby; his fussiness was just another part of his grown-upness come too soon.

The house was comfortable, although to Florence rather too sealed-up and overheated after her own damp and draughty home. Her work was not hard and her loneliness only what she had expected. Cut off from the kitchen by her education, she lacked the feuds and camaraderie, gossip and cups of tea, which make life more interesting for the domestic staff. None of the maids—coming to light the lamp at dusk or laying the schoolroom-table for tea—ever presumed beyond a remark or two about the weather.

One late afternoon, she and Hilary returned from their walk and found the lamps already lit. Florence went to her

room to tidy herself before tea. When she came down to the
schoolroom, Hilary was already there, sitting on the window-
seat and staring out over the park as his father did. The
room was bright and warm and a maid had put a white
cloth over the plush one and was beginning to lay the table.

The air was full of a heavy scent, dry and musky. To
Florence, it smelt quite unlike the eau de cologne she
sometimes sprinkled on her handkerchief, when she had a
headache, and she disapproved so much that she returned
the maid's greeting coldly and bade Hilary open the
window.

"Open the window, dear girl?" he said. "We shall catch
our very deaths."

"You will do as I ask and remember in future how to
address me."

She was angry with the maid—who now seemed to her an
immoral creature—and angry to be humiliated before her.

"But why?" asked Hilary.

"I don't approve of my schoolroom being turned into a
scented bower." She kept her back to the room and was
trembling, for she had never rebuked a servant before.

"I approve of it," Hilary said, sniffing loudly.

"I think it's lovely," the maid said. "I noticed it as soon
as I opened the door."

"Is this some joke, Hilary?" Florence asked when the
girl had gone.

"No. What?"

"This smell in the room?"

"No. You smell of it most, anyhow." He put his nose to
her sleeve and breathed deeply.

It seemed to Florence that this was so, that her clothes had
caught the perfume among the folds. She lifted her palms
to her face, then went to the window and leant out into the
air as far as she could.

"Shall I pour out the tea, dear girl?"

"Yes, please."

She took her place at the table abstractedly, and as she drank her tea she stared about the room, frowning. When Hilary's mother looked in, as she often did at this time, Florence stood up in a startled way.

"Good-evening, Mrs Wilson. Hilary, put a chair for your mamma."

"Don't let me disturb you."

Mrs Wilson sank into the rocking-chair by the fire and gently tipped to and fro.

"Have you finished your tea, darling boy?" she asked. "Are you going to read me a story from your book? Oh, there is Lady scratching at the door. Let her in for mamma."

Hilary opened the door and a bald old pug-dog with bloodshot eyes waddled in.

"Come, Lady! Beautiful one. Come to mistress! What is wrong with her, poor pet lamb?"

The bitch had stepped just inside the room and lifted her head and howled. "What has frightened her, then? Come, beauty! Coax her with a sponge-cake, Hilary."

She reached forward to the table to take the dish and doing so noticed Florence's empty tea-cup. On the rim was a crimson smear, like the imprint of a lip. She gave a sponge-finger to Hilary, who tried to quieten the pug, then she leaned back in her chair and studied Florence again as she had studied her when she engaged her a few weeks earlier. The girl's looks were appropriate enough, appropriate to a clergyman's daughter and a governess. Her square chin looked resolute, her green eyes innocent, her dress was modest and unbecoming. Yet Mrs Wilson could detect an excitability, even feverishness, which she had not noticed before and she wondered if she had mistaken guardedness for innocence and deceit for modesty.

She was reaching this conclusion—rocking back and forth —when she saw Florence's hand stretch out and turn the cup round in its saucer so that the red stain was out of sight.

"What is wrong with Lady?" Hilary asked, for the dog would not be pacified with sponge-fingers, but kept making barking advances farther into the room, then growling in retreat.

"Perhaps she is crying at the new moon," said Florence and she went to the window and drew back the curtain. As she moved, her skirts rustled. 'If she has silk underwear as well!' Mrs Wilson thought. She had clearly heard the sound of taffetas, and she imagined the drab, shiny alpaca dress concealing frivolity and wantonness.

"Open the door, Hilary," she said. "I will take Lady away. Vernon shall give her a run in the park. I think a quiet read for Hilary and then an early bed-time, Miss Chasty. He looks pale this evening."

"Yes, Mrs Wilson." Florence stood respectfully by the table, hiding the cup.

'The hypocrisy!' Mrs Wilson thought and she trembled as she crossed the landing and went downstairs.

She hesitated to tell her husband of her uneasiness, knowing his susceptibilities to the kind of women whom his conscience taught him to deplore. Hidden below the apparent urbanity of their married life were old un-happinesses—little acts of treachery and disloyalty which pained her to remember, bruises upon her peace of mind and her pride: letters found, a pretty maid dismissed, an actress who had blackmailed him. As he read the Lesson in church, looking so perfectly upright and honourable a man, she sometimes thought of his escapades; but not with bitterness or cynicism, only with pain at her memories and a whisper of fear about the future. For some time she had been spared those whispers and had hoped that their marriage had at last achieved its calm. To speak of Florence as she must might both arouse his curiosity and revive the past.

Nevertheless, she had her duty to her son to fulfil and her own anger to appease and she opened the library door very determinedly.

"Oliver, I am sorry to interrupt your work, but I must speak to you."

He put down the *Strand Magazine* quite happily, aware that she was not a sarcastic woman.

Oliver and his son were extraordinarily alike. "As soon as Hilary has grown a moustache we shall not know them apart," Mrs Wilson often said, and her husband liked this little joke which made him feel more youthful. He did not know that she added a silent prayer—"O God, please do not let him *be* like him, though."

"You seem troubled, Louise." His voice was rich and authoritative. He enjoyed setting to rights her little domestic flurries and waited indulgently to hear of some tradesman's misdemeanour or servant's laziness.

"Yes, I am troubled about Miss Chasty."

"Little Miss Mouse? I was rather troubled myself. I noticed two spelling faults in Hilary's botany essay, which she claimed to have corrected. I said nothing before the boy, but I shall acquaint her with it when the opportunity arises."

"Do you often go to the schoolroom, then?"

"From time to time. I like to be sure that our choice was wise."

"It was not. It was misguided and unwise."

"All young people seem slip-shod nowadays."

"She is more than slip-shod. I believe she should go. I think she is quite brazen. Oh, yes, I should have laughed at that myself if it had been said to me an hour ago, but I have just come from the schoolroom and it occurs to me that now she has settled down and feels more secure—since you pass over her mistakes—she is beginning to take advantage of your leniency and to show herself in her true colours. I

felt a sinister atmosphere up there, and I am quite upset
and exhausted by it. I went up to hear Hilary's reading. They
were finishing tea and the room was full of the most overpowering scent, *her* scent. It was disgusting."

"Unpleasant?"

"No, not at all. But upsetting."

"Disturbing?"

She would not look at him or reply, hearing no more
indulgence or condescension in his voice, but the quality of
warming interest.

"And then I saw her teacup and there was a mark on it—
a red smear where her lips had touched it. She did not
know I saw it and as soon as she noticed it herself she turned
it round, away from me. She is an immoral woman and she
has come into our house to teach our son."

"I have never noticed a trace of artificiality in her looks.
It seemed to me that she was rather colourless."

"She has been sly. This evening she looked quite
different, quite flushed and excitable. I know that she had
rouged her lips or painted them or whatever those women
do." Her eyes filled with tears.

"I shall observe her for a day or two," Oliver said, trying
to keep anticipation from his voice.

"I should like her to go at once."

"Never act rashly. She is entitled to a quarter's notice
unless there is definite blame. We should make ourselves
very foolish if you have been mistaken. Oh, I know that you
are sure; but it has been known for you to misjudge others.
I shall take stock of her and decide if she is unsuitable. She
is still Miss Mouse to me and I cannot think otherwise until
I see the evidence with my own eyes."

"There was something else as well," Mrs Wilson said
wretchedly.

"And what was that?"

"I would rather not say." She had changed her mind

about further accusations. Silk underwear would prove, she guessed, too inflammatory.

"I shall go up ostensibly to mention Hilary's spelling faults." He could not go fast enough and stood up at once.

"But Hilary is in bed."

"I could not mention the spelling faults if he were not."

"Shall I come with you?"

"My dear Louise, why should you? It would look very strange—a deputation about two spelling faults."

"Then don't be long, will you? I hope you won't be long."

He went to the schoolroom, but there was no one there. Hilary's story-book lay closed upon the table and Miss Chasty's sewing was folded neatly. As he was standing there looking about him and sniffing hard, a maid came in with a tray of crockery.

"Has Master Hilary gone to bed?" he asked, feeling rather foolish and confused.

The only scent in the air was a distinct smell—even a haze—of cigarette smoke.

"Yes, sir."

"And Miss Chasty—where is she?"

"She went to bed, too, sir."

"Is she unwell?"

"She spoke of a chronic head, sir."

The maid stacked the cups and saucers in the cupboard and went out. Nothing was wrong with the room apart from the smell of smoke and Mr Wilson went downstairs. His wife was waiting in the hall. She looked up expectantly, in some relief at seeing him so soon.

"Nothing," he said dramatically. "She has gone to bed with a headache. No wonder she looked feverish."

"You noticed the scent."

"There was none," he said. "No trace. Nothing. Just imagination, dear Louise. I thought that it must be so."

He went to the library and took up his magazine again,
but he was too disturbed to read and thought with impatience of the following day.

Florence could not sleep. She had gone to her room, not
with a headache but to escape conversations until she had
faced the predicament alone. This she was doing, lying on
the honeycomb quilt which, since maids do not wait on
governesses, had not been turned down.

The schoolroom this evening seemed to have been
wreathed about with a strange miasma; the innocent nature
of the place polluted in a way that she could not understand or have explained. Something new, it seemed, had
entered the room—the scent had clung about her clothes;
the stained cup was her own cup, and her handkerchief
with which she had rubbed it clean was still reddened;
and finally, as she stared in the mirror, trying to re-
establish her personality, the affected little laugh which
startled her had come from herself. It had driven her from
the room.

'I cannot explain the inexplicable,' she thought wearily
and began to prepare herself for bed. Home-sickness hit her
like a blow on the head.   'Whatever they do to me, I have
always my home,' she promised herself. But she could not
think who 'They' might be; for no one in this house had
threatened her. Mrs Wilson had done no more than irritate
her with her commonplace fussing over Hilary and her dog,
and Florence was prepared to overcome much more than
irritation. Mr Wilson's pomposity, his constant watch on
her works, intimidated her, but she knew that all who must
earn their living must have fears lest their work should
not seem worth the wages. Hilary was easy to manage;
she had quickly seen that she could always deflect him from
rebelliousness by opening a new subject for conversation;
any idea would be a counter-attraction to naughtiness; he
wanted her to sharpen his wits upon. 'And is that all that

teaching is, or should be?' she had wondered. The servants had been good to her, realising that she would demand nothing of them. She had suffered great loneliness, but had foreseen it as part of her position. Now she felt fear nudging it away. 'I am not lonely any more,' she thought. 'I am not alone any more. And I have lost something.' She said her prayers; then, sitting up in bed, kept the candle alight while she brushed her hair and read the Bible.

'Perhaps I have lost my reason,' she suddenly thought, resting her finger on her place in the Psalms. She lifted her head and saw her shadow stretch up the powdery, rose-sprinkled wall. 'How can I keep that secret?' she wondered. 'When there is no one to help me do it? Only those who are watching to see it happen.'

She was not afraid in her bedroom as she had been in the schoolroom, but her perplexed mind found no replies to its questions. She blew out the candle and tried to fall asleep, but lay and cried for a long time, and yearned to be at home again and comforted in her mother's arms.

In the morning she met kind enquiries. Nurse was so full of solicitude that Florence felt guilty. "I came up with a warm drink and put my head round the door but you were in the land of Nod so I drank it myself. I should take a grey powder; or I could mix you a gargle. There are a lot of throats about."

"I am quite better this morning," said Florence and she felt calmer as she sat down at the schoolroom-table with Hilary. 'Yet, it was all true,' her reason whispered. 'The morning hasn't altered that.'

"You have been crying," said Hilary. "Your eyes are red."

"Sometimes people's eyes are red from other causes—headaches and colds." She smiled brightly.

"And sometimes from crying, as I said. I should think usually from crying."

"Page fifty-one," she said, locking her hands together in her lap.

"Very well." He opened the book, pressed down the pages and lowered his nose to them, breathing the smell of print. 'He is utterly sensuous,' she thought. 'He extracts every pleasure, every sensation, down to the most trivial.'

They seemed imprisoned in the schoolroom, by the silence of the rest of the house and by the rain outside. Her calm began to break up into frustration and she put her hands behind her chair and pressed them against the hot mesh of the fireguard to steady herself. As she did so, she felt a curious derangement of both mind and body; of desire unsettling her once sluggish peaceful nature, desire horribly defined, though without direction.

"I have soon finished those," said Hilary, bringing his sums and placing them before her. She glanced at her palms which were criss-crossed deep with crimson where she had pressed them against the fireguard, then she took up her pen and dipped it into the red ink.

"Don't lean against me, Hilary," she said.

"I love the scent so much."

It had returned, musky, enveloping, varying as she moved.

She ticked the sums quickly, thinking that she would set Hilary more work and escape for a moment to calm herself —change her clothes or cleanse herself in the rain. Hearing Mr Wilson's footsteps along the passage, she knew that her escape was cut off and raised wild-looking eyes as he came in. He mistook panic for passion, thought that by opening the door suddenly he had caught her out and laid bare her secret, her pathetic adoration.

"Good morning," he said musically and made his way to the window-seat. "Don't let me disturb you." He said this without irony, although he thought: 'So it is that way the

wind blows! Poor creature!' He had never found it difficult
to imagine women were in love with him.

'I will hear your verbs,' Florence told Hilary, and
opened the French Grammar as if she did not know them
herself. Her eyes—from so much crying—were a pale and
brilliant green, and as the scent drifted in Oliver's direction
and he turned to her, she looked fully at him.

'Ah, the still waters!' he thought and stood up suddenly.
"Ils vont," he corrected Hilary and touched his shoulder
as he passed. "Are you attending to Miss Chasty?"

"Is she attending to me?" Hilary murmured. The risk
was worth taking, for neither heard. His father appeared to
be sleep-walking and Florence deliberately closed her eyes,
as if looking down were not enough to blur the outlines
of her desire.

"I find it difficult," Oliver said to his wife, "to reconcile
your remarks about Miss Chasty with the young woman
herself. I have just come from the schoolroom and she was
engaged in nothing more immoral than teaching French
verbs—that not very well incidentally."

"But can you explain what I have told you?"

"I can't do that," he said gaily. For who can explain a
jealous woman's fancies? he implied.

He began to spend more time in the schoolroom; from
surveillance, he said. Miss Chasty, though not outwardly of
an amorous nature, was still not what he had at first
supposed. A suppressed wantonness hovered beneath her
primness. She was the ideal governess in his eye—
irreproachable, yet not unapproachable. As she was so conveniently installed, he could take his time in divining the
extent of her willingness; especially as he was growing
older and the game was beginning to be worth more than
the triumph of winning it. To his wife, he upheld Florence,
saw nothing wrong save in her scholarship, which needed to
be looked into—this, the explanation for his more frequent

visits to the schoolroom. He laughed teasingly at Louise's fancies.

The schoolroom indeed became a focal point of the house —the stronghold of Mr Wilson's desire and his wife's jealousy.

"We are never alone," said Hilary. "Either Papa or Mamma is here. Perhaps they wonder if you are good enough for me."

"Hilary!" His father had heard the last sentence as he opened the door and the first as he hovered outside listening. "I doubt if my ears deceived me. You will go to your room while you think of a suitable apology and I think of an ample punishment."

"Shall I take my history book with me or shall I just waste time?"

"I have indicated how to spend your time."

"That won't take long enough," said Hilary beneath his breath as he closed the door.

"Meanwhile, I apologise for him," said his father. He did not go to his customary place by the window, but came to the hearth-rug where Florence stood behind her chair. "We have indulged him too much and he has been too much with adults. Have there been other occasions?"

"No, indeed, sir."

"You find him tractable?"

"Oh, yes."

"And are you happy in your position?"

"Yes."

As the dreaded, the now so familiar scent began to wreath about the room, she stepped back from him and began to speak rapidly, as urgently as if she were dying and must make some explanation while she could. "Perhaps, after all, Hilary is right and you do wonder about my competence—and if I can give him all he should have. Perhaps a man would teach him more. . . ."

She began to feel a curious infraction of the room and of her personality, seemed to lose the true Florence, and the room lightened as if the season had been changed.

"You are mistaken," he was saying. "Have I ever given you any hint that we were not satisfied?"

Her timidity had quite dissolved and he was shocked by the sudden boldness of her glance.

"I should rather give you a hint of how well pleased I am."

"Then why don't you?" she asked.

She leaned back against the chimney-piece and looped about her fingers a long necklace of glittering green beads. "Where did these come from?" she wondered. She could not remember ever having seen them before, but she could not pursue her bewilderment, for the necklace felt familiar to her hands, much more familiar than the rest of the room.

"When shall I?" he was insisting. "This evening, perhaps, when Hilary is in bed?"

'Then who is *he*, if Hilary is to be in bed?' she wondered. She glanced at him and smiled again. "You are extra-ordinarily alike," she said. "You and Hilary." 'But Hilary is a little boy,' she reminded herself. 'It is silly to confuse the two.'

"We must discuss Hilary's progress," he said, his voice so burdened with meaning that she began to laugh at him.

"Indeed we must," she agreed.

"Your necklace is the colour of your eyes." He took it from her fingers and leaned forward, as if to kiss her. Hearing footsteps in the passage she moved sharply aside, the necklace broke and the beads scattered over the floor.

"Why is Hilary in the garden at this hour?" Mrs Wilson asked. Her husband and the governess were on their knees, gathering up the beads.

"Miss Chasty's necklace broke," her husband said. She

had heard that submissive tone before: his voice lacked authority only when he was caught out in some infidelity.

"I was asking about Hilary. I have just seen him running in the shrubbery without a coat."

"He was sent to his room for being impertinent to Miss Chasty."

"Please fetch him at once," Mrs Wilson told Florence. Her voice always gained in authority what her husband's lacked.

Florence hurried from the room, still holding a handful of beads. She felt badly shaken—as if she had been brought to the edge of some experience which had then retreated beyond her grasp.

"He was told to stay in his room," Mr Wilson said feebly.

"Why did her beads break?"

"She was fidgeting with them. I think she was nervous. I was making it rather apparent to her that I regarded Hilary's insubordination as proof of too much leniency on her part."

"I didn't know that she had such a necklace. It is the showiest trash I have ever seen."

"We cannot blame her for the cheapness of her trinkets. It is rather pathetic."

"There is nothing pathetic about her. We will continue this in the morning-room and they can continue their lessons, which are, after all, her reason for being here."

*   *   *

"Oh, they are gone," said Hilary. His cheeks were pink from the cold outside.

"Why did you not stay in your bedroom as you were told?"

"I had nothing to do. I thought of my apology before I got there. It was: 'I am sorry, dear girl, that I spoke too near the point'."

"You could have spent longer and thought of a real apology."

"Look how long Papa spent and he did not even think of a punishment, which is a much easier thing."

Several times during the evening Mr Wilson said: "But you cannot dismiss a girl because her beads break."

"There have been other things and will be more," his wife replied.

So that there should not be more that evening, he did not move from the drawing-room where he sat watching her doing her wool-work. For the same reason, Florence left the schoolroom early. She went out and walked rather nervously in the park, feeling remorseful, astonished and upset.

"Did you mend your necklace?" Hilary asked her in the morning.

"I lost the beads."

"But my poor girl, they must be somewhere."

She thought: 'There is no reason to suppose that I shall get back what I never had in the first place.'

"Have you got a headache?"

"Yes. Go on with your work, Hilary."

"Is it from losing the beads?"

"No."

"Have you a great deal of jewellery I have not seen yet?"

She did not answer and he went on: "You still have your brooch with your grandmother's plaited hair in it. Was it cut off her head when she was dead."

"Your work, Hilary."

"I shudder to think of chopping it off a corpse. You could have some of my hair, now, while I am living." He fingered it with admiration, regarded a sum aloofly and jotted down his answer. "Could I cut some of yours?" he asked, bringing his book to be corrected. He whistled softly, close to her, and the tendrils of hair round her ears were gently blown about.

"It is ungentlemanly to whistle," she said.

"My sums are always right. It shows how I can chatter and subtract at the same time. Any governess would be annoyed by that. I suppose your brothers never whistle."

"Never."

"Are they to be clergymen like your father?"

"It is what we hope for one of them."

"I am to be a famous judge. When you read about me, will you say: 'And to think I might have been his wife if I had not been so self-willed'?"

"No, but I hope that I shall feel proud that once I taught you."

"You sound doubtful."

He took his book back to the table. "We are having a quiet morning," he remarked. "No one has visited us. Poor Miss Chasty, it is a pity about the necklace," he murmured, as he took up his pencil again.

Evenings were dangerous to her. 'He said he would come,' she told herself, 'and I allowed him to say so. On what compulsion did I?"

Fearfully, she spent her lonely hours out in the dark garden or in her cold and candle-lit bedroom. He was under his wife's vigilance and Florence did not know that he dared not leave the drawing-room. But the vigilance relaxed, as it does; his carelessness returned and steady rain and bitter cold drove Florence to warm her chilblains at the schoolroom fire.

Her relationship with Mrs Wilson had changed. A wary hostility took the place of meekness, and when Mrs Wilson came to the schoolroom at tea-times, Florence stood up defiantly and cast a look round the room as if to say: 'Find what you can. There is nothing here.' Mrs Wilson's suspicious ways increased her rebelliousness. 'I have done nothing wrong,' she told herself. But in her bedroom at night: '*I* have done nothing wrong,' she would think.

"They have quite deserted us," Hilary said from time to time. "They have realised you are worth your weight in gold, dear girl; or perhaps I made it clear to my father that in this room he is an interloper."

"Hilary!"

"You want to put yourself in the right in case that door opens suddenly as it has been doing lately. There, you see! Good-evening, Mamma. I was just saying that I had scarcely seen you all day." He drew forward her chair and held the cushion behind her until she leaned back.

"I have been resting."

"Are you ill, Mamma?"

"I have a headache."

"I will stroke it for you, dear lady."

He stood behind her chair and began to smooth her forehead. "Or shall I read to you?" he asked, soon tiring of his task, "Or play the musical-box?"

"No, nothing more, thank you."

Mrs Wilson looked about her, at the tea-cups, then at Florence. Sometimes it seemed to her that her husband was right and that she was growing fanciful. The innocent appearance of the room lulled her and she closed her eyes for a while, rocking gently in her chair.

*   *   *

"I dozed off," she said when she awoke. The table was cleared and Florence and Hilary sat playing chess, whispering so that they should not disturb her.

"It made a domestic scene for us," said Hilary. "Often Miss Chasty and I feel that we are left too much in solitary bliss."

The two women smiled and Mrs Wilson shook her head. "You have too old a head on your shoulders," she said. "What will they say of you when you go to school?"

"What shall I say of *them*?" he asked bravely, but he lowered his eyes and kept them lowered. When his mother had gone, he asked Florence: "Did you go to school?"

"Yes."

"Were you unhappy there?"

"No, I was homesick at first."

"If I don't like it, there will be no point in my staying," he said hurriedly. "I can learn anywhere and I don't particularly want the corners knocked off, as my father once spoke of it. I shouldn't like to play cricket and all those childish games. Only to do boxing and draw blood," he added, with sudden bravado. He laughed excitedly and clenched his fists.

"You would never be good at boxing if you lost your temper."

"I suppose your brothers told you that. They don't sound very manly to me. They would be afraid of a good fight and the sight of blood, I daresay."

"Yes, I daresay. It is bedtime."

He was whipped up by the excitement he had created from his fears.

"Chess is a woman's game," he said and upset the board. He took the cushion from the rocking-chair and kicked it inexpertly across the room. "I should have thought the door would have opened then," he said. "But as my father doesn't appear to send me to my room, I will go there of my own accord. It wouldn't have been a punishment at bedtime in any case. When I am a judge I shall be better at punishments than he is."

When he had gone, Florence picked up the cushion and the chess-board. 'I am no good at punishments either,' she thought. She tidied the room, made up the fire, then sat down in the rocking-chair, thinking of all the lonely schoolroom evenings of her future. She bent her head over her needlework—the beaded sachet for her mother's birthday present. When she looked up she thought the lamp was smoking and she went to the table and turned down the wick. Then she noticed that the smoke was wreathing upwards from near the fireplace, forming rings which drifted towards the ceiling and were lost in a haze. She could hear a woman's voice humming softly and the floorboards creaked as if someone were treading up and down the room impatiently.

She felt in herself a sense of burning impatience and anticipation and watching the door opening found herself thinking: 'If it is not he, I cannot bear it.'

He closed the door quietly. "She has gone to bed," he said in a lowered voice. "For days I dared not come. She has watched me every moment. At last, this evening, she gave way to a headache. Were you expecting me?"

"Yes."

"And once I called you Miss Mouse! And you are still Miss Mouse when I see you about the garden, or at luncheon."

"In this room I can be by myself. It belongs to us."

"And not to Hilary as well—ever?" he asked her in amusement.

She gave him a quick and puzzled glance.

"Let no one intrude," he said hastily. "It is our room, just as you say."

She had turned the lamp too low and it began to splutter. "Firelight is good enough for us," he said, putting the light out altogether.

When he kissed her, she felt an enormous sense of disappointment, almost as if he were the wrong person embracing her in the dark. His arch masterfulness merely bored her. 'A long wait for so little,' she thought.

He, however, found her entirely seductive. She responded

with a sensuous languor, unruffled and at ease like the most perfect hostess.

"Where did you practise this, Miss Mouse?" he asked her. But he did not wait for the reply, fancying that he heard a step on the landing. When his wife opened the door, he was trying desperately to light a taper at the fire. His hand was trembling, and when at last, in the terribly silent room, the flame crept up the spill it simply served to show up Florence's disarray, which, like a sleep-walker, she had not noticed or put right.

*   *   *

She did not see Hilary again, except as a blurred little figure at the schoolroom window—blurred because of her tear-swollen eyes.

She was driven away in the carriage, although Mr Wilson had suggested the station-fly. "Let us keep her disgrace and her tearfulness to ourselves," he begged, although he was exhausted by the repetitious burden of his wife's grief.

"*Her* disgrace!"

"My mistake, I have said, was in not taking your accusations about her seriously. I see now that I was in some way bewitched—yes, bewitched, is what it was—acting against my judgment; nay, my very nature. I am astonished that anyone so seemingly meek could have cast such a spell upon me."

*   *   *

Poor Florence turned her head aside as Williams, the coachman, came to fetch her little trunk and the basket-work holdall. Then she put on her cloak and prepared herself to go downstairs, fearful lest she should meet anyone on the way. Yet her thoughts were even more on her journey's end; for what, she wondered, could she tell her father and how expect him to understand what she could not understand herself?

Her head was bent as she crossed the landing and she
hurried past the schoolroom door. At the turn of the staircase
she pressed back against the wall to allow someone to pass.
She heard laughter and then up the stairs came a young
woman and a little girl. The child was clinging to the
woman's arm and coaxing her, as sometimes Hilary had
tried to coax Florence. "After lessons," the woman said
firmly, but gaily. She looked ahead, smiling to herself. Her
clothes were unlike anything that Florence had ever seen.
Later, when she tried to describe them to her mother, she
could only remember the shortness of a tunic which
scarcely covered the knees, a hat like a helmet drawn down
over eyes intensely green and matching a long necklace of
glass beads which swung on her flat bosom. As she came up
the stairs and drew near to Florence, she was humming
softly against the child's pleading: silk rustled against her
silken legs and all of the staircase, as Florence quickly
descended, was full of fragrance.

In the darkness of the hall a man was watching the two
go round the bend of the stairs. The woman must have
looked back, for Florence saw him lift his hand in a secretive
gesture of understanding.

'It is Hilary, not his father!' she thought. But the figure
turned before she could be sure and went into the library.

Outside on the drive Williams was waiting with her
luggage stowed away in the carriage. When she had settled
herself, she looked up at the schoolroom window and saw
Hilary standing there rather forlornly and she could almost
imagine him saying: 'My poor dear girl; so you were not
good enough for me, after all?'

"When does the new governess arrive?" she asked
Williams in a casual voice, that strove to conceal both pride
and grief.

"There's nothing fixed as far as I have heard," he said.

They drove out into the lane.

'When will it be *her* time?' Florence wondered. 'I am glad that I saw her before I left.'

"We are sorry to see you going, Miss." He had heard that the maids were sorry, for she had given them no trouble.

"Thank you, Williams."

As they went on towards the station, she leaned back and looked at the familiar places where she had walked with Hilary. 'I know what I shall tell my father now,' she thought, and she felt peaceful and meek as though beginning to be convalescent after a long illness.

Hare Park

AT an early hour, the pale deer moved down from the high slopes of the park towards the lakes. Sunlight gilded the stone deer on the piers of the main gates, where the steward stopped his horse and shouted to the lodge-keeper to take in a line of washing. As he rode on up the great avenue he could not see a twig that was out of place; on either side, stretches of water—one harp-shaped, one heart-shaped—glinted as if they had been polished. The landscape might have been submerged all night and now risen, cleansed and dazzling, as new as the beginning of the world, this April morning.

Along the avenue, the clear shadow of the man and horse slanted across the gravel. To the steward this was a wonderful hour of the day. His master, the Duke, slept late, shut away in the great house, and until the moment when he rose and came out on to the terrace, his steward claimed his possessions for himself, watched *his* pheasants fly up in a flurry disturbed by the horse, as he passed, *his* hare leaping through the grass. When he met any of the estate men, he lifted his crop as affably as the Duke himself.

Farther up the hill, the road forked. The avenue with its lime-trees continued up towards the stables, and the second road, treeless, austere, led over the Palladian bridge which spanned the narrow end of the harp lake; and there the house came into view.

The steward took this road, and, looking up at the great

building, felt his sense of ownership lessening. The stained, brown sandstone was crowned with a vast green dome. In some weathers it could look frightening; but this morning the sun mellowed it.

The grassland swept right up to the terrace. There were no flowers, no shrubs to spoil the formality. Even the runs along the terrace were empty. Stuck rakishly among the hundreds of chimneys were three television aerials. Holland blinds made blanks of rows of windows, but at one window on the second storey the curtains were parted and a young boy, still in his pyjamas, was looking out.

*   *   *

Arthur was watching his father's steward riding along before the house. The horse dancing like a race-horse seemed to be trying to shake off his own shadow. There was a tremendous certainty about the weather, unlike the apprehensions which had gathered about the day itself. The sun went up in triumph and drenched the park-land with gold. Arthur had a feeling that he was looking down upon an empty stage, awaiting the development of a drama which he wondered if he would ever understand. He imagined, later in the day, cars coming up the drive; the invasion, as his mother named it, beginning—the great house, Hare Park, thrown open to the enemy at half-a-crown a ticket, exposed for the first time in its history to shuffling sightseers, sullied, cheapened. So the Duchess protested. Her husband was robust enough to laugh at her charges and she could not goad him with the sharpness of her tongue. Upon all his money-raising schemes she had poured her scorn. "You could let them be photographed in our bed at twopence a time," she cried. "Or I could pose stark naked on a plinth in the Orangery. I should be no more exposed than I shall be."

"What would your Mamma have said to that?" he asked gravely.

"What would Mamma have said?" had been her theme for months. Once upon a time, Mamma and her friends had supposed that she had married well. Yorkshire had thought it a staggering match. She had gone from the manor house near Harrogate to the great ducal seat in the south; had gone, as now was shown, from gentility and decency, to vulgarity, publicity and flamboyance. Mamma was dead, though, and spared knowledge of such an indecorous trapesing about her daughter's home, of pryings and pokings, ribald comments, names scribbled, souvenirs stolen, germs breathed out.

All the preparations were made. Red ropes made passage-ways through the rooms, heirlooms were brought out and personal possessions put away. The dogs and their baskets were moved from the library to the gun room. A stall for picture postcards and ice-cream was built in the courtyard, and upon two of the doors hung notices printed 'Ladies' and 'Gentlemen.'

"Ladies! Gentlemen!" said the Duchess. "What lady or gentleman would wish to spy upon us just because we are poor?" She could hear all the tea-cups of Harrogate tinkling as the cries of pity passed above them, eager and energetic as cries of pity are. "How dreadful for her! Imagine one's own feelings!" And the coronet and the seat in the Abbey would be forgiven.

Arthur had felt the air about him riven with expectation and dissent. The staff had split apart, as his parents had. The steward, the wood ranger—but not the gardeners—stood close to the Duke. Footmen and housemaids were excited; the butler saddened, but understanding. The housekeeper was in a frenzy of indignation and the Duchess's maid aligned herself fully with Harrogate and almost outdid the Duchess herself in sensibility and distaste. Arthur's tutor, who had begun to see his present employment coming to an end as talk of Eton grew more frequent, was wondering if he might not make himself indispensable in other ways: his attachment to the house, and the knowledge of its history he had come by, fitted him beautifully for the task of Guide or Lecturer. Perhaps Guide and Librarian would be a pleasant combination and might keep him settled for the rest of his life. He became as eager as the Duke to bring in the half-crowns and to have the ice-creams sold. He had written a little guide-book and Arthur's lessons were neglected while he polished up his commentary.

"When they are about the place, you are to keep to the schoolroom or play in the walled garden," the Duchess had told her son. As for herself, her pianoforte, her painting materials, her tapestry canvas with enough wools to last five years or more, were carried to her sitting-room. She gathered her possessions about her, as if to withstand a long siege.

With feelings totally curious and expectations muddled, Arthur had awaited the day. He sensed surveillance lifting from him, authority rising away from him, as indifferent as the sun going up in the sky. He was sure that neither schoolroom nor walled garden should play any part in his day.

His father now came out on the terrace below. He stood looking across the lakes, his hand resting on the winged foot of a stone Mercury, whose shadow mingled with his own. All along the front of the house the sun was bleaching the statues. Rain-pitted, damp from the dew-fall, with mossy drapery and eye-sockets, they held out their shells and grapes and cornucopias to dry.

* * *

"Nothing gives me more pleasure than the notion that

every little helps," the Duke had told the steward. This feeling had led him to what his wife called 'excesses of vulgarity' and which had even slightly estranged those who were sympathetic to him. The steward was obliged to turn his eyes from the litter of paddle-boats on the harp-shaped lake.

The first cars to drive in when the gates were opened came very slowly and looked purposeful and menacing to Arthur—like a funeral procession—but soon the atmosphere became jollier; the car-park filled up; the crowds spread about the terrace, invading the house from all sides, like an army of ants, penetrating in no time the stables and court-yard and lining up for the house itself. The tutor, Mr Gilliat, soon collected his first batch of sightseers and fluently and facetiously began his description of pictures and cabinets and carvings.

Arthur had wandered round into the courtyard. Helpers from the village, selling postcards and refreshments, might have recognised him and he dared not buy an ice-cream and so risk being identified and imprisoned in the walled garden for the afternoon. When the steward came through the courtyard, people looked at him respectfully. A boy beside Arthur nudged him and whispered: "That's the Duke."

"No, it isn't," Arthur said.

"How do you know? He's got a badge on with the coat of arms."

The boy was running his tongue over his ice-cream cornet, long, slow licks which Arthur watched with increasing irritation. They leant against the warm stone wall. The sun in this enclosed place made them feel drowsy.

"I've shaken my lot off. Gave Dad the slip," the boy said. He was about Arthur's age. He wore a school blazer with a row of fountain-pens clipped to the pocket. His lapels were covered with little enamel badges. Ice-cream, melting

fast, dripped on to his trousers, and he spat on his handkerchief and wiped it off.

"I gave mine the slip, too," Arthur said.

"They get my goat," said the boy.

"And mine."

"Once they're safely inside we might get on a boat.
What say?"

The afternoon now seemed to Arthur to have expanded
with brilliant promise.

They moved on together as if by a silent arrangement
and came to the Orangery which was apart from the house.
Crowds shuffled through it, looking at the rows of statues
and busts, and nymphs and goddesses and broken-nosed
emperors.

"Might as well have a look round as it's free," said the
boy. "What's your name?"

"Arthur Blanchflower."

"You're kidding."

"No I'm not."

"Well, rather you than me. I bet it takes some living
down at school. My name's Derek Beale," he added with
simple pride.

The Orangery smelt of damp stone and a chalky dust
filtered down through the sunlight over all the mutilated
and dismembered sculpture.

"What a lot of rubbish," said Derek, and in fact this was
so. The statues had become a burden and problem,
accumulating through the centuries, breaking and flaking;
crumbling, but never quite away. Until today, no one had
glanced at them for years. Now they were the object of
derision and ribaldry. Laughter echoed round as the crowds
drifted through the building.

"Look at this one! He's had his knocked off," said Derek.

Arthur felt vexed. He had begun to toady to Derek, who
had taken the initiative from the start, but he wondered if

he was prepared to toady to the extent of disloyalty towards his home.

"Some of the best statues have bits knocked off," he said. "Everyone knows that."

But Derek only went eagerly ahead and now was testing the strength of the armature upholding a disintegrating torso of Aphrodite.

"You're not supposed to touch them," Arthur said nervously.

"I should bloody care," said Derek.

*   *   *

Difficulties arose all the afternoon. On the lake, taking turns to manage the little boat, Arthur felt exposed to view from the house.

"What will happen when your father finds you?" he asked Derek.

"I shall tell him where he gets off."

"Won't he mind that?"

"What he minds or doesn't mind's up to him, isn't it?"

"Yes, I suppose it is."

"Let's go and chase those deer," said Derek, when they got out of the boat.

Arthur could see the deer-keeper riding up the avenue. "There's . . . a man's watching." He sat down on the grass with his face turned away.

"He can't do anything to you."

"Yes, he can. He did once before," Arthur said truthfully.

"What, for chasing the deer?"

"Yes."

"What did he do?"

"He told my father."

"What of it? I thought you meant he had used that whip on you."

Arthur's wits were exhausted with all the day's evasions and the risks he had run. A girl from a nearby riding-stables was walking his pony round at the edge of the lake, giving sixpenny rides to the children—since every little helped, His Grace had said.

"Want a ride?" Derek asked.

"Not much."

"I'm going to. I've only ever been on a donkey. I shall tell her where she gets off, if she thinks she's going to walk round with me, though. You go first."

"I don't want to go at all."

"She'll hold you if you're afraid."

He was forced to go up and pay his sixpence and the pony recognised him if the girl did not. She insisted on walking beside him.

"They're my orders," she said. "I'm responsible. You can take it or leave it."

He was led round the lake's edge in humiliation. His face burning with embarrassment, he dismounted and threw himself on to the grass while Derek had his turn. Yet, despite the anxieties and indignities, he clung greedily to this casual encounter, his first meeting with another boy, free of the incidence of hovering adults. He tried to make the most of the opportunity to discover a great deal that he needed to know, and doggedly asked his questions and listened with respect to Derek's terse replies.

"You swear a lot, don't you?"

"Yep."

"Do you like school?" (He could not ask, "What is school like?")

"No."

"Do the bigger boys bully you?"

"They better not try it on."

Derek's father, mother, and auntie were now seen coming away from the house. The boys hid behind a tree until they had disappeared into a tunnel of wistaria which led to a grotto.

"Now they've come out, we can go in," said Derek. "You don't have to pay extra so we might as well take a quick butcher's."

A 'quick butcher's' sounded vaguely brutal to Arthur but he would not demean himself by asking for translations of slang.

"I'll stay out here," he said. "It's too hot to go inside. I'm not interested in houses. My father might be in there."

"If he is, he'll have gone to the front by now. We can hang about at the back so no one sees us."

"I'd rather not."

"Are you afraid of your father?"

"No."

"Well then . . ."

He went towards the house as if hypnotised by the older boy. Waiting wretchedly for the appalling moment when he would meet his tutor's eye, and to delay his discovery and disgrace, he stood behind two fat women and tried to merge with their swarm of children.

Mr Gilliat had become rather tangled up and confused with the queue and most people were simply drifting through at their own pace, not listening to him. The group which he had gathered about him stayed only from courtesy and listened with a sense of rebellion, eyeing with envy and reproach those who had escaped. Too slowly they were taken down the long gallery, past one Duchess after another, by Romney, by Gainsborough, by Sargent.

"The mistress of the Third Duke, by Lely," said Mr Gilliat, standing coyly before the portrait.

"That means they weren't married," Derek whispered. "She was breaking the law all right. What a mug, I ask you! She looks like a bloody horse."

"Lady Constance Considine, the present Duchess, before

her marriage," said Mr Gilliat. They all gazed up at Arthur's mother. "Lovely gold tints in her hair," one fat woman said. "The lace is quite life-like." "She looks half asleep," said someone else, and Arthur bowed his head.

Mr Gilliat drew them on. He was almost hysterical with fatigue and with the failure of all his little jokes. Like cows they herded together, his unworthy audience, gazing blankly, mute and stupid. He felt like taking a stick and whacking their rumps. His domed and nearly bald head glistened with sweat, his hands flapped and gesticulated and he smiled until his face was stiff.

"Proper pansy," one young woman murmured to another.

All the time Arthur managed to conceal himself behind the fat women; but Mr Gilliat was no longer looking at the crowd, could meet the bovine stares no more.

The Haunted Bedroom with its legend of scandal and tragedy interested only Arthur from whom such frightening stories had been kept. The others stared dully at the worn brocade hangings and at the priedieu where some wanton forebear had been strangled while she was praying—presumably for the forgiveness of her sins. A burden of vice and terror was descending upon poor Arthur. The best that any of his ancestors had done was to be arrogant in battle. They were painted against backgrounds of carnage, standing, with curls blowing and armour shining, among contorted and dying horses.

Mr Gilliat now brought them to the partition chambers. Here, he explained, was an ancient, creaking apparatus which could lift one wall in its entirety so that eighteenth-century house-parties might be diverted by having a curtain as it were, raised without warning to disclose their friends' discomfiture and deshabille. Arthur felt shame to hear of such behaviour and he did not wonder that these rooms were usually locked. Scenes of cruel embarrassment he could imagine, obscene hordes of mockers in night-caps and ruffled wraps jeering at sudden exposure, invading the privacy of their fellows' undressing or praying or making love.

This last possibility Mr Gilliat did not suggest. He merely dwelt laughingly upon the picture of an imaginary lady discovered without her wig—bad enough, thought Arthur.

Derek moved closer to him and murmured: "Yes, and people might be . . . you know."

"Rather childish," someone said. "They might have had something better to do with their time."

Arthur felt stifled and frightened.

"My feet!" a woman complained.

They were nearly at the end, had wound through the core of the house and now were to descend the other side of the horse-shoe staircase.

"Fancy keeping it clean," one of the fat women said. She stopped to run a finger along the carved banister and Arthur drew up close behind her.

"Very tiring," they said, coming out into the fresh air again.

"Where the dickens have you been?" shouted Derek's father, pushing into the crowd. "Wasting our time; worrying your mother? Don't answer me back, my lad, or you'll get a taste of my hand."

Disillusioned, Arthur watched the boy pushed on ahead, nagged and ranted at. He took it in silence. He did not tell his father where to get off, but kept his eyes averted. "Where have you been?" cried his mother, "we've been beside ourselves." He straightened the row of fountain-pens in his pocket, looked nervous and meek, did not glance back at Arthur, who could not bear to witness this sudden change in him and turned away in the opposite direction.

*   *   *

The Duchess went to her bath as the last visitors departed. Although she had kept to her room, she felt bruised and buffeted and contaminated. "The noise!" she said, pressing her fingers to her temples and thrusting back her beautiful golden hair. "I tried to be brave," she told her maid.

The Duke was exhilarated as he walked in the grounds with his steward. "A good day," he said. "A nice crowd and no litter."

The steward picked up an empty cigarette packet.

"I wonder what they all think and why they come, and do they resent my having such a place as this, I wonder?"

The steward could not say: "No, your Grace, they pity you, and go back to their own homes in relief."

*   *   *

As the last cars went down the drive, Arthur, watching from the schoolroom window, felt a sense of isolation coming over him. In the new silence a cuckoo called. Two other birds in a bush below him carried on a boring exchange. He was loth to explore his own loneliness. It was distasteful to him, and the day had done too much.

He did not turn from the window, when Mr Gilliat came in.

"What a day!" fussed the tutor. "Oh, dear, my head! The hoi polloi! One despairs. Have you done your Latin?"

"I couldn't find the book."

"But"—his voice rose hysterically—"you should have asked me for it."

"I couldn't find you either."

"Someone could have done so. I was not entirely inaccessible. So you have idled your day away? It is too vexing for words. You will have to put your back into it tomorrow to make up. Yes, you really will. To take advantage at a time like this when we all have so much to cope with! More than enough on our hands. All of us tired and trying to do our best, and this is to be our reward, is it? You have fallen short of all your Papa would expect of you."

Arthur stood quite still, watching the deer moving across the park, up towards the wooded slopes for the night. "I should bloody care," he said.

You'll Enjoy It When You Get There

"SHYNESS is *common*," Rhoda's mother insisted. "I was never *allowed* to be shy when I was a girl. Your grandparents would soon have put a stop to *that*."

The stressed words sounded so peevish. Between each sentence she refreshed herself with a sip of invalid's drink, touched her lips with her handkerchief, and then continued.

"Self-consciousness it was always called when I was young, and that is what it is. To imagine that it shows a sense of modesty is absurd. *Modesty*. Why, I have never known a *truly* modest person to be the least bit shy."

The jaundice, which had discoloured her face and her eyes, seemed as well to wash all her words in poison.

"It's all right for you, mother," Rhoda said. "You can drink. Then anyone can talk."

Mrs Hobart did not like to be reminded that she drank at all: that she drank immoderately, no one—she herself least of all—would ever have dared to remind her.

Rhoda, who was sitting by the window, nursing her cat, stared down at the gardens in the square and waited huffily for an indignant rebuke. Instead, her mother said wearily:

"Well, you will have a drink, too, before the banquet, and no nonsense. A 'girl of eighteen'."

"I hate the taste."

"I, I, I. I hate this; I loathe that. What do you think would have happened if *I* had considered what *I* liked through all these years. Or the Queen," she added. "The poor girl! The rubbish she's been forced to eat and drink in foreign countries. And never jibbed."

"You and the Queen are different kettles of fish from me," Rhoda said calmly. Then she threw up the window from the bottom and leant out and waved to her father, who was crossing the road below.

"Please shut that window," Mrs Hobart said. "Leaning out and waving, like a housemaid. I despair." She put the glass of barley-water on one side and said again: "I despair."

"There is no need. I will do my best," said Rhoda. "Though no one likes to be frightened in quite such a boring way."

*   *   *

She sat in the train opposite her father and wedged in by business-men. In books and films, she thought, people who go on train journeys always get a corner seat.

In a corner, she could have withdrawn into her day-dreaming so much more completely; but she was cramped by the fat men on either side, whose thighs moved against hers when they uncrossed and recrossed their legs, whose newspapers distracted her with their puzzling headlines— for instance 'Bishop Exorcises £5,000 Ghost,' she read. Her father, with his arms folded neatly across his chest, dozed and nodded, and sometimes his lips moved as if he were rehearsing his speech for that evening. They seemed to have been in the train for a long time, and the phlegmy fog, which had pressed to the windows as they left London, was darkening quickly. The dreadful moment of going into dinner was coming nearer. Her father suddenly woke up and lifted his head. He yawned and winked a watery eye at her, and yawned and yawned again. She sensed that to be taking his daughter instead of his wife to what her mother called the Trade Banquet made it seem rather a spree to him and she wished that she could share his light-heartedness.

Like sleepwalkers, the other people in the compartment, still silent and drowsy, began now to fold their newspapers, look for their tickets, lift down their luggage from the racks. The train's rhythm changed and the lights of the station came running past the windows. All that Rhoda was to see of this Midlands town was the dark, windy space between the station entrance and the great station hotel as they followed a porter across the greasy paving-stones and later, a glimpse from her bedroom window of a timber-yard beside a canal.

When she was alone in the hotel bedroom, she felt more uncertain than ever, oppressed by the null effect of raspberry-coloured damask, the large intolerable pieces of furniture and the silence, which only sounds of far-away plumbing broke, or of distant lifts rising and falling.

She shook out her frock and was hanging it in a cavernous wardrobe when somebody in the corridor outside tapped on the door. "Is that you, Father?" she called out anxiously. A waiter came in, carrying a tray high in the air. He swirled it round on his fingers and put down a glass of sherry. "The gentleman in number forty-five ordered it," he explained. "Thank you," Rhoda said timidly, peeping at him round the wardrobe-door, "very much," she added effusively.

The waiter said "Thank *you*, madam," in a quelling voice, and went away.

Rhoda sniffed at the sherry, and then tipped it into the wash-basin. 'I suppose Father's so used to Mamma,' she thought. She knew the bedroom imbibing that went on, as her mother moved heavily about, getting dressed: every time she came back to her mirror, she would take a drink from the glass beside it.

The hotel room was a vacuum in which even time had no reality to Rhoda. With no watch to tell her, she began to wonder if she had been there alone for ten minutes or an hour and in sudden alarm she ran to the bathroom and turned on taps and hurriedly unpacked.

She put on a little confidence with her pretty frock; but, practising radiant smiles in the looking-glass, she was sure that they were only grimaces. She smoothed on her long white gloves and took up her satin bag, then heard a distant clock, somewhere across the roofs of high buildings, strike the half-hour and knew that she must wait all through the next, matching half-hour for her father to come to fetch her.

As she waited, shivering as she paced about the room, growing more and more goose-fleshed, she saw the reasonableness in her father's thought about the sherry and wished that she had not wasted it and, even more, that she had lain twenty minutes longer in her warm bath.

He came as the clock struck out the hours and, when she ran and opened the door to him said: "Heavens, ma'am, how exquisite you look!"

They descended the stairs.

In the reception-room, another waiter circled with a tray of filled glasses. Four people stood drinking by the fire—two middle-aged men, one wearing a mayoral chain, the other a bosomful of medals; and two middle-aged women, stiffly corseted, their hair set in tight curls and ridges. Diamonds shone on their freckled chests and pink carnations slanted heads downwards across their bodices. They look as if they know the ropes, thought Rhoda, paralysed with shyness. They received her kindly, but in surprise. "Why, where is Ethel?" they asked her father, and they murmured in concern over the jaundice and said how dreary it must be to be on the waggon. 'Especially for her', the tone of their voices seemed to Rhoda to suggest.

A bouquet was taken from a little side table and handed to Rhoda, who held it stiffly at her waist where it contended fiercely with the colour of her dress.

The six of them were, in their importance, shut off from a crowded bar where other guests were drinking cocktails: on this side of the door there was an air of confidence and expectation, of being ahead of the swim, Rhoda thought. She wished passionately, trying to sip away her sherry, that she might spend the entire evening shut away from the hordes of strangers in the bigger room but, only too soon, a huge toast-master, fussing with his white gloves, brought the three couples into line and then threw wide the doors; inclining his head patronisingly to guest after guest, he bawled out some semblance of the names they proffered. As the first ones came reluctantly forward from the gaiety of the bar, Mr Hobart leaned towards Rhoda and took the glass from her hand and put it on the tray with the others. "How do you do," she whispered, shaking hands with an old gentleman, who was surprised to see that her eyes were filled with tears. "You are deputising for your dear mother?" he asked. "And very charmingly you do it, my dear," he added, and passed on quickly, so that she could brush her wet lashes with her gloved hand.

"Good-evening, Rhoda," The bracing mockery of this new voice jolted her, the voice of Digby Lycett Senior, as she always called him in her mind—the mind which for months had been conquered and occupied by Digby Lycett Junior. This unexpected appearance was disastrous to her. She felt indignantly that he had no right to be there, so remotely connected was he with the trade the others had in common. "Nice of you to come," her father was now telling him. They were old business friends. It was Digby Lycett who sold her father the machinery for making

Hobart's Home-made Cookies. It was *loathsome* of you to
come, Rhoda thought, unhappily.

She took one gloved hand after another, endlessly—it
seemed—confronted by pink carnations and strings of pearls.
But the procession dwindled at last—the stragglers, who had
lingered over their drinks till the last moment, were rounded
up by the toast-master and sent resignedly on their way to
the banqueting-hall, where an orchestra was playing "Some
Enchanted Evening" above the noise of chairs being scraped
and voices mounting in volume like a gathering wave.

In the reception-room, the Mayor straightened the chain
on his breast. One duty done, he was now prepared to go on
to the next. All of his movements were certain and auto-
matic; every evening of his life, they implied, he had a hall
full of people waiting for him to take his seat.

As she moved towards the door a sense of vertigo and
nausea overcame Rhoda, confronted by the long walk to her
place and the ranks of pink faces turned toward her. With
bag and bouquet and skirt to manage, she felt that she was
bundling along with downcast eyes. Before a great heap of
flowers on the table, they stopped. The Mayor was humming
very softly to the music. He put on his spectacles, peered at
the table and then laid his hand on the back of a gilt
chair, indicating that here, next to him, Rhoda was to be
privileged to sit.

At the doors, waitresses crowded ready to rush forward
with hors-d'œuvres. The music faded. Without raising her
eyes, instinctively, wishing to sink out of sight, Rhoda slid
round her chair and sat upon it.

Down crashed the toast-master's gavel as the Mayor, in a
challenging voice, began to intone Grace. Mr Hobart put
his hand under Rhoda's elbow and brought her, lurching,
as she could not help doing, to her feet again. The gilt chair
tipped, but he saved it from going over, the bouquet shot
under the table and Rhoda prayed that she might follow it.

"Please God, let me faint. Let me never have to look up again and meet anybody's glance."

"*Now* you can, young lady," the Mayor said, helping her down again. Then he turned quickly to the woman on his other side and began a conversation. Rhoda's father had done the same. Sitting between them, she swallowed sardines and olives and her bitter, bitter tears. After a time, her isolation made her defiant. She lifted her head and looked boldly and crossly in front of her, and caught the eye of Digby Lycett Senior, just as he raised a fork to his mouth, and smiled at her, sitting not far across the room, at right angles to her table, where he could perfectly observe her humiliation and record it for his son's interest and amusement later. "Poor old Rhoda"—she could hear the words, overlaid with laughter.

She ate quickly, as if she had not touched food for weeks. Once, her father, fingering a wine-glass restlessly, caught and held as he was in conversation by the relentless woman at his side, managed to turn his head for a moment and smile at Rhoda. "All right?" he asked, and nodded his own answer, for it was a great treat for a young girl, he implied— the music, the flowers, the pretty dress, the wine.

Someone *must* talk to me, she thought, for it seemed to her that, through lack of conversation, her expression was growing sullen. She tried to reorganise her features into a look of animation or calm pleasure. She drank a plate of acid-tasting, red soup to its dregs. Chicken followed turbot, as her mother had assured her was inevitable. The Mayor, who went through the same menu nearly every evening, left a great deal on his plate; he scattered it about for a while and then tidied it up: not so Rhoda, who, against a great discomfort of fullness, plodded painstakingly on.

At last, as she was eating some cauliflower, the Mayor turned his moist, purple face towards her. She lifted her eyes to the level of the chain on his breast and agreed with him that she was enjoying herself enormously.

"It is my first visit to Norley," she said gaily, conscious of Digby Lycett Senior's eyes upon her. She hoped that he would think from her expression that some delicious pleasantry was in progress. To keep the Mayor in conversation she was determined. He should not turn away again and Digby Lycett, Senior or Junior, should not have the impression that she sat in silence and disgrace from the beginning to the end.

"But I have a cat who came from here," she added.

The Mayor looked startled.

"A Burmese cat. A man in Norley—a Doctor Fisher— breeds them. Do you know Doctor Fisher?"

"I can't say that I do."

He was plainly unwilling for her to go on. On his other side was feminine flattery and cajolery and he wished to turn back for more, and Rhoda and her cat were of no interest to him.

"Have you ever seen a Burmese cat?" she asked.

He crumbled some bread and looked cross and said that as far as he knew he never had.

"He came to London on the train all by himself in a little basket," Rhoda said. "The cat, I mean, of course. Minkie, I call him. Such a darling, you can't imagine."

She smiled vivaciously for Digby Lycett Senior's benefit; but, try as she might, she could not summon the courage to lift her eyes any higher than the splendid chain on the Mayor's breast, for she shrank from the look of contempt she was afraid he might be wearing.

"They are rather like Siamese cats," she went on. "Though they are brown all over and have golden eyes, not blue."

"Oh?" said the Mayor. He had to lean a little nearer to

her as a waitress put a dish of pistachio ice-cream over his left shoulder.

"But rather the same natures, if you know what I mean," said Rhoda.

"I'm afraid I don't care for cats," said the Mayor, in the voice of simple pride in which this remark is always made.

"On all your many social commitments," the woman on his other side said loudly, rescuing him, "which flavour of ice-cream crops up most often?"

He laughed and turned to her with relief. "Vanilla," he said jovially. "In a ratio of eight to one."

* * *

"Enjoying yourself?" Rhoda's father asked her later, as they danced a foxtrot together. "I daresay this is the part of the evening that appeals to you—not all those long-winded speeches."

It appealed to Rhoda because it was nearer to the end, and for no other reason.

"You seemed to be getting on well with the Mayor," Mr Hobart added.

The Mayor had disappeared. Rhoda could see no sign of his glittering chain and she supposed that he disliked dancing as much as he disliked cats. She prayed that Digby Lycett Senior might not ask her to do the Old Fashioned Waltz which followed. She was afraid of his mocking smile and, ostrich-like, opened her bag and looked inside it as he approached.

Another middle-aged man stepped forward first and asked to have the pleasure in a voice which denied the possibility of there being any. Rhoda guessed that what he meant was 'May I get this duty over and done with, pursued as it is as a mark of the esteem in which I hold your father.' And Rhoda smiled as if she were enchanted, and rose and put herself into his arms, as if he were her lover.

He made the waltz more old-fashioned than she had ever known it, dancing stiffly, keeping his stomach well out of her way, humming, but not saying a word to her. She was up against a great silence this evening: to her it was the measure of her failure. Sorting through her mind for something to say, she rejected remarks about the floor and the band and said instead that she had never been to Norley before. The observation should have led somewhere, she thought; but it did not: it was quite ignored.

"But I have a cat who came from here," she added. "A little Burmese cat."

When he did not answer this, either, she thought that he must be deaf and raised her voice. "There is a doctor here who breeds them. Perhaps you have come across him— a Doctor Fisher."

"No, I can't say that I have."

"He sent the kitten to London by train, in a little basket. So pretty and gay. Minkie, I call him. Have you ever seen a Burmese cat?" She could not wait for his answers, lest they never came. "They are not a usual sort of cat at all. Rather like a Siamese in many ways, but brown all over and with golden eyes instead of blue. They are similar in nature though, if you can understand what I mean."

He either could not, or was not prepared to try and at last, mercifully, the music quickened and finally snapped off altogether. Flushed and smiling, she was escorted back to her father who was standing by the bar, looking genial and indulgent.

Her partner's silence seemed precautionary now. He handed her over with a scared look, as if she were some dangerous lunatic. Her father, not noticing this, said: "You are having quite a success with your Mayor, my dear."

"My Mayor?"

She turned quickly and looked after the man who had

just left her. He was talking to a little group of people; they all had their heads together and were laughing.

"He took that chain off then?" she said, feeling sick and dazed. It was all she had had to distinguish him from the rest of the bald-headed and obese middle-aged men.

"You couldn't expect him to dance with that hanging round his neck—not even in your honour," her father said. "And now, I shall fetch you a long, cool drink, for you look as if the dancing has exhausted you."

VIRAGO MODERN CLASSICS

The first Virago Modern Classic, *Frost in May* by Antonia White, was published in 1978. It launched a list dedicated to the celebration of women writers and to the rediscovery and reprinting of their works. Its aim was, and is, to demonstrate the existence of a female tradition in fiction which is both enriching and enjoyable. The Leavisite notion of the 'Great Tradition', and the narrow, academic definition of a 'classic', has meant the neglect of a large number of interesting secondary works of fiction. In calling the series 'Modern Classics' we do not necessarily mean 'great' — although this is often the case. Published with new critical and biographical introductions, books are chosen for many reasons: sometimes for their importance in literary history; sometimes because they illuminate particular aspects of womens' lives, both personal and public. They may be classics of comedy or storytelling; their interest can be historical, feminist, political or literary.

Initially the Virago Modern Classics concentrated on English novels and short stories published in the early decades of this century. As the series has grown it has broadened to include works of fiction from different centuries, different countries, cultures and literary traditions. In 1984 the Victorian Classics were launched; there are separate lists of Irish, Scottish, European, American, Australian and other English speaking countries; there are books written by Black women, by Catholic and Jewish women, and a few relevant novels by men. There is, too, a companion series of Non-Fiction Classics constituting biography, autobiography, travel, journalism, essays, poetry, letters and diaries.

By the end of 1986 over 250 titles will have been published in these two series, many of which have been suggested by our readers.

OTHER WORKS BY
ELIZABETH TAYLOR

IN A SUMMER SEASON

First published in 1961, this is one of Elizabeth Taylor's most subtle and satisfying novels. Kate Heron is a wealthy attractive widow who lives with her son, her daughter, and her aunt Ethel in their early Victorian house outside London. She meets and marries Dermot: ten years her junior, he is charming and feckless. Their relationship is special – strong enough to withstand their neighbours' disapproval – but there appears an enemy within which threatens to tear the marriage apart . . . In a moving and powerful climax Elizabeth Taylor reveals human loving to be the thing it is: tragic and often piercingly funny.

'. . . swings, like the deftest weathercock, between humour, tragedy and ironic observation; most of it is quite exceptionally funny, and bright with the author's acute susceptibilities . . . It would be hard to find a novel more consistently accomplished and entertaining.' – *Sunday Times*

'I have long loved Elizabeth Taylor's novels' – Brigid Brophy, *New Statesman*

'Elizabeth Taylor writes like an angel' – Iain Hamilton, *Daily Telegraph*

OTHER WORKS BY
ELIZABETH TAYLOR

THE SOUL OF KINDNESS

The soul of kindness was what Flora believed herself to be, and made almost everyone else believe. Tall, blonde and beautiful as a Botticelli girl, she appeared to have everything under control – her household, her baby, her husband Richard, her all-too-loyal friend Meg, Meg's brother Kit who has always adored Flora, and Patrick the novelist and domestic pet. Only the painter, Liz, refuses to become a worshipper at the shrine . . .

In this novel, first published in 1964, Elizabeth Taylor gives us a study of deception, all the more telling for the deceptively gentle way in which it unfolds. The varied characters are delicately drawn; the irony is light as a feather: but only the Floras of this life will close the book without understanding more clearly the disease of self-love.

'I have always admired Miss Elizabeth Taylor's quietly distinguished novels . . . [*The Soul of Kindness*] is an unobtrusive book, full of detail, elegant and gentle . . . skilful and subtle' – Susan Hill

'This wonderfully observant and feeling writer is at her very best in this novel' – Angus Wilson, *Observer*

OTHER WORKS BY
ELIZABETH TAYLOR

ANGEL

Angelica Deverell is fifteen years old at the turn of the century. She is the daughter of a widow who keeps a grocery shop in a dreary provincial backstreet, working hard to pay for Angel's education so she can "better herself". But Angel rejects the drabness of her daily life and, retreating into a world of romantic dreams, she begins to write stories remarkable for their extravagance and fantasy. To those around her it is simply *folie de grandeur*, but Angel knows better. She knows she is different, that she will grow up to be a fêted authoress, owner of great riches and of the mysterious Paradise House . . .

OTHER WORKS BY
ELIZABETH TAYLOR

A GAME OF HIDE AND SEEK

During those summer games of hide-and-seek Harriet falls in love with Vesey and his elusive, teasing ways. When he goes to Oxford she cherishes his photograph and waits for the letter which doesn't come. Then Charles enters her life, a solid and reliable solicitor, and Harriet stifles her imaginings. With Charles and their daughter, she excels at respectability: its crimson-papered walls, remembered birthdays and jars of lilac. But when Vesey reappears, her marriage seems to melt into nothing. Harriet is older, it is much too late, but she is still in love with him. First published in 1958, this is Elizabeth Taylor's subtlest and finest work.

OTHER WORKS BY
ELIZABETH TAYLOR

PALLADIAN

Young Cassandra is alone in the world, her father has just died. When she goes to Cropthorne Manor as a governess, its weary façade and crumbling statues are all that she could hope for. And Marion Vanburgh is the perfect employer – a widower, austere and distant, with a penchant for Greek. But this is not a nineteenth-century novel and Cassandra's Mr Rochester isn't the only inhabitant of the Manor. There's Tom, irascible and discontented, Margaret, pregnant and voracious, the ineffectual Tinty and the eccentric, domineering Nanny. Just as Jane Austen wittily contrasted real life with a girl's Gothic fantasies in *Northanger Abbey*, so Elizabeth Taylor subtly examines the realities of life for a latter-day Jane Eyre in this sharply observed work, first published in 1946.

OTHER WORKS BY
ELIZABETH TAYLOR

THE SLEEPING BEAUTY

Vinny Tumulty is a quiet, sensible man. When he goes to stay at a small English seaside resort his task is to comfort a bereaved friend, Isabella. A past master at sympathy, Vinny looks forward to a solemn few days of tears and consolation. Then, on the evening of his arrival, he looks out of the window at sunset and catches sight of a mysterious, romantic figure: a beautiful woman walking by the seashore. Before the weekend is over Vinny has fallen in love, completely and utterly, for the first time in his middle-aged life. But Emily is a sleeping beauty, her secluded life hiding bitter secrets from the past: how can this unlikely Prince Charming break the spell and rouse her from her dreams?

OTHER WORKS BY
ELIZABETH TAYLOR

THE WEDDING GROUP

Cressy has grown up in an artistic community, presided over by her eccentric Grandfather who bears more than a passing resemblance to Augustus John. Rebelling against this existence she leaves home, taking a job in an antique shop. Here she meets David, a self-satisfied journalist, and they marry. But as Cressy cannot fend for herself and David is securely tied to his mother's apron strings, this act of escape for both of them proves a powerful form of bondage. First published in 1968, this quietly ironic exploration of the ways in which the parental mould is not easily broken is one of Elizabeth Taylor's most ambitious novels. Combining fresh observation with disinterested understanding, it is 'a beautifully telling comedy by one of our foremost novelists – *Angus Wilson*

OTHER WORKS BY
ELIZABETH TAYLOR

MRS PALFREY AT THE CLAREMONT

One rainy Sunday in January Mrs Palfrey, recently
widowed, arrives at the Claremont Hotel in the Cromwell
Road. Here she will spend her remaining days. Her fellow
residents are a magnificently eccentric group who live off
crumbs of affection, obsessive interest in the relentless
round of hotel meals, and undying curiosity. There is Mrs
Burton with her mauve-rinsed hair, her costume jewellery
and her drinking; Mrs Arbuthnot, bossy and arthritic; Mr
Osmond with his risqué stories, his endless stream of letters
to the press. Together, upper lips stiffened, teeth gritted,
they fight off their twin enemies: boredom and the grim
Reaper. And then one day Mrs Palfrey encounters the
handsome young writer, Ludo, and we learn that even the
old can fall in love. . .

OTHER WORKS BY
ELIZABETH TAYLOR

THE DEVASTATING BOYS

Lonely in middle age, a well-meaning Oxford professor and his anxious wife, Laura, decide to take in two unknown Black boys from London's East End for a summer holiday. What happens when Benny and Sep actually arrive surpasses all imagination: difficult, funny, touching, they are like two small tornados, shattering the rural peace, upsetting forever the settled order of their home – and lives.

This moving and hilarious tale leads this collection of Elizabeth Taylor's greatest short stories. Varied in their settings and characters – from the lonely, ascetic immigrant in ''Tall Boy'', to brassy, good-natured Phyl of ''Flesh'' – they are nevertheless the quintessence of all that is most distinguished, and witty, in her art. We meet women, children and men, often ostensibly ordinary, who follow their paths of ruthlessness and ambition, each in pursuit of happiness, love, or power – each a classic creation.